John Ackworth

Clog Shop Chronicles

John Ackworth

Clog Shop Chronicles

ISBN/EAN: 9783743358799

Manufactured in Europe, USA, Canada, Australia, Japa

Cover: Foto ©Andreas Hilbeck / pixelio.de

Manufactured and distributed by brebook publishing software (www.brebook.com)

John Ackworth

Clog Shop Chronicles

To

The Memory

of

My Mother

CONTENTS

An Atonement

An Atonement

WHEN " Barbary " Royle returned to Beckside
to live, it was generally understood that she had
had a misfortune, but that as it was something
for which she was more to be pitied than blamed
no person with any " dacency " would ever think
of making inquiries about it. Besides, everybody knew everything about everybody else in
Beckside, and if they only waited Barbara would
" tell " of herself.

But she never did. And nothing could be
gathered from the little girl she brought back
with her, who reminded the old people so much
of the Barbara of long ago.

She had lived in a big place a long way off,
she said. Her mother had told her that she
had a " daddy," but she had never seen him,
and she was called Royle like her mother—and
that was all that could be elicited.

" When a child's cawd after its muther,"
drawled Long Ben, picking a chip out of
the Clog Shop fire and lighting his pipe
with it, " there's summat wrong wi' its fayther
and "—

" If all t' childer i' Beckside as had faythers wi' summat wrung abaat 'em had to be renamed after their muthers," interrupted old Jabe the clogger, lifting a very red face from over a disabled clog, "there'd be a bonny christenin' at yo'r haase."

" An' I tell thee summat else," he continued, rising to his feet and brandishing a well-worn knife; "if t' mon as talked abaat puncing a chap when he wor daan 'ad cum to Beckside he'd find them as 'ud do it to a woman."

Jabe's rejoinder being unusually fierce, even for him, it was clear that he disapproved of curiosity in this direction, and that the subject had better be dropped.

Dropped at the Clog Shop, it was soon dropped everywhere else, for that establishment and its proprietor were the centres of public opinion in the village.

Beckside scarcely was a village; it was just two or three clusters of cottages, dotted here and there with bigger buildings stationed on the left slope of the clough, having a little Methodist chapel at one end of it and a mill at the other. There was no street in the village, the road that ran slantwise down to the Beck-bridge at the bottom of the clough and up again towards Knob Top, as the farm on the opposite side of the clough was called, being the only provision of the nature of streetage which Beckside possessed.

The Clog Shop stood on the left, just past the chapel, at the point where the road turned down towards the Beck, so that it commanded a full view of the road right down to the bridge, and it was the main object in sight when you came up the road from the bridge. The Clog Shop itself was merely a lean-to standing against the end of Jabe's cottage, and having a big window facing the road, and a little one looking into the garden behind. The fireplace stood with its back to the cottage. Though of comparatively modern construction it was very ancient in style, and was as nearly like an oldtime ingle-nook as the imagination of Jabe and the ingenuity of the local builder could produce. The remains of two or three clog-benches and two long, low stools provided the furniture of this primitive, cosy corner, which was all the year round, and almost all the day long, occupied either by customers who waited for clogs that were being "spetched," or by old Becksiders, to whom it served as club-room and hotel.

Jabe himself was a bachelor and a confirmed woman-hater. His apprentice for the time being was usually both cook and housemaid, except when Aunt Judy came in to "fettle up." "Independent o' boath men *and* women," Jabe used to say, with a tremendous emphasis on the "and."

Jabe had a short leg and a long one, the

shorter one being used as a sort of indicator of feeling, much in the same way as a dog uses his tail, and the sudden jerking out of the abbreviated member and its being flung violently over the other was taken as an unfailing sign that something was coming.

Barbara Royle had been one of Jabe's special trials in days gone by. A laughing, teasing, black-eyed beauty who, even after her conversion, was suspected of " carrying on " with the lads, she would come into the Clog Shop to have her clog mended as demurely as she went to class, except that she was usually humming some popular Sunday School tune.

" I want to be an angel," she was murmuring on one of these occasions whilst Jabe put on her clog iron.

" Ay, but ther'll ha' to be a vast change if iver th'art an angel, wench," said Jabe.

And there had been a change. Barbara had gone away from Beckside, and was supposed to be doing well in a distant town. Suddenly, however, she had returned—a sad-eyed, shrinking woman, whose every action proclaimed that she wanted to be let alone.

" Goa when th'art axed," Jabe said to those who " thowt o' cawin' on her," but as Barbara never asked anybody they had to be content as they were. Jabe himself was strongly suspected of having been to see Barbary, for Peter Twist, bending his head down as he sat in the nook and speaking under his breath whilst Jabe served a customer, communicated to two or three of the "chaps" that owd Jabe had been to him to speak for a "couple o' looms" for Barbara, and that when he came he "looked as if he'd been skriking."

So Barbara was allowed to settle down quietly among her own. She had no near relatives. The more distant ones had known little about her whilst she was away, and kept carefully aloof when she returned, and so she and her child were allowed to follow their own devices and settle in a small cottage down by the Beck-bridge.

Except to gratify their curiosity, the Beckside women had taken no interest in Barbara, and only showed their nature by a characteristic hardness to one who had seen misfortune. Some of them, indeed, owed her a grudge of long standing for her flirting triumphs of other days, and affected to be astonished when Jabe received her as a full member of his "class."

"Barbary Ryle's Barbary Ryle," said Aunt Judy, who, in virtue of her relationship to Jabe, was a sort of a leader of opinion amongst the women; "Barbary Ryle's Barbary Ryle, an' if hoo isna settin' her cap a sumbry afore hoo's bin here mony wik my name's not Judy Jabe."

As a matter of fact this was not Mrs. Judy's name at all. She had been married for a few months only, and as her late husband had been nobody in particular, people had never got into the habit of calling her by his name. Surnames were always somewhat of a difficulty in Beckside. In most cases they were superfluous, and were also considered to be pretentious, and so in the nature of things it came about that Aunt Judy became known as Judy Jabe—the Judy of Jabe.

Whether Barbara ever heard of Judy's prediction or not, she seemed to take particular pains to avoid the society of men, and when Ned Royle, the new overlooker, came to the mill, and Aunt Judy and her gossips were "sartin sure" she'd try to catch him, they were perplexed to find that Barbara avoided Ned even more carefully than she did other men.

Ned turned out to be a Methodist, and one Monday night went to the prayer-meeting. He must have been a little early, for the room was empty. Presently the door opened, and Barbara entered. But she stopped suddenly, turned deadly pale, and, wheeling round, nearly flew down the chapel flags.

Long Ben met her rushing away, and declared over the Clog Shop fire that night that it was a "regular queer do." "Aw seed her go in, and Aw seed her come aat, and hoo' looked as if hoo'd seen a boggart; and when Aw geet inta th' vestry, theer wor Ned lookin' moar like a boggart nor even Barbary did."

Ned Royle was something of a mystery. The fact that he bore the same surname as Barbara attracted no attention, for Royle was the commonest surname in the district. Nobody seemed to know where the new overlooker came from, although a slight difference in his "twang" made it clear that he was not of Beckside origin. The "super" had told Jabe that he had received a note of removal for Ned, and that he had been a Sunday School teacher. At the mill he was regarded somewhat suspiciously, as he had introduced several useful but very unpopular changes. The fact that he was a teetotaler was against him, and his neglect of the flagrant weed disfranchised him as far as the Clog Shop Club was concerned.

He had joined the Sunday School, of which Jabe was perpetual superintendent. Ned showed, however, a most decided preference for teaching girls, but as such a thing was only allowed in cases of emergency, his opportunities did not occur very often. However, he was soon immensely popular with the "little wenches," and at tea-parties foraged for them in the provision room, and waited upon them with untiring zeal. His special favourite was little Emmie Royle, Barbara's daughter. The women said he was simply kind to the child to get at the mother—an opinion openly denied, but privately accepted by Jabe.

When, however, one dark Sunday afternoon

as school was " loosing," and Jabe was limping home a little behind the rest, he saw little Emmie in front of him, and was just noticing how she walked " straight " like her mother, when he saw a man start out of a " ginnell," snatch Emmie up in his arms, kiss and hug her passionately, and then, putting her tenderly down again, hurry away in Jabe's direction. Jabe was excited, and had just prepared a hot blast for this offender when, meeting him face to face, he discovered it was Ned Royle, and that tears were in the man's eyes, and he was visibly agitated.

Jabe's gruff " 'Ow do " in return to Ned's salutation was evidently intended to be addressed to the pole-star, judging by the direction in which he looked as he uttered it. And the following evening over the Clog Shop fire, Jabe, whilst not making the slightest reference to what he had seen, expressed a very decided opinion that " Yon mon 'as had childer of his own some time."

About this time the mill began to run short-time, and eventually stopped altogether. Trade was bad, and hard times were come again. Considerable surprise was expressed in Beckside that Barbara Royle, one of the newest of the weavers, should be almost the last to be stopped, and the women folk took it as another sign that Ned was " after " Barbara.

Jabe suppressed all murmurings in his presence by quoting the text about the widow and the fatherless.

"Widow, indeed," sniffed Mary Meadows, an angular, hard - faced old weaver of grasping habits. "Hoo's as mitch a widow as "—

But Jabe had jumped to his feet, and was kicking aside a small heap of clog tops which had accumulated around his bench as if he wanted to get at the speaker, and the look on his face was so threatening that Mary forgot to pay for her new heel irons in her haste to depart.

It was noticed also by the members of the Clog Shop Club, and by several quite ordinary people as well, that Ned Royle, who had nobody to keep but himself, was one of the first to feel the pinch of the stoppage. What made it more perplexing was that Ned was commonly supposed to have declined at least two offers of work since the mill stopped, either of which was better than his present situation. The widow with whom he lodged told Sam Speck, who, of course, told all the Clog Shop cronies that Ned Royle was " fair clemmin' hissel'," which reminded Long Ben that the " super " had lately dropped into the habit of calling Ned *Mister* Edward,—Jabe being the only person in the Methodist Society at Beckside who was considered entitled to be called Mister, even by the superintendent minister.

The Leaders' Meeting at Beckside was also mystified by the fact that the minister always prevented them sending any help during these bad times to Barbara Royle, assuring them with a confidence which greatly excited curiosity that she was amply provided for. And indeed it seemed so, for Barbara was in fact a liberal contributor to the needs of the poor, and might often be seen coming from cottages where poverty was known to exist.

Then the dreaded smallpox came to Beckside, and in a few days poverty was lost sight of in the presence of this more terrifying foe. In a short time half the houses in the hamlet had patients in them. Then, although the welcome news came that the mill was to be restarted, nothing could be done for lack of hands, and strangers would not come near.

The doctor's assistant from Brogden came to live in the place until the plague was over, and the Methodist superintendent was to be seen in Beckside every day. Beyond these no stranger was to be met with. The postman had caught the disease and died, and no one could be got to regularly take his place. Vehicles, instead of driving through Beckside, made a *détour* of nearly two miles round by Stanger Bottom.

A heavy, oppressive silence hung over the place, broken only by the sound of Long Ben's hammer as he worked almost night and day making coffins. The Clog Shop became a sort of relief committee - room, where the self-appointed committee - men sat all day long discussing the situation, and fumigating themselves with tobacco.

A peculiarity of the epidemic was that in Beckside, at anyrate, it was commonest amongst the women, and so many other women were needed to nurse them that a petticoat was scarcely ever seen out of doors during the visitation.

" Has ta yerd as Barbary's little wench has getten it?" asked Long Ben, opening the Clog Shop door one morning, and standing with one hand on the latch, whilst the other held a piece of the now too familiar oak.

"Nay sure!" exclaimed Jabe, and putting on his big spectacles he came to the shop-door, and stared down the street towards Barbara's cottage, as if a sight of that building would help him to realise what he had just heard.

As Jabe and Long Ben stood gazing down the road the minister came round the corner.

" Moor trubbel, moor trubbel, sir," said Jabe, giving the minister's hand a grip which made him wince.

"Who now?" asked the minister, with a jaded look.

"Little Emmie; Barbary's Emmie, you know," said Jabe.

"Ay, and her mother too," said Aunt Judy, as she passed into Jabe's house, on one of her occasional " fettlin' up doos."

" Booath on 'em ? " exclaimed Jabe and Ben together.

" Ay, booath on 'em.   An', O Lord, who's to noss 'em," and poor, hard old Judy actually uttered something which would pass for a sob.

The minister took refuge in his pocket-handkerchief.   Long Ben undisguisedly wept, and Jabe, looking down at Barbara's pest-smitten cottage, blinked his eager eyes with a most suspicious rapidity.

" Well, something must be done," said the minister, with a sort of gasp in his voice. " I'll go and see."

" The Lord goa wi' you," said Jabe, " but there isn't a woman i' t' place as can noss 'em."

" The minister started on his errand, and Jabe went back to his clog-bench.

" Jabe ! Jabe ! does ta see this ? "   It was Long Ben again, and his face had a scared look as he held open the door.

Jabe was at his side as fast as a long leg and a short one could carry him, and, following the direction of Ben's eyes, he saw Ned Royle standing at Barbara's door.

" He met th' minister goin' daan," said Ben, " an' as soon as he spok' to him Ned set off towart Barbary's.   Then he stopt as if he wor feart, and then he started again, and theer he is."

" Why doesn't he goa in ? " asked Jabe.

" Hew con he goa in, an' 'im a single mon?
—see thee! see thee! He *is* goin' in." And,
to the utter amazement of both, Ned, after
hesitating some time and knocking repeatedly,
gently put his hand on the latch, opened the
door, and passed inside.

Ned's hand trembled, and his face was
white and set as he went in. The room he
entered was neatly furnished and spotlessly
clean, but the fire was out and the room
uninhabited. Ned saw nothing. His head
was down and his breath was coming short
and fast.

" Barbary, mun I cum in?" he asked, without looking up, but there was no answer.
Ned tried again, but without success. Then
he raised his head, looked about him, and
finally glancing round at a narrow, much-
bescrubbed and uncarpeted staircase in the
corner behind the door, he stepped towards it
and timidly ascended. He knocked again
when he reached the bedroom door.

" Come in," said a faint voice, and Ned with
a trembling hand pushed open the door. He
did not move, however, but looked wistfully
towards the pink and white bed curtains
behind which Barbara and little Emmie lay,
he said in a humble pleading voice—

" It's me, Barbary, mun I cum in?"

No answer; only the occupants of the bed
seemed to have suddenly stopped breathing.

"Barbary! Barbary! let me cum in, will ta?"

Still no answer, and at last Ned stepped into the middle of the room.

"Barbary!" he said, "I dunnot ask thee to forgive me, but let me noss thee an' Emmie till you're better, and then I'll goa away if tha wants me."

There was a sudden movement in the bed, and one of the occupants turned her face toward the wall and began to sob.

Ned moved gently nearer. Then he tenderly pushed aside the curtains, and the next moment he had taken the plague-stricken woman in his arms and was covering her fevered face with kisses.

"Does ta forgive me? Does ta, Barbary?" gasped Ned.

"Ay, lad!" was the reply slowly and faintly spoken, and then the stricken woman laid her head on Ned's shoulder, and broke out into long sobs of relief.

"Goa away, Ned; yo' shouldn't do that. Yo'll catch it," said little Emmie from the other side of the bed.

"Come here, Emmie," said Barbara from her pillow on the man's broad breast. "Come here, wench; this is thi *fayther*."

.   .   .   .

When the minister returned to the Clog

Shop, he found Jabe and Long Ben in rather heated discussion.

"Haa does ta know as theayre worn't sumbry [somebody] else theer?" Jabe was saying, "an' if tha objects why doesn't tha goa thisell?"

"Haa con Aw goa wi' yon childer i' t' haase?" retorted Ben.

"Brethren," said the minister, drawing the remains of a disused clog-bench near the fire, "I should like to explain this matter to you. Ned Royle is where he has the best right to be, for he is Barbara's husband."

Jabe and his chum looked at each other in amazement.

"They were married at Duxbury," the minister went on, "and were very happy until Ned took to drinking. He is of a very excitable nature, though you wouldn't think it from the quietness of his conduct since he came here. One night, after having endured much provocation, Barbara spoke sharply to him. A quarrel followed, and eventually Ned, losing all control of himself, made a most violent assault upon his wife, and even in his frenzy threw cradle and baby into the street. The magistrates took a serious view of the case, and sent Ned to prison for some months.

"He came out of prison a changed man, and went right away home to ask Barbara's forgiveness. But she had gone, and no one knew where. Ned guessing that she had gone to her native village, and feeling with increasing remorse the blackness of his own conduct, gave up the idea of finding his wife and went away to a distance and got work. Then he got converted at one of our Missions, and engaged himself in good Christian work.

"But his heart was aching for his wife and child, and so hearing of the vacancy at the mill here, he applied for the situation, feeling that though he had forfeited all right to the love of wife and child he would still watch over their welfare, and perhaps some day win back their affection. He has never spoken to Barbara until to-day—except in connection with the work at the mill, and then in the fewest possible words; but just before the bad times he bought the house in which Barbara lives, and Barbara has been very much puzzled because old Croppy, the Brogden rent-collector, refused to take any more rent, and told her she must wait until the landlord asked for it.

"During the bad times Ned kept Barbara well supplied with money, and has in many ways secretly furthered her interests. As soon as the smallpox appeared, he came to me with a proposal for getting his wife and child out of the place, but Barbara refused to move, and now he has broken the ice and gone home to nurse them."

When the minister finished there was a long silence in the Clog Shop, broken only by a sudden falling together of the chips in the fire.

"That's wot I calls Ned's Atonement," said Jabe at last, looking hard into the fire.

"Yes, and his *At-one-ment* too," said the minister.

Billy Botch

Billy Botch

WINDOW dressing was at a discount in the Beckside shops. The largest window was that of the Clog Shop, a short low casement, which made up for lack of height by a quite abnormal width. No partition or curtain separated the window from the shop, except a strong board cocked slantwise at the inside edge of the window bottom which just enabled old Jabe to see over it, and keep an eye on the doings of the world outside.

The window bottom was generally strewn with wax ends, clog irons, small tins of dubbin, bundles of white leather whip-lashes for children's tops, and clog soles in various stages of preparation. Of ready-made boots or clogs there was not a single specimen.

And yet there was, for in the very middle of the window, standing on a little platform a few inches high, stood a pair of handsome specimens of the clogger's craft. Except that there was generally a pretty thick coat of recent dust upon them, these clogs were

always in a high state of polish. The soles
had been varnished, the clasps glittered in
a state of quite arrogant brassiness, and the
tops were resplendent with innumerable coats
of blacking. Woe to the hapless apprentice
who smeared those varnished soles with blacking, or left a speck of dimness on the shining
clasps.

Now, the casual visitor who came to Beckside doubtless concluded that these resplendent clogs were trade emblems, insignia of
the craft.

He was mistaken. To have made a pair of
clogs on stock or for mere show would have
been to make a concession to new-fangled
ways of which the old Clogger was incapable.
No, these clogs had a history which I am
now about to relate.

Jabe once had an apprentice called Billy—
an undersized, sickly-looking little fellow with
unmanageable dark hair, black twinkly eyes,
and a low, broad forehead.

Now, all Jabe's apprentices were supposed to
have done well after they left his training—
in fact there was a feeling in the minds of
the Clog Shop Club that the art of clog-
making depended for its maintenance, as far
as Lancashire was concerned, on the accom-
plished exponents of it who were turned
out from Beckside. Yet whilst they sat at
his bench, Jabe's " lads " were always " leather-

yeds," "numskulls," and the like. And the last one was always the worst.

But Billy seems to have been exceptionally " num," and was emphatically informed about a score times per day—

" Tha'll never mak' a clogger as lung as tha'rt wik."

One evening, owing to some mental abstraction on Jabe's part, the usual terms of raillery were wanting, and once or twice he spoke quite civilly to his apprentice.

This produced a marked effect on Billy, who grew quite light-hearted and had commenced to sing, when Sam Speck from the chimney corner recommended him to " goo i' th' next street." Nothing abashed, Billy continued his tune, and at last, forgetting altogether the presence of Sam in the corner, he turned round upon his bench under the back window, and called across the shop—

" Aw say, mestur, do yo' think Aw'st [I shall] ever be able to mak' a pair ? "

In an instant Jabe was himself again, and realising the danger of further neglect of duty, he replied—

" Thee mak' a pair ! Thee ! Why, tha conna mak' a wax end gradely yet. T'ony thing as ever tha'll be able to mak' 'ull be a-a-a-botch."

There was a great roar from the chimney corner.

"Good, Jabe ; good ! By gum, that's a good un," and Sam smacked his thigh in delight.

Billy flushed, and as he bent over his work a great tear splashed down into the sprig-box before him.

Now, " botch " was quite an unusual word in Beckside, but it sounded so expressive, and seemed so exactly to fit the case, that it was regarded as one of Jabe's greatest inspirations in nomenclature, and when Sam began to call the poor little apprentice Billy Botch, everybody else fell in with the habit, and Billy Botch he continued to be.

The lad was really troublesome. His over-anxious desire to please made him nervous, and he was constantly blundering, but he was so evidently proud of a place in the great cloggery, so humble and penitent when he had failed, and so anxious to make up for his deficiency by harder work, that although Jabe called him "num-yed" twenty times a day, and informed him that " all thy fingers is thoombs " about the same number of times, he hadn't the heart to turn him away.

Billy was worse than an orphan. He was the only child of the village sot. His mother was dead, and Billy and his father lived alone. The drunkard, once a respectable man, had starved and almost killed his wife, and since her death had alternately petted and abused his son. A soft-hearted, harmless man to everybody but his own. And Jabe stuck to Billy all the more on this account, especially after he discovered that neither abuse nor sympathy would induce the lad to say a word against his father.

Billy was rather a timid boy, but on two occasions he had come to his work with a bloody nose, the result of an attack upon some boyish slanderer of his parent, and once, indeed, a dark rumour spread through Beckside that Billy had lifted his hand to throw a clog sole at his master for a similar offence, but as no member of the Club knew anything about it, and the suggestion was so wildly improbable in itself, nobody ever seriously believed it.

One day Sam Speck had been chaffing Billy about his size.

" Mon," he said, leaning his back against the chimney breast, and stretching himself out upon the bench, " tha grows less. There'll be nowt left but thy clugs sumday."

Billy began a reply which threatened to end in a whimper, when Jabe gruffly ordered him to " pike off whoam, and see as tha cums i' time i' t' mornin'."

When he had gone, Jabe put out the brown snuffless candle which was his speciality in dips, drew up to the fire, and filled his pipe.

For a time there was silence, and then Sam, removing his pipe from his mouth, and nodding emphatically as he looked first at Jabe and then at Long Ben, as if to defy even their combined contradiction, said——

" It's trew !   Th' little chap *does* grow less."

" It's moar nor we can say for thy tongue," rejoined Jabe.

There was an inarticulate grunt of amusement from Long Ben far into the ingle-nook, and then a sudden straightening of his face into portentous seriousness and sudden conviction, and he leaned his long body forward and said——

" Aw'll tell thi wot it is, Jabe, that lad's clemm't."

A few days later Billy came to his work limping badly, and making strenuous efforts to conceal his condition.

" Wot's up wi' thi naa ? "

" Nowt."

" Nowt ! why, tha limps like a three-legged donkey.   Wot's to do wi' thi ? "

" Aw tumbled ont' fender and hurt mysel'."

" Cum here and let's look at it."

Slowly and very reluctantly Billy came towards the fire, and, holding up a skinny, blue-hued leg, exposed a frightful bruise.

" That's niver a faw ; that's a punce.   Whoa punced thi ? "

No reply.

" Whoa punced thi, Aw tell thi ? "

" No—noabry " (nobody).

Jabe jumped to his feet. " If tha tells me a lie Aw'll knock thi daan."

By this time Jabe was looking very terrible, and stood over Billy with an unfinished clog sole ready to strike.

" My fayther."

The Clogger's hand dropped to his side instantly, and flinging his weapon back upon the heap it belonged to, he sat down and began glowering into the fire.

That night there was a long confabulation in the ingle-nook, and all next day Sam Speck was running to and from the Clog Shop every few minutes with a look of dark mystery on his face.

In the evening, getting as far into the chimney as they could, and speaking under their breath, Jabe, Sam, and Long Ben had a secret consultation. At the usual time Billy, rising from his bench at the back window, pulling off his apron, and blowing out his candle, was making for home.

" Naa, wheer art goin' ? " demanded Jabe in his raspiest voice.

" Whoam, for sure," answered Billy in dull surprise.

" Theer's going to be a halteration between thee and me," and Jabe pursed out his lips,

knitted his shaggy brow, and jerked his short
leg across the other in a manner that brought
a dingy patch of colour to Billy's cheek.

" Why, wot have Aw dun ? " he was beginning, when Jabe broke in more sternly than
ever—

" Aw'm abaat tiret o' thy gallus ways, so
Aw'm goin' ta have thi livin' in."

" Livin' in ? " murmured Billy in perplexity.

" 'Avin' thy meit here and sleepin'," said Ben
from behind a cloud of tobacco smoke far into
the chimney.

A momentary flush of joy suffused Billy's
dirty cheek, and then it vanished, and in its
place came a hard, desperate expression.

" Aw conna live in; thank yo' kindly,
mestur."

" Tha means tha winna," snarled Jabe.

" He's none goin' ta knock it off thy wages,
tha knows," explained Ben, with a coaxing
cadence in his voice.

Billy only shook his head.

" Aw conna leave my fayther," he said at last.

" Thy fayther ! " cried Jabe, with a look of
infinite disgust.

" It's abaat toime tha did," chimed in Sam
from the other chimney corner. " He's left thi
fur wiks togather, and he's clemm't thi, and
he's threshed thi, and welly [nearly] broken thi
leg. A bonny fayther he is ! " he added
scornfully, after a moment's pause.

"But Aw conna leave him," said Billy, with a weary shake of his head.

"Then tha other leaves him or *me*," shouted Jabe, jumping to his feet and shaking his clenched and waxy fist at Billy.

After an awkward pause, Long Ben asked gently—

"Why conna tha leave thy fayther, lad?"

"Aw—Aw promised my muther Aw wouldn't, when hoo deed," and Billy burst into a great sob.

No more was said to Billy on the question of living in, but from that time things began to occur which prevented him from being spared about meal times, and accepting the evident intention of Jabe, he found himself provided with food at the shop, but at liberty to go home whenever he preferred.

Some time after this Billy was converted, and began to take an eager boyish interest in all chapel affairs. He grew fond of reading, was made school librarian, and revelled in the somewhat heavy literature of the vestry cupboards. Then he fell into the habit of "setting" the preachers home after evening service, and had not been entirely able to conceal from them his own aspirations.

One day a letter came to the Clog Shop which Billy read in a flutter of delight and dismay. It was a request from a sick local preacher that he would take the service at Beckside on the following Sunday night.

Billy was in a fever. He had several discourses prepared, and had frequently rehearsed them in the clough lanes, but now when the opportunity came his heart failed.

Besides, he had never dreamed of commencing at Beckside. How would Jabe take it? His contempt for young men's " forradness " was well known, and then his master and Long Ben were the stewards at the chapel, and there was no telling what view they might take of the case, especially as Billy had no proper authorisation.

All day on Friday and also on Saturday Billy was brooding over the coming ordeal, and watching for a favourable opportunity of telling the Clogger. But none occurred, and Billy went home on Saturday night with his fearful secret locked in his own breast.

Sleep was impossible, and when Sunday came he went to chapel with the fixed resolution of telling his master after the service. But the preacher was billeted with Jabe that day, and being an old friend would stay to tea. So Billy's last chance was gone.

As the stumpy fingers of the hair-of-the-head clock hanging in the chapel vestry drew near to six, there was anxiety in the minds of those who occupied the apartment. Long Ben was watching the clock and gently rocking his long body to and fro as a vent for his nervousness. Jabe strode from end to end of the vestry with his most pronounced unevenness of gait, and Jonas Tatlock the "leading singer" sat at the end of the table tapping impatiently on it with his finger ends, and glancing expectantly every now and again at the door.

"He doesn't use be'en this lat!" said Long Ben apologetically.

"He's ne'er bin nowt else sin' Aw knowed him," snapped Jabe, glad of an outlet for his growing wrath, "but we'st begin at toime, preicher or no preicher."

"Whoa'll begin?" asked Long Ben cautiously.

"Whoa? Why, thee."

"Me, Aw oppened aat t' last toime."

"Tha did nowt at sooart."

"Ya, bur 'ee did," Jonas broke in.

Jabe was just preparing a fearful blast for these contrary spirits when the door was opened, and Billy, as white as the vestry wall, stepped in.

"Wot's *tha* want?" cried Jabe at the intruder.

"Aw've come to tak' t' sarvice," stammered Billy.

There was a dead silence. Jabe stood glaring at his apprentice in speechless amazement. Jonas became deeply absorbed in his tune-book, and Long Ben fixed his eyes upon the ceiling as if he expected some explanation from it.

"Out of the mouths o' babes," he murmured

at last, drawing out the "babes" as long as possible in a sort of pathetic emphasis.

The fiery eye which Jabe had fixed on Billy was now turned upon Ben, who seemed under the glance to become lankier than ever.

After transfixing him for some time with a terrific glare, Jabe turned suddenly on his heel, snatched his hat from the peg against the wall, and exclaiming mockingly, "Then tha can coodle thy ba-abes," limped into the chapel with his short nose very high in the air.

In a few moments he was followed by Billy and the rest, and a buzz of suppressed astonishment arose as the young clogger walked into the pulpit.

Billy trembled until the pulpit wax candles shook in their sockets. Then in a husky, tremulous voice he gave out the hymn. The former part of the service was got through without anything that needs comment, except that Long Ben, who was not usually very demonstrative in his worship, kept up a constant fire of responses during the prayer. There had never, within living recollection, been any moment of stillness in that chapel so awful as that in which Billy prepared to announce his text.

"Prepare to meet thy God," read the preacher.

A long pause, in which Long Ben, sitting

near the vestry door, declared afterwards he heard every tick of the vestry clock.

" Prepare to meet thy God," repeated Billy.

The superintendent minister had a way of announcing his text twice before he began to preach, and so, detecting an ambitious imitation, Sam Speck gave a significant and resounding sniff from behind the choir curtain.

" Prepare to meet thy God," reiterated the preacher with a perceptible quaver in his voice.

Another painful pause and a silence that was deathly, broken at last by Jabe in the back pew throwing his expressive leg about, and kicking the pew front as he groaned audibly, and in a tone of insufferable disgust.

" Hay, dear ! "

The young women tittered, the boys in the gallery over Jabe's head suspended their preparations for fun, and were breathlessly attentive. All over the chapel there was a bending down of bonnets, and Jonas in the singing pew began to clear his throat to start a verse. Then Billy, gripping the sides of the pulpit to hold himself up, began—

" Christian brethren, along the path of life there are many strange meetings. . . ."

Having got started, the preacher divided his sermon into the orthodox three parts and an application. When he had been going several minutes he seemed to get the upper hand of his work.   There were a few people, at any-rate, who were all eye and ear.   The exhortation proved to be longer than the sermon, and when Billy sat down bathed in perspiration there was many a shining face and not a few glistening eyes in the little Beckside congregation.

On Sunday nights the Clog Shop Club sat in Jabe's parlour.   The day's sermons were, of course, the chief subjects of discussion, but the debate was conducted by a strict and well-understood method.

Supper of oatcake, cheese, and small beer or coffee having been partaken of, the critics drew round the fire.   It would have been nothing short of a misdemeanour for any one to have broached the sermon during supper,—only strangers ever attempted it,—and for any one to have led off the conversation without waiting for Jabe would have been simply rank treason.   When the pipes had been lighted, and no sound could be heard except the regular p't, p't of the smokers' lips as they poured forth expanding columns of smoke, Jabe would turn to Long Ben and commence the discussion with the invariable formula—

" Well, wot dost reacon off yon mon ? "

On the night of Billy's sermon, however, there was a hitch.

P't, p't, went the pipes—Jabe was a long time beginning.

P't, p't, p't, but he never spoke. Two or three of the cronies fidgeted in their chairs.

"Little David wi' a sling an' a stoan," said Long Ben at last, in a hesitant, musing way.

"Ay, an' plenty thick-yed Goliaths to throw 'em at," answered Jabe.

The chairs creaked loudly, and Jonas had a fit of coughing.

Another long silence. Jabe's rejoinder gave no clue whatever as to his mental whereabouts on the subject of the evening, and the first thing to do was to solve that problem. So Sam Speck presently tried the other side, but very cautiously—

"It tak's moar nor memory to mak' a preicher."

"That's why they wouldn't ha' thee, Aw reacon," said Jabe—in allusion to a long by-gone attempt of Sam's to get upon the Plan.

Sheepish grins flitted for a moment on two or three countenances, and Jonas' cough came on again, and after a time he said: "This 'bacca's mortal strung."

It was no use. The conversation would not flow—Jabe could not be drawn; and in spite of several attempts to start other topics, the conversation hung fire. The Club broke up earlier than usual therefore, and Jabe was left to himself. As he was filling his pipe with the nightcap charge, however, the parlour door opened an inch or two, and Long Ben, holding the door open without coming into sight, said with unnecessary loudness—

" Jabe ! "

" Well ? "

" Deal gently, for my sake, with the young man," and bang went the door, and Ben's long steps were heard retreating down the road.

The night following, however, the ice was broken, and after Sam had retailed all the gossip of Beckside relating to Billy's sermon, and Jabe had elicited from his cronies by such tortuous byways of conversation as were peculiar to them that they were pleased with the effort, Jabe dropped his mask, and whilst sternly repressing all extravagance of praise, he conceded in what was regarded as one of his few weak moments that " Th' lad met [might] mak' a hexhorter i' time."

But Billy improved rapidly, was made a local preacher, became in request, and was, withal, exceedingly studious and modest.

The " super " had been " planned " all day at Beckside one Sunday, and though not billeted with Jabe, he was known to have visited him and had a long conversation during the day.

The gathering in the parlour was therefore unusually large at night in expectation of news. Supper over and the pipes lighted, Jabe, leaning back in his chair until it stood on its back legs only, and looking hard at the brass candlesticks on the high mantelpiece, puffed out a volume of smoke and remarked in the most indifferent voice he could command—

" Th' ' super's ' wot Aw caw a far-seein' mon."

Six pipes were taken out of six mouths, and six pairs of inquiring eyes were turned on Jabe, but nobody spoke. Somewhat disconcerted at not receiving the spoken question, Jabe went on—

" A gradely commonsense chap."

Another long silence; and then Sam Speck, looking across at Jonas as if addressing him particularly, said—

" Queen Anne's deead."

Foiled again, Jabe went on another tack, and after a suitable pause remarked, with the same exaggerated assumption of indifference—

" Aar Billy's bin axed to preich t' charity sarmons at Clough End."

Now, most of those present were already in possession of this piece of information, and as every one felt that this was only preliminary skirmishing, which was being unnecessarily prolonged, they still maintained their taciturnity.

Jabe fidgeted in his chair, threw his short leg over one arm of it, then took it down again, and at last, turning to his nearest neighbour, who happened to be Long Ben, he said—

" Th' ' super ' wants aar Billy to cum aat."

" Aat into t' ministry, does tha mean ? "

" Ay ! "

There ; the cat was out of the bag now, and in a few minutes they were talking one against the other in a manner bewildering to any but a native Beckside.

Sam Speck had " expected nowt else sin' he preiched his fust sarmon."

Jonas told Jabe: " Tha'll see that lad Cheermon of a District afore tha dees."

Lige (Elijah), the road-mender, wanted to know " wot th' circuit ud think o' Beckside when it turn't aat a 'traveller,'" and Long Ben sat back in his chair with an exhausted pipe between his lips and beamed in silent satisfaction.

When the conversation was loudest, and two or three had risen to their feet to get a better hearing, the door opened and in walked Billy.

In a moment there was a great hush, and those who were standing slunk back into their chairs as if they had been suddenly detected in stealing.

Billy looked round with curiosity and surprise.

" What is the matter ? " he asked ; for he had been out preaching, and had not yet dropped back into his work-a-day vernacular.

Jabe was informed afterwards that it would have been more becoming if he had held his tongue on this occasion, a criticism which his own judgment endorsed, but he was excited, and so he blurted out—

"Th' 'super' says tha hes to goa aat."

The colour went from Billy's cheek. The hand which rested on Jonas' chair shook. A soft light came into his eyes, and he sank quickly into a seat. But nothing could be got out of him. As the others talked with a rude eloquence about his future, Billy looked steadily and abstractedly into the fire, a sadness settling on his face which cast its chill over all the company. When they were all gone except Ben, Jabe, who was evidently waiting, turned to his apprentice and demanded—

"Well; has tha nowt to say abaat it?"

"Mestur," was the reply in tones of anguish, "even if Aw wor fit Aw conna goa."

"Tha conna goa! Wot's to hinder thi?"

Billy was still gazing into the fire.

"Ay! why conna tha goa, lad?" added Ben.

"Aw conna tak' my fayther wi' me," was the slow reply in tones of deep dejection.

"Whoso loveth father or mother more than Me," cried Jabe, in evident pain and anger.

"If my fayther were a gradely mon," began Billy again, and then he bent his head down upon his knees and heaved a heavy, struggling sob, for he was relinquishing the one great dream of his life.

Billy's father, it should be said, had been converted under one of his son's sermons, and for more than a year had kept himself respectable. But a few weeks before the night we are speaking of he had broken out again, to Billy's great grief. Moreover, steady or otherwise, he was no longer able to sustain himself.

Next day Jabe was unusually quiet, and when Billy, who had been quite as dull as his master, was leaving for the night, Jabe called him back and said, in a voice subdued with unwonted emotion,—

" Howd on, lad, Aw want thee."

Rising from his bench, he went and locked the shop door, and then pulling Billy down upon a stool inside the ingle, he said in a choking voice—

"Will tha goa, lad, if Aw'll tak' cur on him ? "

They were only simple Lancashire men, those two; but they fell into each other's arms, and when they parted Jabe had arranged for " t'owd chap " to live with him, and Billy was pledged to offer himself as a candidate for the mission-field, for it was understood that his heart was set upon that kind of work.

Billy became a candidate for the Wesleyan ministry, was accepted, and, as there was great demand for men just then, was appointed immediately to the West Indies.

The day of the young missionary's departure from Beckside was one of the most memorable in the history of the village. The farewell really began the day before. Billy, having finished his packing and made his last calls, felt the time hang heavily on his hands, and so sat down at his old bench by the back window to make one last pair of clogs.

As he was getting towards the end of his work a great lunge came against the shop door. Jabe, who generally disdained to leave his bench for any such purpose, jumped up hastily and opened the door. As he did so a huge chest, apparently borne by invisible hands, but really held up from the outermost end by Long Ben, came sailing into the shop, and was suddenly dropped with a bang upon the floor opposite the fireplace.

Although only early autumn, a chip fire was burning, and Ben, after taking his breath, made a pretence of warming his hands as he said, looking up the shop towards Billy.

" Theer, Aw reacon that 'll be big enough for thee."

Now, as nearly all Billy's belongings had already been packed, this box seemed to the young missionary to be a kind of " day behind the fair " sort of thing, but he was soon undeceived, for before he could speak Sam Speck, who had been sitting in the nook

for some time with a mysterious and somewhat impatient air upon him, suddenly ducked
down, and dragging a carefully wrapped
parcel from under the stool he had been
sitting on, cried——

"Theer, if them b¹acks starts on thi, give
'em a taste of thooas," and loosing the string
he revealed a pair of silver-mounted pistols,
which even then were antique, but were
Sam's dearest bits of earthly property.

All this had evidently been arranged, for
whilst Sam was still speaking Aunt Judy
came in with her arms laden with home-
made hosiery of the very thickest Beckside
make: a number of pairs of stockings, a
"comforter" of bewildering length, a heap of
mittens of almost all colours and patterns,
and a long, red, knitted nightcap with a
big bobbing tassel at the top of it.

"Why, Judy," cried Sam, "India's a whot
country; he'll ne'er need them things."

"Good cloas keeps th' heat aat as well
as t' cowd," answered Judy, a little dashed
at this failure of her grand *coup*.

Then others came. Jonas brought a pedi-
gree fiddle, which had been his grandfather's,
and had made music at innumerable local
"sarmons" and tea-meetings.

Presently the box was full, and Ben began
to rearrange the articles for their long journey.

Jabe insisted on helping him, and the two

bent double over the side of the huge case, seemed to take most excessive pains to see that all was safe. And it was only when Billy stood in a West Indian mission-house, with the thermometer at over 90°, and held two greasy money-bags containing gold in his hands, that he understood the sweet kindness of this mysterious packing.

Next morning the Clog Shop was occupied very early by six solemn-looking men dressed in their Sunday best. An extra coach had been chartered to take them to Duxbury, whence the new railway was to carry Billy and his belongings to London.

Billy's father, in a state of nervous collapse, sat looking on at the preparations in a dazed manner. Jabe was scarcely less disturbed, though he attempted to get up a conversation on the state of the high roads they were going to travel on, just to conceal his own condition—a device that deceived nobody. Billy's successor was stationed in the road to give the signal when the coach and cart for the luggage hove in sight.

" It's cummin'," shouted the new apprentice at last.

" It's cummin'," passed from lip to lip, and then with a white face and lips all awork, Jabe limped to the door and locked it, and the company, without any prompting but instinct, fell to their knees. One after the other the

humble souls commended their " lad " to
" Him who holds the winds in His fists."
And then Billy prayed a broken, hesitant,
mixed sort of prayer, beginning with the
minister's English and ending in the Lancashire 'prentice boy's broad dialect, with a
great sob for the last " Amen."

" Tak' care o' my owd fayther, my dear,
dead muther's husband. Tak' care, O Lord,
o' my second fayther, and all my dear owd
frien's, and if we never meet again below,
may we all meet in he-e-e-ven and ' niver,
niver part again.' "

Then they dried their eyes and went to
the coach. All Beckside was ready by this
time, for Ned Royle had stopped the mill
for half an hour to give Billy a good send off.

Then all the Clog Shop cronies got inside
the coach as solemnly as if they had been
going to a funeral, and as a big cheer went
up from the crowd Billy bade farewell to
his native village.

It was a mournful company that gathered
round the Clog Shop fire that night. Everybody was dull and weary as well as sad.
Presently the shop-door opened, and a man
came in.

" Is them clogs dun?" asked the newcomer.

" Wot clogs?" said Jabe, in no mood for
mundane matters.

" Them as Billy said he'd finish fur me afore he went."

Jabe looked at the customer with a long, steady stare, during which it was evident something was passing in his mind. At last going to Billy's bench and picking up a pair of new clogs, he put them on the little counter. The man was picking them up, but Jabe snatched at them before him, and holding them at a safe distance from the customer, he asked—

" Is thoas 'em ? "

" Ay ! "

Then Jabe drew a long breath, and, surveying the would-be purchaser from head to foot, he said—

" An' has tha th' impidence to want t' last pair o' clogs as aar Billy iver made or iver will mak' ? "

The man was speechless with astonishment.

" Sithee," Jabe continued, " theer isna brass enoo i' all Lancashire, neaw, nor i' all England, to buy them clogs."

Next morning Long Ben had orders to make a little stand, and when it was finished the last specimens of Billy's handicraft were placed on the top of it.

And that is the story of Billy Botch.

"Hanging his Hat up"

" Hanging his Hat up "

THE doctor had given " Owd 'Siah " (Josiah) up, and humanity and ordinary neighbourliness, to say nothing of higher considerations, required a becoming manifestation of concern on the part of Becksiders. But it was uncommonly difficult to do—in fact, it required constant self-repression to conceal the presence of quite opposite feelings ; and when Sam Speck related to Jabe and Long Ben how that the doctor—a rather hot-headed young fellow—had stamped his foot and sworn because he had not been sent for sooner, declaring at the same time that nothing could save the patient now, the news was received with looks which came suspiciously near to malicious satisfaction.

This neglect to call in the doctor was so exactly characteristic of " Owd 'Siah " and his miserliness that its fatal termination was recognised as retributive, and everybody in Beckside believed in retribution.

Old Josiah had begun life as a farm-labourer. Then he got on to keeping a few cows. Then he had taken Gravel Hole farm, and one day he surprised everybody by buying—actually buying outright—a small milk-farm called the Fold, which stood on the opposite side of the road to the Clog Shop as you turned the corner to go down to the Beck.

But thrift had degenerated into penuriousness, and then into miserliness, and finally into every kind of meanness in 'Siah. He gave up his pew at the chapel, and sat on the free seats. He was only present on Sundays when there was no collection. A fourpenny bit was the highest contribution he had ever been known to give to any subscription, and when he withdrew from the Beckside string and reed band Sam Speck declared he " gien up fiddlin' to save th' expense o' rozzin." When his wife died, Aunt Judy declared that she had been " nattered to death wi' his cluseness." His two sons had both run away from home, and were dead, and his only daughter Nancy had left home and was a weaver at the mill.

When 'Siah died, though every tongue was still in the presence of death, and the women all sighed as they talked of it, from sheer force of habit, nobody pretended to any particular regret, and some, ignoring the immediate cause, expressed their satisfaction that Nancy would be " weel off naa."

When at the tea after the funeral old Jabe absent-mindedly started " Praise God, from whom," etc., instead of " Be present at," etc., nobody saw the grim humour, except perhaps the young doctor, who went out rather hastily with a very red face.

Nancy was just bordering on thirty, a rather tall, straight young person, whose homely, comfortable face was sharpened by a hard line or two about the mouth. Everybody had sided with her in her rebellion against her father, and everybody felt a sort of relief from moral responsibility when it became known that her father had not carried his resentment to his grave, but had left her sole legatee.

Before old Josiah had been long dead, people began to speculate about Nancy's future husband ; for though they had treated with mild surprise the fact that such a " likely wench " had not got married whilst she was a mere weaver, now she had become a freehold farmer single blessedness was not to be thought of. With " beeasts " to care for and a farm to manage, marriage was at once a necessity and a duty.

A few weeks after the funeral Aunt Judy was " takkin' a soop o' tay " with Nancy, but though full of the subject of the young woman's future, she feared to venture far until assured that it would be agreeable. She led several times, but Nancy somehow would not follow.

" Ay, well ! " she said with quite a demonstrative sigh, looking steadily into the fire, " life's full o' changes, wench. We doan't

knaw wot a daa nor an haar may bring forth,
as th' Beuk says."

" Neaw," said Nancy in a most provoking
non-committal tone.

" An' there'll be moar changes afoor t'year's
aat," hinted Judy with the smallest catch of
significance in her tone.

" Aw reacon ther' will," asserted Nancy, but
she went no farther.

" Well ! Aw mun goa, wench," said Judy,
rising from her seat. " Tha mun keep thy
'art up, tha knows. Ay, dear," she continued,
fixing her eye on the wooden partition near the
door she was approaching, and looking directly
at something she saw there, " Aw see thy
fayther's owd hat's hanging on t'peg here yet,"
and then, with a significant sidelong glance at
Nancy, " Aw expect there'll be a young felley's
billycock hanging up theer afoor we're mitch
owder. But mind wot th' art doin', wench.
Aw expect tha'll no spend thy haupenny at
fust staw'."

" Neaw, neaw, Aunt Judy. The mon as
hangs his hat up o' that peg 'ull ha' ta *be* a
mon, Aw con tell yo'." And Nancy smiled a
quiet, humouring smile as she opened the door
for Judy, as if hastening her departure.

After Judy had gone the quiet smile still
lingered on Nancy's face, and she sat down
before the fire, and was soon in a brown study.

Very soon all kinds of rumours flew about

Beckside anent Nancy's matrimonial prospects, and as there was a rather large proportion of eligible bachelors and widowers, the supposed competitors for her hand were many.

Now it was Luke Knowles who was the happy man. He was " rather owd," but, as a substantial yeoman, was in every way suitable; and then it was Billy Bumby, the coal-dealer, who was the only man in Beckside who had shares in a bank. But as Billy kept flying pigeons (that is, homers), it was a moot point whether Nancy wouldn't be rather bemeaning herself; for though Billy was very well off, to keep pigeons was to be a publican and a sinner.

Then it was confidently stated that the young doctor was " after " Nancy, and a day or two later the doctor was supplanted by " the mestur's " son from the mill.

Now, as old Jabe was a confirmed bachelor, and at all times cynical and abusive on the subject of women; as Sam Speck (who was in matters of opinion a mere echo of Jabe) was a widower, whose marital experiences were supposed to have given him ample grounds for sympathising with Jabe's extreme views; and as Long Ben was known to everybody as a woeful example of the henpecked husband, it will be supposed that the Clog Shop Club took little or no interest in Nancy's prospects.

And perhaps under ordinary circumstances it would not have done. But, then, Nancy's farm stood nearly opposite the Clog Shop door, and the front of the house, as well as one end, and the road leading down the Fold to the farm premises were right before you, a little to the right as you looked through the Clog Shop window, and could even be easily seen as you sat by the shop fire.

Besides, Nancy had long been a member of Jabe's class, and was the leading "seconds" singer in the chapel choir, which, of course, laid some responsibility on our friends as to her future happiness.

Whatever the reason, Nancy's prospects were a matter of curious interest at the cloggery. Never a trap turned the corner into "the Fowt"; never a creak was heard at Nancy's garden gate; never a bang of her front door, but the old Clogger lifted his bald, grey-fringed head over the low board that separated the window bottom from the shop, and Sam Speck stepped nimbly to the window end nearest the counter to look.

Sam, as a sort of henchman to Jabe, always spent a considerable amount of time at the Clog Shop, but about the period of which I write he seemed to be constantly there. He also took to slipping on his "Saturday afternoon" coat on ordinary days, and greatly scandalised his sister by putting on "shoon" which were always supposed to be especially reserved for Sundays and festivals.

Sam was a short, small-made, but very "natty" man, and always neat in his appearance. Just at this time, however, he became quite vain, but was so busy gathering and discussing the village gossip about Nancy and her future, and so animated, not to say excited, in his discussion of it, that the change in his get-up passed unnoticed by his chums.

Early one afternoon, when Jabe had just finished his after-dinner pipe and resumed his work, Sam sat on the end of the long stool that jutted out from the ingle-nook, lost in profound meditation.

Presently he began to hug his knees with his hands, leaning back as he did so, and looking at Jabe as if he were making some intricate calculation of which Jabe was the subject. At length he said—

" Hoo's mooar nor an ordinary wench, hoo is."

"Who art talkin' abaat?" asked Jabe gruffly.

" Aw'm talkin' abaat 'Siah's Nancy, an' wot Aw say is as hoo's mooar nor a common woman."

This was said with such unnecessary warmth that Jabe took a sort of hesitant glance at Sam as he asked—

" Whoa said hoo worn't ? "

" Th' felley as hes her 'ull have a fortin *in* his wife as well as *wi'* her," continued Sam meditatively and ignoring Jabe's question.

" Tak' her thysel', then," was the rejoinder.

" Well," he replied, hesitating as if he knew he was giving himself away, but didn't see how to avoid it, " Aw met dew wor."

" Wot ! " shouted the Clogger, enlightened at last, and rising to his feet in his indignation and scorn. " Th'art theer are ta ? thaa yorney ! " " At thy age tew," he continued after a pause.

" Aw'm nooan sa owd," snapped the would-be bridegroom, suddenly sensitive on the point of age. " Aw'm twenty year younger nor thee."

" Ay, an' a hundred year i' sense Aw wop [hope], thaa meytherin' owd maddlin' thaa."

Finding no sympathy or even encouragement to talk, Sam left in a huff, and for the rest of the week the Clog Shop saw him not.

On Monday, however, he was back in his place, and confided to Jabe and " Owd Lige " over the fire that " Marriage wor a big risk efter aw. Them's t'best off as hes nowt to do wi' it."

This and his resumption of clogs and ordinary wearing apparel created the suspicion that Sam had " axed " Nancy and had been refused, which was confirmed by Aunt Judy, who was supposed to be in Nancy's confidence, and who reported that Sam had been in Nancy's on Sunday afternoon and had " cum away wi' a flea in his ear."

A few days after Sam's discomfiture, and

whilst he still wore a pensive and chastened air, Job Sharples sidled into the Clog Shop. Job was a sharp-nosed man with a hard little mouth and red eyes that were suggestive of chronic catarrh. He had a clean-shaven face, was quite fifty years of age, and was a pork-butcher and cattle-jobber by trade. He took snuff, and had a hesitating manner, which was supposed to conceal a dogged, tenacious will.

He stood for a few moments before the short counter pretending to take a survey of the contents of the window bottom, but in reality he was counting Nancy's cows as they were being driven into the Fold to milk. Presently he remarked—

"Them clugs Aw had t'other day has split, Jabe."

"T'other day," cried Jabe, always on the alert where Job was concerned, and never greatly in love with him; "it's six munths sin tha had 'em if it's a day."

"Eh, is it so lung?" replied the visitor, whose cue it was to conciliate rather than pro-voke. "Haa tolme flies!" "But," he added, unable entirely to repress his natural weakness, "nowt lasses [lasts] naa as it used do."

Saying this he sauntered to the fireplace, and was soon comfortably seated on one of the stools. Then he began to balance the poker on one of his fingers, whilst Jabe, with a darkening countenance, became suddenly very violent amongst his tools, banging them about and making a most unnecessary clatter.

Job waited a moment or two, took another pinch, and then, setting the poker carefully into one corner as he spoke, said—

" Aw reacon tha knows Aw've bowt Sally's haases."

" Ay ! " answered Jabe shortly, and in a tone of strong reluctance, as though he were acknowledging something to which he objected, but which he could not help.

Job took up a handful of chips from the corner, sprinkled them slowly on the fire, dusted his hands one against the other, and then proceeded in a conciliatory tone of voice—

" Aw'm nooan so badly off, tha knows, Jabe, for a Becksider."

Now the pig-dealer was noted for a constant cry of poverty, and Jabe was therefore uncertain whether to take this unwonted admission as a mark of special confidence or as an introduction to something yet to come, so he was silent.

Job blew his nose, scraped together the chips scattered on the hearthstone with his feet, walked to the end of the counter nearest the window, and took another long look at Nancy's house and yard.

Walking back to the fire, but sitting down on the stool nearest to Jabe, he leaned forward and said in a low coaxing tone—

"Dost think Owd 'Siah's property had owt on it?"

And Jabe laid up mental lacerations for himself by answering—

"Aw knaw nowt abaat it."

"Le'ss see. They'n five caas, an' a bullock ha' na they?" And the clogger suffered further inward humiliation as he replied—

"Aw tell thi Aw knaw nowt abaat it."

"Naa, Jabe, nooan o' thy fawseniss."

But Jabe had perjured himself sufficiently, and commenced hammering an obstreperous clog top as though he would knock a hole through it.

Job had recourse to the snuff-box again, and turning to the fire sat looking into it and ruminating deeply. Then he got up once more, stepped behind the counter and over to the clog-cutting bench, which stood against the wall at Jabe's right hand. Sitting down uneasily on this he said in a loud whisper—

"Jabe, owd lad, Aw'm goin' to put up for Nancy."

Jabe looked dangerously like hitting Job's bullet head with his hammer, but he checked himself, and was about to speak, when a new idea seemed to strike him, and after clearing his throat he said, with a very poor attempt at a smile—

"Tha'll ha' ta be sharp abaat it."

That was enough; and whilst the Clogger

was struggling with the fear that he had added fresh sin to his soul, Job was pressing him with eager questions—

" Wot dost meean by that ? Whoa's t'others ? Am Aw i' time, dost think ? "

" Th'art i' time if tha goas naa," was the answer.

Job started to his feet to go. At the door, however, he hesitated, took another long look at the Fold through the window, playing nervously the while with the latch. At last he said—

" Hoo's a soft-spokken soart o' wench, isn't hoo, Jabe ? "

" Soa, soa," was the reply.

The pig-dealer slowly opened the door and stepped into the road. In a moment he was back, however—

" 'Siah left it aw to her, didn't he, Jabe ? "

" Whoa else could he leave it tew ? "

Away went Job, sidling past the window, and going a few steps up the road before he crossed it, so as not to appear to be going direct ; whilst Jabe, dropping his hammer, rose to his feet and stood back a little, so that he might see his visitor go into Nancy's without being seen himself.

Just as Job reached the garden gate Sam Speck stepped into the Clog Shop.

" Hay ! " cried Jabe in a stage whisper, " cum here ; sithee ! sithee ! " and pointing through the window at Job fumbling with a refractory gate latch, he drew Sam behind the counter and into the shade where he could see without being seen.

By this time the pig-dealer had reached Nancy's door, and when he was admitted Jabe began to hop on his unequal legs about the shop, crying—

" Aw wodn't ha' missed this ; Aw wodn't ha' missed this for aw t' brass owd 'Siah ever had."

Sam seemed to enjoy the situation quite as much as Jabe, though probably for a different reason, and when in a few minutes they saw Job emerge from Nancy's door and stalk down the short garden path, looking so abstractedly before him that he nearly fell over the gate, and then from their vantage point, standing back, saw Nancy's comely face, all beaming with fun, peep out from behind the curtain at the retreating form of her would-be husband, the two sat down and guffawed and grinned with unalloyed satisfaction—Jabe taking off his apron and adjourning to the chimney corner to discuss the matter in all its details.

Something strange must have been in the air that day, for, drawn by some occult influence, first one and then another of the Clog Shop cronies dropped in until the ring round the fire was complete, and the host had to tell his tale over again each time a newcomer arrived.

Job being heartily disliked by nearly all Becksiders, his discomfiture was the tit-bit of every feast of gossip for some time, and, in fact, it was only forgotten when another piece of news had put it out of people's heads.

Soon after the event just recorded, there sprang up in the village a rumour that Nancy was going to be married. Nobody seemed to know how it had originated, but Jimmy Juddy (Jimmy, son of George), who was only an occasional occupant of the ingle-nook stools, happened to be there when Sam Speck brought the news to the Clog Shop, and he immediately adduced confirmatory evidence in the fact that he had just come from the Fold, and had received orders to " fettle th' place up inside and aat, upstirs an' daan."

But who was the happy man? And here rumour was absolutely silent. That there was to be a wedding was now certain, for Aunt Judy had taxed Nancy with it, and she had not denied it, but all attempts to get at the name of the bridegroom had utterly failed.

Once, indeed, when Aunt Judy and Sally Walters had cornered Nancy, and there did not seem any possible escape for her, she evaded it by saying, as Judy reported, that " Hoo worn't gradely sure ; hoo hadn't axed him yet," but as this was clearly a joke nobody paid much heed to it.

Sam Speck declared himself out of all

patience with Jimmy Juddy, because night after night during his labours at Nancy's, where he must perforce be in constant contact with that lady, he assured the members of the club that he'd " nayther seen nowt nor yerd nowt."

This was all the more remarkable because, though the men spoke of Jimmy as soft-hearted, he was known to be a great favourite with women : his quiet, almost womanly, ways procuring for him a great share of the feminine confidences of the locality.   Jabe and the rest, though not so severe on Jimmy as Sam, yet were fain to confess that he certainly hadn't made the most of his opportunities.

But it was like Jimmy. He was too mild for anything, and whilst all gave him more than the average share of personal affection most were ready to subscribe to Jabe's oft-repeated declaration that " He'd a getten on better i' life if he'd had a bit mooar spunk in him." Jimmy was a social failure ; beginning life with something more than average oppor-tunities he had made nothing at all out. A middle-sized, mild-mannered fellow, with an arm partly disabled by rheumatism, he was already going down the hill of life, in spite of hard work and a great personal popularity.

He began life as the bookkeeper at the mill, which gave him a status amongst the better end of the Beckside population, especially as he would do their private bookkeeping for them. At that time he was considered to have excellent prospects, and no one was surprised when a boy-and-girl courtship sprang up between him and 'Siah's Nancy.

But one day Jimmy was dismissed without notice, and no explanation of the matter was forthcoming, either from the masters or from the bookkeeper himself, but it was said that old 'Siah had put his foot down concerning Nancy and Jimmy, and I am now revealing for the first time a secret when I state that Jimmy in a painful interview would give no explanation to Nancy, and so there was an end, too, of that.

All this was years ago, and since then much had happened. Jimmy was considered to have wiped out his disgrace by rescuing a little piecer from the top room of the mill during a fire at the risk of his own life. On this occasion the excitement of his effort, and the drenching he got with the water used for extinguishing the flames, threw him into bed with rheumatic fever, and permanently injured his health, unfitting him for hard work.

Then the smallpox came, and Jimmy, who had become a sort of handy man—white-washer, jobbing painter, and even chimney-sweep for those sufficiently well off to afford the luxury—served as Long Ben's assistant in coffin-making and undertaking until he went down himself with the plague, and barely escaped with life. Altogether, Jimmy's had been a sad career; but he was a cheerful, willing, kindly fellow, and in a quiet way a general favourite, whilst his old mother and paralysed sister simply worshipped him.

Jimmy was busy cleaning, whitewashing, and painting Nancy's premises for several days, and at last worked his way down into the front kitchen, which for general convenience had been left to the last. The kitchen had formerly been larger, but it was now divided into two, the end nearest the Clog Shop being partitioned off to make a small "best parlour." Attached to the partition was a thick peg, ornamented at the front with a short cow's horn.

"Mun Aw tak' this peg daan?" asked the painter as he prepared to paint the partition.

"Neaw, tha munnot. Th' mon as is comin' here 'ull want ta hang his hat theer," replied Nancy.

Now, Jimmy had been several times on the point of sounding Nancy on the mystery of her approaching marriage, and here was a direct challenge. But after stealing a long sidelook at her, and forming his lips two or three times as if to speak, he lapsed into silence and went quietly on with his work.

During his labour at the Fold he had not

seen much of the proprietor, but now as he was in the general living place they seemed constantly together, and anybody but Jimmy would have noticed that though she bustled about a great deal Nancy was really doing next to nothing, and was constantly hovering about him in a quite suggestive way. Once or twice, indeed, in explaining her wishes, she had come very close to him, and had brushed his whitewash-spotted cheek with her frizzy brown hair.

But Jimmy was used to women, and his mind was rather preoccupied by a little domestic anxiety of his own, and so he thought nothing about it.

A stranger listening to their fragments of conversation would have thought that Nancy was trying to draw Jimmy, but the poor fellow saw nothing, and the questions he had previously asked were intended more to furnish information for the Clog Shop inquisitors than to gratify his own curiosity, though that was not quite dormant.

It drew near to tea time, and Nancy became really busy; in fact, Jimmy could not help noticing that her preparations were much too extensive for a party of one. She had brought in a great piece of cheese, toasted several slices of bread, reached down a plateful of oatcake from the rack over her head, and was searching the depths of a cupboard for what turned out to be a large pot of blackberry jam, when the painter began wiping his brushes on the edge of his paint can, saying as he did so——

"Aw'll goa to my baggin [tea], an' cum agean i' t' morn."

"Tha'll do nowt o' t' soart; corn't tha see Aw'm makkin' sum tay, tha'll ha' ta finish ta-neet. Dost think Aw want thi here till Chresmass ? "

Jimmy looked surprised, but the women were all kind to him, so he resigned himself to the inevitable.

When they had " said a blessin'," and Jimmy was pouring his tea out of his cup into his saucer, as was the correct thing at Beckside, he nearly upset it upon his paint-stained trousers as Nancy abruptly commenced——

"Tha hasn't axed me whoa Aw'm goin' t' have ? "

The painter smiled sheepishly, and answered, " Neaw."

Somehow the pause that followed felt rather awkward, and it struck Jimmy that his silence might be taken for lack of interest, so he ventured——

"Noabry [nobody] seems to know whoa it is."

"Let 'em find it aat then," was the reply, and Nancy's eyes began to dance with fun.

Jimmy was stuck again, but as Nancy

seemed to be expecting him to go on, he said—

"He's not a stranger, is he?"

"Neaw, he'er [he was] born i' th' clough."

"But not a Becksider?"

"Ya,—a Becksider," and Nancy laughed out.

"Has ta known him lung?"

"Ya, aw my life."

Jimmy felt uneasy, and would gladly have stopped—he scarce knew why; but Nancy was so evidently pleased to be questioned, and so openly invited him by her manner to go on, that there was no help for it. So he resumed—

"Do Aw knaw him?"

This question really did seem to disturb Nancy, for a crumb went down the wrong throat as she swallowed her tea and led to a violent fit of coughing, and the painter felt absolutely compelled to get up and slap her between her shapely shoulders to help her.

When she had recovered and heaped Jimmy's plate with muffins again, she came back to the interrupted conversation with—

"Well, Aw doan't think tha does knaw him gradely; at ony rate, tha doesn't think mitch abaat him."

Jimmy was simply bewildered. It wasn't like Nancy to have anything to do with a doubtful character, so at last he said—

"Well, Aw wop he's a gradely mon."

"Gradely!" and her flashing eyes suddenly softened into a strange tenderness. "He *is* that. He's a hero!"

"Th' woman's i' luv wi' him at ony rate," thought the painter. But Nancy hadn't done.

"He's wun o' them scarce chaps as conna get on for helpin' other folk ta get on." And there was a curious break in her voice, and she got up to seek something on the high mantelpiece which she never found.

"A-y," said Jimmy, with slow incredulity, and he began to run his mind over all the eligible Beckside males who could be said in any sense to be heroic.

"A hero, tha says?" he queried.

"Ay, as owt to 'a hed t' Royal Society's medal mooar nor wunce to my knowledge. He's no mitch to look at, and he's welly [nearly] lame wi' th' rheumatiz ; Aw—aw "— and there were tears in Nancy's voice—" Aw'd rayther have him nor t' Prince o' Wales."

Jimmy was sitting straight up in his chair, and looking at her as if he had fears for her reason. He had heard many women's confidences before now, but this—. But Nancy was speaking again.

"He's clemm't hissel' for mony a year for th' sake of an owd craytur and her badly dowter at th' Beck Bottom yond."

But Jimmy had jumped to his feet, his mouth wide open, and his face bathed in sudden perspiration, whilst the smothered, buried but ever living, love of a lifetime came welling up in his heart.

"Nancy! Nancy! tha doesn't mean me?"

And there the two stood: Nancy with blushing, tearful face buried in her hands; and Jimmy looking about him as if he were expecting an earthquake.

Then he took a step or two back, and shaking his head with solemn earnestness, said—

"Neaw, neaw, Nancy! Aw'm fain to see th'art same as tha allis were; but it munno be, it munno be?"

"Why munno it be?" she said, lifting her head out of her hands with a look of sudden fear and anger.

"Tha'rt young and bonny, an' weel off, and Aw'm poor, and my arm's welly stiff wi' rheumatism, an' Aw's soon be dun for."

"If tha talks like that abaat bein' dun for, Aw'll—Aw'll smack thi i' th' faace," and Nancy really looked like doing it.

"Then theer's my owd muther, and aar Alice, an'—"

"Well, Aw want them mooar nor Aw want thee," and Nancy looked quite triumphant at her own double-barreled retort. There was silence, during which Jimmy stepped slowly backwards.

" Tha knows, Nancy, if theer wor nowt else, theer wor that other thing tha knows on."

" Wot thing ? "

" It's past twelve ye'r sin', as tha tow'd me when Aw geet sacked [discharged], niver to think o' thee till Aw'd cleared mysel'; an' Aw niver have, tha knows."

" Cleared thysel' ! Cleared thysel' ! " and Nancy flew across the floor and seized him by the shoulder as she cried : " Jimmy, *tha* knows ; an' Watty knows ; an' when he left for Australia a fortnit sin', he told me in this varry kitchen as tha's carried his shawm [shame] for twelve ye'r ta save him fro' jail, and his wife and childer fro' th' bastile [workhouse].   Aw've never thowt o' noabry else, an' when Aw yerd that Aw said Aw'd mak' thi ha' me.   An' Aw will !   Aw will ! "

And the push she gave him by way of emphasis sent him spinning against the cupboard door.

What they said and did after that is nothing to you and me, gentle reader, but they talked a long time, a great happiness filling poor Jimmy's heart, such as he had never felt before.

When he rose to go, for there was no chance of being able to finish that night, Nancy called him back.

" Jimmy," she said.

" Wot ? "

" Tha's never kissed me yet."

Kissing was reserved for children at Beckside, and was, at the best of times, a very rare thing, but Jimmy made up for twelve years of enforced and bitter abstinence before he let his sweetheart go.

Once more Jimmy began to collect his paint cans to depart.

" Jimmy."

" Wot ? "

" Is that t' hat tha allis wears ?'

" Ay."

" Hang it up o' that peg then.

Giving a Man Away

Giving a Man Away

WHEN Jimmy Juddy left his sweetheart on the night of their engagement, he walked like a man in a dream. He crossed the road into Mill Lane, which ran parallel with the Clog Shop, and led down to the mill, and thence on to Beck Bottom, where it joined the road to Clough End. Jimmy passed the mill without noticing it, and never heard the two or three "How do's" that were addressed to him by passers-by. His head was bent, and he was muttering to himself.

Presently he entered the field beyond the mill, and approached a clump of young trees in a corner at the side of the lane. Here he dropped upon his knees under the shadow of the trees, crying as he did so—

"*Tha's* done it, Lord, it's noabry but Thee —but it's like Thee. Ay! it's like Thee. Aw've waited twelve ye'r an' Aw gav' up hope lung sin, but Aw see naa 'at it *is* good boath to hope and to wait for the salvation of the Lord."

Jimmy spent several minutes on this broken

ejaculatory prayer, and then quietly picking up his cans and brushes he made for home.

As he approached, new thoughts forced themselves upon him. What would his mother and sister think of these things? Since his disappointment of twelve years ago, he had given up all thought of marriage, and latterly he had come to regard his duty to his woman-kind as precluding it.

The state of his mind was very clearly understood by both mother and daughter, and in their womanly inconsistency they began to evince a most anxious desire that he should take to himself a wife. But Jimmy was not deceived. He knew that the certainty they felt of his remaining a bachelor encouraged them in their banterings.

But his heart told him this was only one of the little self-deceptions which do so much to sweeten life. He knew that the reality would be terrible.

Moreover, though old Matty his mother was really healthier than either he or his sister, they had persuaded themselves that her heart was weak, and they had become fertile in inventing devices to prevent her ever being suddenly startled.

This was an occasion, however, which taxed Jimmy's love-quick inventiveness to its utmost. He knew how difficult it was to conceal any-thing from them. One or other would find him out in no time, and they both boasted they could read him "like a book." It was no use, therefore, to attempt concealment; only he must break the news gently, for the old woman's sake.

By this time he had reached their cottage, a little low house standing between the mill lane and the Beck, and having a garden in front that ran to a point at the bridge where the road crossed the Beck.

Hastily putting away his cans and brushes in the little workshop behind the house, and washing himself, he hurried in, and in his eagerness to get a lead in the conversation lest he should be cornered, commenced at once—

"Well, Aw hav'n't finished after aw, but "— and then he broke off.

"Hay, muther, yo' do look bonny. Yo' getten younger. If Aw wor a bit younger, Aw'd start o' courtin' yo'."

"Bless thee, lad! tha's ne'er done nowt else sin' Aw know'd thee," was the reply. But this turn to tenderness did not suit Jimmy's purpose at all, so he sat down to his porridge, preparing to talk.

"Hoo's spending a lot o' brass o' yon haase," he remarked.

" Hast yerd yet whoa hoo's goin' to have ? " asked Alice, who sat with her crutch by her side on the opposite side of the table.

Jimmy's heart gave a great leap.

"Have?" he cried, "hoo's having sumbry, that's sartin; everybody's gettin' married na'adays. Aw'st be goin' off mysel' some fine mornin'."

Jimmy had made so many threats of this kind to amuse his mother that both women smiled with a sweet sense that their mirth was safe, and Alice was encouraged to pursue the subject by receiving a gentle kick on her crutch from Jimmy's foot under the table. So she said in gentle raillery—

"Well, dunna brag sa mitch; its leap ye'r, tha knows."

"By th' mon it is!" exclaimed Jimmy, "Aw ne'er thowt o' that. Aw'st ha' to look aat, Aw con see. Some on 'em 'll happen ax me."

But the effort to keep excitement out of his speech was a little overdone, and Alice shot at him a glance of quick inquiry, but his mother, noticing nothing, answered—

"Well, theer's plenty on 'em 'ud do that if they thowt ther' wor ony chance for 'em," and the old woman's face beamed with quiet pride in her son's popularity as she continued, "But theer's nooan on 'em good enough for aar Jimmy."

"Naa, mother, yo'll mak' him mooar consated nor he is," broke in Alice, "but if ony on 'em axed him he couldn't say neaw, especially if hoo wor owd or i' trouble."

Jimmy bent his head over his porridge,

and gave another kick under the table as he answered, in a shamed sort of way—

" Well, they'an axed me."

" Wot! Whoa ? " cried both women at once.

Jimmy took a long, careful look at his mother and shook his head with a smile as he answered—

" Ay; yo'd like to know, wodn't yo' ? "

" Whoa is it ?   Hoo's an impident jade whoever hoo is," cried Alice with sudden misgiving, which brought fear into her face. But Jimmy was watching his mother.

" Howd thy bother, Jimmy," she said, with a quiet smile, " th' art nobbut gammin'."

And Jimmy felt like dropping through the floor as, watching old Matty's face very narrowly, he answered, with an assumption of nonchalance which was ridiculously overdone—

" It's reet.   Aw've been axed this varry day."

There was a dead silence.   Both women turned pale ; the older one gripped the arms of her chair, and Alice stood up and leaned on her crutch.

At last the mother said, almost under her breath, " Whoa is it, lad ? "

But Jimmy was alarmed.   There was no reason that he could see why his words should have produced so sudden a change. So he got up and fussily rearranged his mother's chair cushions as he answered, in a tone of gaiety—

" Nay; yo' mun guess."

Neither woman had any heart to do this, for

though Jimmy's words were innocent enough, his manner justified the gravest conclusions. To gratify him they began to select. They guessed all the marriageable women they could think of, eligible or ineligible, but chiefly the latter.

" Neaw ! neaw ! " Jimmy cried, with growing excitement at each guess.

" Well, whoa con it be ? " cried Alice, in perplexity, the pain at her heart making her doubly impatient ; " Wheer has ta bin to-day ? "

" Aw've bin noawheer but th' Fowt."

A pale, sickly light shot across old Matty's face as she asked—

" It's not Beck—Becky o' Tom's, is it ? "

Becky was the handsome, strapping, but somewhat aggressive, maidservant at the Fold farm.

" Becky ? Neaw," and Jimmy laughed and danced on the sanded floor with gleeful anticipation of the next question, crying as he did so, " Yo're warm, muther ; yo're warm."

" Jimmy ! " cried Alice, " it's no "—but she stopped, and took a long look at her brother's face, and then she turned and hugged her mother and burst out in a great sob of relief as she cried—

" It *is*, mother ! it is ! it's Nancy."

Both these women knew of Jimmy's old-time attachment to Nancy, and the look on his quiet face spoke so eloquently of the love that had never been really dead, that they both felt glad for his sake, but with a wistful, dumb sort of gladness.

They sat on each side of the fire, and made the painter sit down on his favourite low stool between them and tell them all about it.

As Jimmy talked with glowing face and brightening eyes, they laughed, rather loud laughs for them, laughs which had odd catches in them, and which once or twice nearly ended in sobs. Whilst Jimmy was looking up into either of their faces they smiled with hard-forced but very passable smiles, but if he turned to speak more particularly to one, the one not addressed turned her face hastily and brushed away a tear.

Jimmy talked much about the goodness of God, and God moving in mysterious ways, and they answered " Ay, lad ! " And then he talked about it always being darkest before daylight, and they smiled and nodded and said " Ay " again, but it almost choked them, for a future without Jimmy would be perpetual midnight at Beck Bottom.

The painter was so radiant, so eloquent on the subject of Nancy, and so constantly blending all his utterances with ejaculations of praise to God, that the women seemed for a time to catch his spirit, and drank Nancy's health with quite a respectable show of gladness in warm, home - made elderberry wine, which smelt strongly of cloves.

But somehow old Matty tired sooner than usual that night, and after conducting family prayers herself, she rose to retire.

" Well, good neet, lad !   Hay ! who'd a thowt o' this when tha went aat this morning ?   But we doan't know what a day nor an haar may bring forth.   Good neet, an' God bless thee."

When she had reached the top of the stairs, however, Jimmy called to her, and as she stood with one hand on the bedroom door-latch whilst she held a candle in the other, he told her about Nancy saying she wanted mother and daughter more than she wanted the son, and as Jimmy laughed old Matty laughed,— quite a demonstrative attempt for so quiet a person,—but when her bedroom door had been closed behind her the wreathed smile disappeared, darkness and tears came into those old eyes, and the face became white and woeful as she dropped heavily on her knees, crying under her breath as she did so—

"Aw connot do it, Lord ; Aw connot do it. Lord, help me."   And then, after a long pause, " Thy will—Aw dunnut *mean* it, but Aw'll say it till Aw *con* mean it—Thy will be done."

.   .   .   .   .

Beckside was amazed when the name of Nancy's bridegroom became known, as it did next day, and for a time the verdict seemed doubtful.

The surprise was so complete as to be

aggressive and awaken resentment. And then everybody felt that it was so natural a thing to have come about that their never having thought of it was a reflection on their intelligence. But this was only momentary; very quickly the current set steadily in favour of the arrangement, and in twenty-four hours Jimmy and his bride were more popular than they had ever been in their lives.

The Clog Shop cronies gave Jimmy "a wiggin'" for what they called his "fawseniss," and would perhaps have kept up a show of disapproval but that a better occupation was found for them.

On the second day after the engagement, Jabe, happening to look up from his work at the click of Nancy's garden gate, saw that young lady and Aunt Judy, with shawls over their heads, making for the Clog Shop with "serious business" writ large on their faces.

"Jabez," began Judy, as soon as they were inside, assuming an attitude of uncompromising non-surrender, and giving her brother his full name, as she always did when very much in earnest, "Aw want to knaw wheer this poor wench is for t' be married?"

This was said with slow and weighty deliberation, and Jabe, lifting his head, asked—

"Wheer?"

"Ay, wheer? Hoo wor chesened at th' chapel, and hoo's bin browt up at th' chapel, an' hoo wor born agean at th' chapel, an' aw her fowks is buried i' th' chapel yard, an' Aw reacon hoo'll ha' ta goa to a church two mile away wheer hoo's ne'er bin in her life to be married."

" An' sarve her reet if hoo's soft enough ta get married," said Jabe; but though the words were rough the sound was not very dreadful.

" Wot Aw want for t' know is why hoo conna be married at th' chapel ? " demanded Judy.

" 'Cause hoo conna."

" Why, Jabe ? " chimed in Nancy.

" 'Cause it's no licensed."

" An' why isn't it licensed ? Wot's trustees doin' not ta hav' it licensed all these years ? " asked Judy.

" 'Cause it'll cost ta mitch."

" Haa mitch will it cost ? " asked Nancy again.

But something had just entered Jabe's head. He sat straight up on his stool and looked directly through the window as if he were thinking rapidly. Presently he answered, looking hard and musingly now at Nancy—

" Bless thee, wench, Aw dunnut knaw. But," and here he leaped to his feet and smote his hard fist on the counter, as he cried : " Aw'll tell thee wot. Tha *shall* be wed at th' chapel, if th' licence cosses [costs] twenty paand !"

Three days later Jabe and Long Ben sat at the Clog Shop fire in their Sunday best, reporting to the assembled magnates the result of their excursion to Duxbury.

The short of it was that the chapel was to be licensed forthwith, and all would be in time for Nancy's wedding. The deputation, big with the importance of their mission and contact with authority, legal and ecclesiastical, were unusually communicative.

The " super " had informed them that it was customary to present a Bible and Hymn-Book to the first couple married in the chapel. That was considered a most becoming idea, and was enthusiastically adopted for the approaching occasion.

Then Long Ben mentioned that the " super " said he thought the chapel ought to be cleaned and decorated, and in a short time a scheme was sketched for the whitewashing, painting, and cleaning of the chapel by a band of volunteers superintended by Ben himself.

Then it was suggested that all the Sunday School scholars should attend the ceremony, the girls to be dressed in their white anniversary frocks, but as the married men present hesitated to commit themselves before consultation with their home-rulers, this question was deferred.

When conversation began to flag, and Ben had glanced once or twice window-wards as if meditating departure, Sam Speck, who, as the most juvenile member of the Club, was considered to have a somewhat dangerous inclination to novelties, asked whether it was not customary to have music at weddings.

Jabe had "ne'er yerd on't." Ben thought he had "read about it i' th' papper," and Jethro, the knocker-up, gave it as his opinion that "they on'y hed music when royalty were married." But Sam stuck to his point, calculating with cunning confidence that an opportunity for the band to display its talents would greatly tempt the members of that organisation, and he was right, and easily carried the day.

But what sort of music was it to be ? Sam had heard something about wedding marches ; but marches were worldly, and nothing but sacred music could be played in the chapel.

Lige, the road-mender, suggested his in-variable selection for all times and seasons, "There'll be no mooar sorra there," but as Jabe vetoed that as inappropriate, Long Ben named the hymn—

> "Two are better far than one,
> For counsel or for fight."

to the tune *Asylum*. But nobody supported the idea, and at length Jonas Tatlock, the leader of both band and chapel choir, was sent for, and by the time he had smoked two pipes at a furious rate, arguing and demonstrating all the time, he had convinced the company that the " Hallelujah Chorus," which they had been rehearsing intermittently for years, was the correct thing, and it was resolved to go into hard practice at once.

.   .   .   .   .

Never a brighter day dawned than the one on which Jimmy and Nancy were to be married. All nature smiled, and human nature, at any-rate in Beckside, put on its very best. The Amateur Painting Committee had done its work, and the chapel was resplendent and very redolent of whitewash and paint. Nancy's Sunday School class, in their white frocks, and carrying "posies," occupied the front pew. The band had taken possession of the singing pew in the left hand corner, and overflowed into the adjoining pews, as on "Sarmon" days. The villagers, even including Job Sharples, had packed every available inch of space, the gallery being reserved for the children. The registrar was in the vestry, and the "super" was walking about in the aisles exchanging greetings with his people.

Presently the vestry door opened, and the registrar beckoned the minister. Arrived in the little sanctum, the "super" found an old woman with a black poke bonnet, and a face almost as white as the frill in her bonnet front.

"Good morning, Mrs. Crawshaw; this is a happy day for you," said the minister.

"Happy! My heart's welly broken; but he's bin a good lad, an' Aw've come to give him away."

"To give him away, Mrs. Crawshaw?"

"Ay; Aw've nowt else to give her."

"But it is the lady who is given away, you know, not the gentleman."

But just then there was a commotion in the chapel. The bridal party was coming. There were no cabs in Beckside, and even the *very* respectable thought it no dishonour to walk to their wedding, and at that moment the weddingers were coming arm in arm up the hill, and the front of the somewhat long procession had reached the chapel door. The minister hastened to his place within the communion-rail, and amid a buzz of excitement the party walked up the aisle.

Jimmy, with a huge blush-rose in his coat, looked warm, but quiet and radiantly happy. Nancy, flushed and proud as any duchess, glanced around as she reached the communion-rail as if in search of something, but the minister was commencing, so she had to give attention to the business in hand.

When they had got about halfway through the service, and the happy couple stood with clasped hands, there was an interruption.

The vestry door opened, and Jimmy's mother, calling out "Wait a minute," hobbled to the front, and, placing her hands on the heads of the bride and bridegroom, cried out—

"God bless thee, lad! May thy childer be as good to thee as tha's been to me. God bless thee, Nancy. God's gien thee a good 'art an' a bonny face, and thy fayther's gien thee th' farm, but Aw'm givin' thee aw as Aw have. God bless yo' booath."

There was a perfect chorus of quavering "Amens," accompanied by a display of handkerchiefs and a wiping of eyes, for this staid, still old woman, who during a lifetime had never spoken in chapel before,—not even at those great Beckside institutions, the Lovefeasts,—had touched a chord in every heart.

Then the service was finished, and the "super," in a neat speech, presented the Bible and Hymn-Book to the happy pair, after which the people clapped, and the boys in the gallery set up a thunderous stamping. Then the bridal party adjourned to the vestry to sign the register, during which there was such a tuning of instruments and resining of fiddle-bows as was not heard even at the anniversary in Beckside.

Jonas Tatlock, mounted on a high stool at one corner of the singing pew, watched the vestry door as for dear life, and as it opened he cried excitedly—

"Naa, lads, brast aat — Wun, two, three, fower!"

And they did "brast aat." Handel's grand chorus probably never received so entirely original a rendering, and it certainly was never produced with more whole-hearted earnestness and meaning than by the perspiring, but joyful, Beckside band.

Tatty Entwistle's Return

Tatty Entwistle's Return

A STERN, lowering look sat on the minister's face as he lifted the Clog Shop latch. He had come to Beckside on very serious business. That very forenoon a woman, agitated and tearful, and with a slight bruise on her forehead, had called at the manse in Duxbury, and had complained that her husband had struck her, and that she could no longer live with him. And this husband turned out to be none other than Nathan Entwistle, the Beckside blacksmith, who was chapel steward and trustee in the Beckside Methodist Church.

The good " super " was grievously shocked. A humane and chivalrous man himself, he was scandalised to think of such an act being committed by a church steward. What a disgrace it would be if it got abroad. What a scandal would be caused, and what injury would be done to the name of religion ! The thing must be hushed up and the two brought together again; and if that could not be brought about, then such measures of discipline must be taken as would make it clear to all outsiders that the Church condemned, repudiated, and punished such conduct.

What a beast that Nathan must be! And he had always thought him such a quiet, decent fellow. And so deeply attached to the cause, too! He was very much afraid that the morals of these rough north-country folk were very lax. It was very painful, but he must do his duty. Unless Nathan repented and made full amends, he must be expelled, if only as a warning to the rest. And even if Nathan was contrite, he must be relieved of his offices. Such conduct could not be passed over. He must be faithful at all costs.

These were the thoughts which were passing through the minister's mind as the venerable horse he hired jogged lazily along towards Beckside. As he entered the village, the glances and nods and winks which the villagers made to each other as he passed them confirmed him in his fears that the thing had become a public scandal; and so, after putting up his horse at the Fold farm, he came across to the Clog Shop in a stern and resolute frame of mind.

Long Ben and the Clogger, who were alone, rose with joyous surprise at this unexpected call, but the look on the minister's face checked them.

"Well, brethren, this is a serious matter," he said, with a sigh, as he pulled off his gloves and stuffed them into his overcoat pocket, and then turning up his coat tails sat cautiously down on an old clogging-bench near the fire.

The faces of the two friends formed themselves into notes of interrogation. They glanced with quick inquiry at their visitor, and then at each other, and then Jabe inquired—

"Wot dew yo' meean, Mester 'Shuper' ? "

"I mean about Nathan. Such conduct is infamous for a Christian man, and a member, too. But you don't mean to say you know nothing about it ? "

"We knaw nowt wrung abaat Nathan," said Jabe slowly and decisively, "and wot's mooar, there's noabry can tell nowt nother."

" If they'll speik th' truth," added Ben, whose face wore an emphatic and almost defiant indorsement of Jabe's remark.

"But haven't you heard?   Is it possible you don't know what he has done ? "

" He's dun nowt as he needs ta be shawmed on, Aw'll back," cried the Clogger doggedly.

" Ashamed," cried the "super," beginning to feel that Beckside morality was laxer even than he had expected. " It's not a matter for shame, it's a matter for punishment. The law of the land punishes it, and the Church certainly cannot be below that. If all I hear be true, we shall be compelled to expel him."

" Hexpel!   Ay, yo'll ha' plenty of hexpellin' ta dew if yo' starten wi' Nathan. Yo'll ha' t' hexpel us aw woll yo're abaat it."

" But, Mr. Jabez, it is a misdemeanour; you cannot know what he has done, to talk like that."

" Well, wot *has* he done?" shouted the Clogger petulantly, whilst both his face and that of Ben became dark with gathering storm-clouds.

" Done?   Why, he has struck his wife."

The anger-puckers suddenly straightened themselves out on the faces of the two friends. An amused mischievous light leapt into their eyes, and after a momentary effort to control themselves they burst into a low chuckling laugh.

The " super " was indignant.   Had these men no sense of shame in them?   And, besides, their laughter was insulting.

" An' han yo' cummed aw th' way fro' Duxbury abaat that ?" asked Jabe, when he could check himself.

" Certainly! and I am pained and humiliated to see that you think so lightly of the matter. It may be Beckside morality, but it is not mine, and it's not the morality of the New Testament either."

But even this sharp sally could not disturb the serene good temper into which the two cronies had laughed themselves, and after enjoying another broad grin, Jabe said—

" Bless yo', Mester ' Shuper,' yo' dooan't knaw Beckside yet, an' Aw'm feart yo' dooan't knaw

women fooak nother.   Naa, tak' yo'r coit off
and hang it upo' that peg on th' parlour dur,
an' come an' sit yo' daan, woll Aw tell yo' a
thing or two."

After getting the minister an old leathern
cushion to lean his back upon against the
chimney jamb, he continued—

"Women, Mestur ' Shuper,' are loike dogs;
the woss yo' sarve 'em the better they loike
yo.'   Han yo' niver noaticed as aw th' scamps
i' th' country has good wives as 'ull welly dee
for 'em?   But if yo' foind a felley as is a
gradely dacent chap, a bit better nor common,
he's sartin ta be henpecked.   Well, its o'
thatunce wi' Nathan.   Hoo's a dacent hard-
workin' woman, but that nattering, an' unyessy,
an' discontented, ther's noa biding near her.
A felley as has lived wi' her i' this loife 'ull
need noa purgatory i' th' next, Aw con tell
yo.' "

Having thus got fairly going, Jabe proceeded at length to give the minister a full
and particular account of the marital experiences of poor Nathan, interspersed with
sententious moralisings on the ways and wiles
of women.

Nathan, it appeared, had been married into
the teens of years.   He and his wife were
both members of the Church at the time of
their marriage, but about three years after
Nathan fell into drinking habits, driven to

it, Jabe averred, by the " nattering " of his wife. However that may have been, in Nathan's drunken days Tatty was a model wife, patient and still-tongued, loyal to her husband, and ready to quarrel with anybody who spoke a word against the blacksmith. Everything that womanly ingenuity could devise was done by Tatty to shield her husband and preserve his character.

During this time, also, she was most diligent at all the means of grace, took great interest in all chapel affairs, and prayed incessantly at class and prayer meetings for her husband's reclamation.

After a while, Nathan came to his senses, chiefly through the good offices of the Clogger and his friends. Tatty was, of course, greatly delighted and thankful, and Nathan was never tired of proclaiming how much he owed to the patience and kindness of his wife in his wild days.

Gradually Nathan was drawn into Church work, and as he could write better than most of his associates, was installed chapel steward, which office he had held ever since. But as Nathan's zeal waxed warm, Tatty's grew cold. It soon required all Nathan's persuasive powers to keep her going to chapel at all. She ceased altogether to attend class and prayer meetings, and whilst willing for Nathan to attend the sanctuary, she ceased to see any particular reason for doing so herself.

In course of time she discovered that Nathan had too much to do at the chapel. As they had no living children, she complained of her loneliness, and in swearing, nagging tones rated Nathan, saying again and again, "Tha'rt allis aat o' th' haase."

The Clog Shop, however, became her most particular aversion. Its owner and his friends were denounced without measure or mercy, and though Nathan was one of the least regular visitors to this favourite village resort, he came in for more abuse about it than all the other transgressors put together.

Nathan played the bass viol in the band, which, of course, brought that cherished institution into ill repute with his wife, and latterly the practice nights before the "Sarmons" had been times of tribulation for the blacksmith. More than once he had found the strings of his instrument cut when he reached it down from the joists to take it to the practice, and when, on the third occurrence of the kind, he bluntly charged his wife with doing the damage, she flew into a "tantrum," flounced out of the house, and went away to Duxbury to her sister's.

Poor Nathan, deeply attached to his wife, and full of grateful memories of her bygone faithfulness, was perplexed and alarmed when she did not come home that night. And next morning he was at Duxbury by break-fast-time, humbly begging Tatty's pardon and coaxing her to come back again.

But something of the same kind occurred again not long after, and Mrs. Nathan went off again; and since then, at every little tiff, Tatty might be seen sitting like a statue at the far end of the coach on her way to Duxbury, and Nathan was certain to follow in a few hours or days at most, to get forgiven and bring her back.

Of course such proceedings soon became common property, and whenever Nathan's wife was absent from home, the blacksmith was quizzed by his customers at the smithy as to when he was going to fetch her back.

Another element of difficulty between the two and, perhaps at bottom the cause of all the rest, was that they were childless. Three of their four little ones had died in infancy, and the fourth—little Nathan, a wee fragile bit of humanity—lived to be about four years of age and then quietly faded out.

Some time before his death, however, Nathan had taken him into the smithy one afternoon against his wife's wishes, and whilst there the little fellow trod upon the head of a long-shafted hammer, which tilted up quickly and struck the little fellow on the temples. He dropped on the floor like a dead thing, and Nathan with a wild cry snatched him up and carried him into the cottage. He soon recovered, and seemed all right; the doctor, in fact, said that he was very little the worse, but as he died about a month after, although the doctor scoffed at the idea of the accident having anything to do with the child's decease, its mother evidently had her own opinion on the subject, and in moments of anger of late had darkly hinted that but for Nathan she might still have had " one comfort i' loife."

To a man pining for child-love, this was hard to endure, and on the day of the now notorious quarrel, Tatty, carried beyond all restraint, had openly charged her husband with responsibility for the death of the little one. Nathan, smarting with a sense of cruel injustice and white with indignation, lost all control of himself, and struck his wife a smart slap on the face. Upon which Tatty had taken her usual excursion, adding this time, the serious step of going to tell the minister.

This, and much more, was told to the "super" as he sat toasting his shins before the Clog Shop fire, and by the time that Jabe had finished, he had veered round decisively to Nathan's side of the question, and proposed to go down to the smithy and offer Nathan his sympathy, suggesting also that he should go and persuade Tatty to return home.

"Yo' mun dew nowt o' th' sooart. Let her bide, an' come whoam when hoo's ready. An' leave Nathan ta uz; we'll poo' him through, yo'll see."

When the minister had gone, the two stewards fell into close consultation on the case in hand, and decided that this time, instead of avoiding the subject carefully, out of respect to Nathan's feelings, they would wait their opportunity and persuade him to bring things to a crisis by letting his wife stay away until she came back of her own accord.

Two or three nights later, Nathan sauntered into the Clog Shop in that restless, absent manner which always came upon him when his wife was away. Jabe, still at his bench, followed the blacksmith with his eyes as he passed up the shop, and having previously resigned his position of chief spokesman to Ben for this occasion only, he motioned to him that now was the time, and then turned round again and went on with his work with much unnecessary demonstrativeness.

Ben silently handed his tobacco-box to the newcomer. The two smoked on for some moments without speaking; and then Ben leaned forward out of the nook and said in a low voice, which was not quite so steady as it ought to have been——

"We've bin killin' a pig; wilt come an' ha' thy dinner wi' us o' Sunday?"

Nathan's lip quivered, tears swam in his eyes, and he stared steadily before him without speaking.

Ben took several long draws at his pipe,

and then, touching Nathan gently on the knee, he said soothingly—

" Every heart knoweth its own bitterness."

Nathan seemed shaken by a sort of internal convulsion. He bent forward, propped his chin on his knees, and sat staring into the fire, whilst great tears splashed down upon the chip ashes at his feet.

Jabe, at his bench, had suddenly stopped working, and was holding his breath to listen, though his eyes were still fixed on his work.

Presently Nathan faltered: " Hay, bud Aw dew loike aar Tatty. Aw'll fetch her whoam i' th' morn."

" Tha'll dew nowt o' th' sooart," shouted Jabe from his bench ; and, dropping further pretence of work, he threw down his hammer, and, unable any longer to keep out of the business, came and joined them at the fire, and plunged at once into hot discussion on the hitherto forbidden topic.

Ben and he insisted that Nathan had made his own trouble by always being so anxious to get his wife back ; that he would have no peace of his life until she was cured of this habit, and that as she was " a dacent woman enough i' mooast things," it was his duty to make one supreme effort to bring her to her senses. They prophesied that she would be sure to come back soon, and that, if once she had to come of her own accord, there would be an end to her vagaries, at anyrate in that direction.

Nathan took a great deal of persuading, and both his advisers realised that their task was only commenced, for, as Jabe said, the blacksmith would "tak' a lot o' keeping to it."

And indeed he did. Lonely at home, save for the occasional presence of a girl who came to do the housework, he spent his evenings at the Clog Shop, and often when the rest had left for the night all the arguments had to be gone over again, and all the objections once more answered.

Slowly Nathan settled down to a dogged endurance of his troubles, praying almost night and day that the Lord would forgive him for his part in the trouble, and soften the heart of his absent wife toward him.

Meanwhile Tatty gave no sign, and as everybody avoided naming her to the blacksmith, he did not even hear the bits of news of her that did reach the village.

It was reported at the Clog Shop that Tatty was looking "ter'ble bad"; and whilst some of the cronies cried, "Sarve her reet," Long Ben remarked softly, "Hoo'll be whoam afoor lung, yo'll see."

One night Nathan, heavy of heart and out of love with all the world, pulled the sneck out of his cottage door and strolled wearily towards his favourite resort.

As he approached, he heard a number of voices raised in animated discussion, and, opening the door, he came upon a rather odd scene.

There, on a clog stool behind the counter, sat Lige, the road-mender, with a face beaming with mystery, importance, and delight, holding on his knees a bundle of old clothes containing a very young baby; and standing over him, scarcely less excited, were several others of the Clog Shop fraternity.

"Aw wor comin' whoam fro' my wark up th' Brogden Loan [Lane], an' Aw yerd it skriking i' th' hedge bottom," cried Lige, in answer to Nathan's look of amazement.

"It'll be some poor wench's chance-chilt, Aw reacon," said Long Ben, in pitying tones.

"It's a bonny un, chuse wot it is," said Jabe, with unwonted music in his voice as he turned back the edge of the old Paisley shawl in which it was wrapped, and looked intently into its face.

The child gazed up at him with owl-like solemnity, and then puckered its mouth as if it would have spoken if it could, and the hard, crusty, misogamous old Clogger beamed upon it with delight as he murmured—

"Bless thi, tha'rt ta pratty for a chance-chilt."

Just then Nathan came round the corner of the counter, and bent down over the baby.

After gazing at it a moment he stepped back, and surveying the little bundle of rags and humanity, he asked—

" Wot art goin' ta dew wi' it, Liger ?

Before we could answer, Jabe broke in—

" Aar Judy can tak' cur on it ta-neet, and i' th' morning Aw—Aw—reacon it'll ha' ta be ta'n to th' bastile [workhouse]."

There was silence for a moment or two, every man looking a strong protest, but feeling that he could think of no better thing to do.

" Has ony on yo' ony idea whoase it is ? " asked Nathan, still looking hard at the little one, which was just beginning to cry.

" It's noabry's abaat here," said Sam Speck, who, through his sister Lottie, knew all the secrets of the village.

" Then, Aw'll have it," cried Nathan, and before Lige could object he had snatched the baby from his knee, and was dandling it up and down to stop its crying.

" Thee tak' it ? " objected Lige, taken aback, and not too pleased to be thus summarily robbed of his treasure; " wi' thy wife "—

But he stopped, and could have bitten his tongue off as he remembered what he was saying; but Nathan took it up.

" Ay! wife or noa wife, Aw'll tak' it. Aw mun ha' summat i' th' haase ta talk to."

Others were raising objections, but a new idea had evidently struck Long Ben, and, motioning and winking at the rest, he gently encouraged Nathan in his purpose, and in a few moments a small procession started for the smithy, led by the blacksmith proudly carrying his new-found joy.

Arrived at the cottage, Nathan held the baby whilst Lige went upstairs to fetch the long-disused cradle, and Sam Speck put a pan of milk on the fire to provide the little one with food.

In a few minutes Long Ben turned up, bringing his buxom wife, who, after expressing lofty scorn of the blundering ways of men folk, took the baby from Nathan, and, after cuddling and kissing it, pulled out a bundle of old baby clothes, and soon had it washed, dressed, fed, and asleep in the cradle.

When the others departed, they left Nathan pulling the cradle string and humming " Rock of Ages," as he had done so often in days gone by, and musing pathetically over his former experiences, now so vividly brought back to his mind.   It was arranged that Mrs. Ben should fetch the baby presently for the night, until some other arrangement could be made.

Nobody claimed the little one, and Nathan, to his great delight, remained in undisturbed possession of it.   The baby came on famously, and crept so deep into Nathan's heart that Mrs. Ben began to fear it would take the place of the absent Tatty.   One night Ben was the victim of a severe curtain lecture, and next day being market day, Mrs. Ben set off in the coach to Duxbury.

After doing her business, she made her way into a quiet part of the town, and in a few moments was sitting talking confidentially with Nathan's wife.

Tatty, looking thin and pensive, made all sorts of inquiries about Beckside and its doings, but carefully avoided any reference to the smithy.

Mrs. Ben tried several times to draw her, but it was of no avail, until at last, growing desperate, she blurted out—

" Hast yerd wot yo're Nathan's getten ? "

" Neaw."

" Whey, he's getten a babby."

Tatty turned and looked with a long, wistful, sidelong glance at her friend, and then with a great sigh changed the subject, and could not be brought back to it.

But Mrs. Ben knew what she was about, and next night after dark, the tall, wan form of Tatty Entwistle might have been seen stealing down the darker side of the Beckside road toward the smithy.

The blacksmith's shop stood sideway on to the road, and the cottage was behind it, facing into the smithy yard, Tatty stole quietly up amongst heaps of old iron, cart hoops, and disabled agricultural implements, and was soon at the side of the house. Nathan, man-like, had lighted the lamp, but had forgotten to draw the blind.

Tatty drew softly near, stole along the house side until she was close to the window, and then, standing on a broken pulley, which enabled her to see over the curtain, she peered round the corner of the window into the house.

There sat Nathan in the rocking-chair, with the baby in his arms, talking to it as he rocked it. Her heart smote her as she saw how thin her husband's face had become, but that pain gave way to another of a quite different kind as she saw how happy he seemed to be with the little one.

It began to rain, but Tatty never felt it. Presently the baby dozed off, and Nathan put it into its cradle and made it cosy. The cradle stood where she could see all this, and as she watched there came into her eyes that hunger of child-love which only a childless mother knows.

Then Nathan took something down from the mantelpiece, and began to look earnestly at it, whilst the firelight flickered up into his face. It was a little glass photo of Tatty, taken at the last Brogden wakes, and the watching woman almost cried out as she saw him looking at it so intently.

Suddenly he fell to his knees with the likeness still in his hands, and though she could not quite hear what he said, yet the way he held up the little photo as if showing it to his Maker told her all she wanted to know.

Then Nathan got up, and after glancing at the cradle he put on his coat and went out. Tatty crept back into the shade of the coal house to avoid being seen as her husband crossed the yard. When she was sure he had gone, she stepped out of her hiding-place, picked up a bit of old iron, which she could see on the ground by the light through the window, and inserting it into the hole of the sneck, gently lifted the latch and went inside.

The first thing she did was to go to the mantelpiece and make sure that it was her likeness that Nathan had been looking at. Then she turned to the cradle, half smiled as she noted how clumsily the baby had been put into it, and then, turning down the coverlet, she stood looking down on the sleeping infant.

It was certainly pretty. What if it had crept into her place in Nathan's heart! Oh, what a fool she had been, and what a sinner too!

But just then a step at the door made her start. A smothered exclamation told her that Nathan had returned. But she did not move. Her back was to him, but she felt he was looking at her. There they both stood for quite a long time, until at last, slightly turning towards him, she asked—

"Whoa's is this babby, Nathan?"

"It's moine."

"Tha'rt no' it's fayther."

"Neaw, bud Aw'm goin' ta be, if God helps me."

There was silence again for most of a minute, and then Tatty turned her back full upon her husband again, and dropping her head, murmured—

"Aw—Aw'll be its muther, if tha'll let me."

Then she heard a sob behind her, felt herself being drawn down into a chair, and in a moment more was held fast in the tight, silent embrace of the now happy blacksmith.

Hours after, as Nathan was picking up the cradle to carry it upstairs, baby and all, he noticed that the child's clothes had been changed, and it was wearing the night-gown of the little Nathan they had lost. As he made toward the staircase, his wife said—

"Has t'baby a name, Nathan?"

"Neaw, no' yet."

"Then we'll caw him Nathan, shall us?"

And that was how Tatty Entwistle came home.

Coals of Fire

Coals of Fire

FOUR dusky figures sat toasting themselves at the Clog Shop fire. Long Ben occupied the ingle-nook nearest the door, and Sam Speck the other, whilst Jabe and Jethro, the knocker-up, were in front. A heavy thaw was going on outside, and the fire was therefore so large that those who did not enjoy the shelter of the nook, were, as Jethro remarked, " frizzled o' wun side an' frozzen o' t'other."

Evidently something serious was under discussion. Jabe's bristly brows were drawn together, his lips pursed out grimly, and his tell-tale leg was riding up and down over the end of the other knee at a furious rate. Sam's small face seemed to have sharpened under some internal feeling, and Jethro sat in his favourite attitude, with his chin propped on his knees, glowering into the fire. Long Ben's flabby and hairy face was drawn up into that pathetic pucker suggestive of imminent weeping, which it always assumed when anything mentally disagreed with him.

"Ther'll be a ter'ble judgment for aw this,"

said Jethro, moving his head round solemnly in his knee-propped hands.

" Well, if there isna, Aw'st give o'er believin' i' Providence, that's aw abaat it," said Sam, with great emphasis.

" Dunna thee meyther thysel'," answered Jabe. " Aw've lived a good while naa, an' Aw ne'er seed it miss yet. If ther's owt trew i' th' Bible it's th' owd text, ' Be sure your sin will find you out,' an' it allis docs—an' especially sins o' this soart."

" Why, dust think as th' Almighty's wuss daan o' this mak' o' sins nor ony other ? " asked Jethro.

" Aw meean to say as Aw've known a tooathre [two or three] chaps i' my time as hez played fawse wi' women, but Aw hav'n't known wun case wheer it didn't cum back on 'em ten times wus. Neaw," he added, after a moment's reflection, " not th' *odd* un."

The general principle laid down by Jabe obtained unanimous acceptance in Beckside, but this particular application of it was new, and so his friends sat in silence for a few moments meditating on the law thus expounded, and ransacking their memories for examples confirmatory or otherwise.

" If Jimmy Juddy hed as mitch pluck as a maase " (mouse), began Sam presently—but just then the shop door opened, and in stepped a man, stamping his slushy clogs as he did so.

He was a stumpy fellow with a rough red face, a slight cast in one eye, and a fringe of straight red hair under his chin.

Jabe and Jethro, as soon as they saw who the visitor was, made pantomimic facial signals to those in the nook, and looked hard for a moment at each other, and then at their pipe bowls.

" Cowd neet, chaps," said the last comer, but nobody spoke, and Sam muttered something under his breath about " impidence."

" Hast ony 'bacca ? " said the stranger to Jabe, pulling out his pipe ; but Jabe, usually generous in his distribution of dark shag, neither moved nor spoke.

The intruder perched himself on the protruding end of the bench on which Long Ben sat, and after glancing round with a slightly perplexed look slapped Jabe on the sleeve and said, with a show of triumph—

" Naa, tha sees ; wheer should Aw ha' been if Aw'd wed yond' wench ? Aw should a' leuked weel wi' a paralysed wife, shouldn't Aw ? Aw wor nobbut just i' time, tha sees ; bud maa luck "—

But he never finished his tale of self-gratulation, for he was suddenly seized from behind by the coat collar, jerked to his feet, and then lifted up and thrown across the Clog Shop counter, as a schoolmaster throws a boy over a bench, and Long Ben, with white, quivering face and blazing eyes, stood over him, and picking up an unfinished clog sole held him tightly down, and belaboured him, schoolmaster fashion, until he kicked and bellowed and even cursed.

Laying on until the victim's howl became a shriek, Ben suddenly stopped, opened the shop-door, and flung the sufferer out into the dark road, where he landed in a heap of slushy snow.

Quietly closing the door and putting down the catch, so that the offender could not return, Ben lounged back to his seat in the nook in a somewhat breathless condition.

After the first little start of surprise, the assembled friends had watched Ben's proceedings with considerable satisfaction, and now— though not a muscle of their faces moved—they listened to the evicted visitor's curses outside without a single sign that they heard; and the next remark that was made was on a totally different subject, which gives an opportunity of explaining the meaning of what had just happened.

The man whose ignominious expulsion has been described lived at the other—that is, the Mill Lane—end of the irregular little row of cottages in which the Clog Shop stood. He kept a sort of store, and, disclaiming all such distinctions as usually obtain amongst tradesmen, seemed to have adopted the most profitable branches of each business, and was something of a grocer, something of a draper, did a little in the hardware and ironmongery, with a blending of chemistry, butchering, greengrocery, and tailoring. It was even darkly hinted in certain quarters that he was not above a little illicit trade in clogs.

The building he occupied had been left to him by his father, but so disposed of that he could neither sell nor forfeit it. For a short time the father of the present occupant had got the premises licensed, under the name of the Bull Inn; but as Beckside could not sustain two public-houses, and the Bridge Inn was well established, the speculation failed, but ever afterwards the villagers associated the owners with this unfortunate venture, and so the present occupant was known, not as Hiram Crompton, but as Hiram Bull, or, by the older people, as Hiram Bill Bull.

Hiram possessed strong, rude health, which gave him a good flow of animal spirits, and developed in him the habit of loud, blustering laughter; but that this was not good nature was made abundantly clear by the fact that he manifested an unscrupulous directness as to his own interests, a total disregard for the feelings and interests of others, and a keen enjoyment of misfortune or suffering in his fellow-mortals.

There was also a certain rough smartness

about him and a sublime self-confidence, which made the oracular Jabe say again and again that " Brains is nowt wheer brazzenness cums."

Some time before the episode above described, Alice Crawshaw, Jimmy Juddy's sister, who at that period was a sweet, fair-haired girl of about four-and-twenty, amazed everybody by accepting an offer of marriage from Hiram.

That Jimmy disapproved of the union goes without saying. There was a series of painful scenes at Beck Bottom, first between Jimmy and Hiram, and then between Jimmy and his sister, but Hiram carried the day, and Alice seemed infatuated. In his loud way the storekeeper was proud of his conquest, but more because it was a triumph over others than because he had any extraordinary attachment to Alice.

Becksiders never became reconciled to the arrangement, for every few days some new story of Hiram's greed or cruelty was circulated, and people pitied Alice when it was known that the wedding-day was fixed, and the bride-elect was making her wedding-dress and bespeaking the guests.

One night about this time Long Ben went to the Clog Shop with a face that was a flag of distress. Jabe, who was alone, perceived it, and knew better than to ask any questions. Presently, after many relightings of a pipe, which somehow would not keep in, Ben applied a blazing chip to his clay, and remarked, between the resultant puffs in his slow way—

"'Bill Bull' 'ull ne'er be deead while his son lives."

It sounded as though he had finished, but Jabe knew better, and so commenced picking wax from his horny fingers, and Ben pulled a nail out of his pocket and poked it down the still refractory pipe-bowl as he resumed—

"Aw seed him clippin' (embracing) Tom Plum's widder o'er th' caanter as Aw went past this forenoon."

An exclamation broke from Jabe's lips, but he checked himself as Ben continued.

"Tha'll see, there'll be noa weddin' at th' Beck Bottom yond'."

And so it proved. For though poor Tom Bibby, generally known as Tom Plum, had only been dead a few weeks, Hiram had already shown quite extraordinary energy in obtaining the widow's smile, and as Tom had left her £1200 nobody looked far for the reason. Alice Crawshaw heard of the matter pretty early, of course, but laughed at the idea of it, and went gaily on with her bridal pre-parations.

She wanted a little dress lining of some sort one day, and slipped up to Hiram's as the nearest shop to procure it.

After a little playful talk during her selection of the material, she turned to go, when Hiram called her back and said with smiling brutality—

"Ther' mun be noa moar marlocking between thee an' me, Alice. Aw'm goin' t' marry Tilly Plum next week."

Alice gasped, but the entrance of a customer set Hiram off in a garrulous conversation with the last arrival, and poor Alice, with white face and whiter lips, held her hand to her side and fled home.

A few days later Hiram and Tilly went away to be married, and returned home on what should have been Alice's wedding-day. Alice had never been seen in the village since.

Quiet Jimmy, her brother, not yet recovered from the disgrace of his dismissal from the mill, went about with his head down, and old Matty, their mother, had fainted in the class-meeting, and Long Ben had had to take her home in his spring cart.

Next morning news passed from loom to loom in the mill weaving-shed that the doctor had been seen going in great haste to Beck Bottom, and by noon everybody knew that Alice Juddy had had a stroke.

This last event was the one under discussion when Hiram entered the Clog Shop, and the details now given will explain what then took place.

But Hiram continued to prosper, and the prophecies with which this story commenced remained unfulfilled. But they were not forgotten. Hiram was not the sort of person to hide his light under a bushel, and every now and again some fresh act of hard, brazen greed brought him vividly before people's minds, and evoked fresh crops of fateful prediction.

Then Tilly died, and Hiram, after making a scene of blubbering emotion at the grave which caused Silas the chapel-keeper to declare, " Aw welly picked him into th' hoile," dismissed the mourners without the customary tea, and was seen out the same evening at his favourite sport of rabbit-shooting.

In a few weeks the storekeeper brought another wife home, a stranger, but as he was disappointed in his expectation that she was well off,—her money going from her on her re-marriage,—she was, as Jabe put it, " nattered ta deeath i' noa time."

Then Hiram by some trickery got possession of a bit of land at the end of Long Ben's property, and immediately set up a most unscrupulous claim as to the right of light, and proceeded on resistance to put up " spite and malice boards " outside Ben's end windows. This drove the quiet carpenter into most distasteful litigation, from which he finally withdrew at the eleventh hour, leaving Hiram to gloat over an expensive victory.

Besides these more prominent episodes, " Th' Bull," as he was now invariably called, kept himself in people's minds by numberless acts of petty cheating and oppression, aggravating the feeling against him until the Clog Shop Club gave up prediction in despair; and Sam Speck became so cynical in his remarks about Providence, that Jabe declared it was " nowt short o' blasphem*i*ous."

Then Hiram began to gamble, and became the chief patron of the pigeon-fliers and foot-racers who frequented the Bridge Inn, greatly angering Jabe and his friends by exploiting one of the most promising youths at the Sunday School, and turning him into a sprint-runner under the title of " the Lancashire Deerfoot."

When Jimmy Juddy was married, and came with his sister and mother to live at the Fold farm, Hiram had the effrontery to try to patch up the long estrangement, but Jimmy's wife undertook the matter, and so " cooamed his yure " (hair) for him that he was glad to get away, and revenged himself by mocking poor Alice's lameness as she went past on her crutch.

This last offence was still burning in the breasts of the confederates of the cloggery, when most startling news came to Beckside. Old Croppy, the Brogden rent and debt collector, brought it, and told it to the first person he met, who happened to be Sam Speck.

Without waiting for full details, Sam hurried to the Clog Shop and electrified Jabe by opening the door and shouting: "It's cum at last," and then rushed out to fetch Ben, picking up Jethro as he returned.

It was a proud moment for Sam, and after banging the door to, and setting his back against it, as if afraid someone would escape before he could tell his tale, he exclaimed: "'Th' Bull's' busted."

After a moment's pause to get his breath, he descended to such details as he knew. Hiram had embarked some three years before in a coal-mine speculation at Yardley Woods, beyond Duxbury. Suddenly there had been a collapse, and as his co-speculators were men of no substance, and the liability was unlimited, the creditors, who had been shamefully robbed, came down on Hiram.

Croppy's report turned out to be substantially correct, and when the sale came every member of the Club attended, and seemed to derive grim satisfaction from watching the gradual despoilment of the oppressor's residence.

Hiram himself was there in his shirt sleeves, pretending to render obsequious assistance to the auctioneer and his clerks, and laughing his hoarse laugh over sundry jokes of his own. Towards evening, however, he grew quiet, and a haggard, desperate look sat on his face.

When the sale was over there was an adjournment to the usual council chamber. There was only a small, make-believe fire, as it was early summer, but the friends gathered round it from sheer force of habit, and soon every available seat was occupied, and the Clog Shop full of smoke. Everybody saw retribution in the circumstances of the day; everybody admitted the ampleness of the "judgment"; and everybody had his own particular wise saw or text of Scripture to confirm his opinion.

"We con run fast and run fur, as wun o' th' owd ministers used for t' say," said Lige, the road-mender, "bud theer's Wun aboon as 'owds th' reins, and He can bring us daan ta aar marraboanes ony minnit, if it suits Him."

"Ay," sighed four or five, through pipe-embarrassed lips, and the irrepressible Sam gave a new turn to the conversation by observing—

"Aw wundur wot he'll dew for a bed ta-neet; he'll ha' ta lie upo' th' boards, Aw'm thinkin'."

A rather lengthy silence followed, during which each seemed to be occupied with his own particular mental picture of the ruined man in the empty house.

Long Ben, who had never spoken during the discussion, now began to manifest signs of uneasiness. After puffing out several volumes of smoke in rapid succession, he heaved a deep sigh, and then said meditatively—

" He used dew my sums for mi at th' schoo'."

" Ay, an' he's bin doin' sums for folk ever sin', as plenty knows ta the'r sorra," rejoined Sam, and the rest, attracted by the first word not condemnatory which had been spoken of Hiram that night, turned their eyes on Ben in mild surprise.

Ben fidgeted in his seat; and just when the inquiring eyes were turning away from him, he brought them back with wide open astonishment as he murmured—

" When Aw wor i' bed wi' th' maysles, he brought me a brid's neest wi' four eggs in— just ta bree-breeten me up a bit," and Ben's voice quivered most strangely as he recalled this boyhood reminiscence.

" He's moastly spent his time robbin' neeses (nests) sin' he grew up," said Sam again.

Ben made an impatient gesture with his pipe, and Jabe, his eyes gleaming with a look of injured justice, said—

" Why, tha'll want ta whitewesh owd Scratch next."

There was an awkward pause, and presently Ben took his pipe out of his mouth, carefully and deliberately reared it in the extreme corner of the nook, and then, rising to his full height, and buttoning his coat as a preparation for departure, he said—

" Chaps, wot yo' say's reet enouff, bud Wun as yo' aw know said, ' If thy enemy hunger, feed him,' and Ben Barber's no' goin' t' sleep in a warm bed ta neet while wun of his fellers lies o' bare boards. Neaw, not even if his name's Hiram Bull."

With an agitated gesture Ben strode to the door. As he got opposite the window, however, he suddenly pulled up, whilst the rest all heard the Fold farm garden gate click.

Ben, peering through the dusty glass, made an exclamation which instantly brought every man in the shop to his side, and, following the direction of his eyes, they saw Jimmy Juddy looking cautiously up and down to see that nobody was about. Then he stepped lightly back into the house, and almost instantly returned carrying a single bed and a pillow, whilst Alice stole quietly after him carrying in her free hand a basket of provisions.

Not a man in the shop drew his breath as Jimmy and his sister crossed the triangle toward Hiram's ; but when they had passed, every man turned and looked into his neighbour's face with an expression on his own of wonder, admiration, and rising shame.

" Naa, that *is* religion," cried Long Ben at last, struggling to keep back a rush of tears, and then flinging open the door, and crying in a choking voice, " Aw'll ne'er be byetten (beaten) wi' a lame woman," he plunged into the twilight in the direction of home.

Hiram, under the combined influence of drink and desperation, was attempting to sing a public-house song, accompanied by two pigeon-fliers who had come to offer him a bed for the night, when Jimmy and his sister, white and trembling, knocked at his door.

"Cum in," he shouted, and Jimmy stepped into the middle of the almost empty room and threw down the bed and pillow, whilst Alice, her heart beating almost into her ears, followed him.

"It's nobbut a flock un, but tha'rt welcome to it, Hiram," stammered Jimmy, straightening himself, and Alice added, "An' heer's a tooathre vittles fer—fer th' sake o' owd toimes!" And then she broke down and began to cry.

And then there came a bang at the half-opened door, and Jabe came limping in with a three-legged table, followed by Lige carrying some fire-irons and an old copper kettle. Sam Speck came next with a collection of crockery, and in a minute or two afterwards Long Ben brought a hand cart on which was a wooden bedstead which he had actually taken from under one of his own children.

By this time Hiram's sporting friends had sidled off, and Hiram was sitting leaning his head on one arm, which was laid across the arm of his chair. One or two spoke to him, but he never answered ; and so, at a signal from Jabe, the visitors stole quietly away, and Hiram was alone with the tokens of a human kindness in which he had never believed.

Early next morning Jethro going his knocking-up rounds, found the storekeeper pulling down the "spite and malice boards" outside Ben's side windows. And on the following Sunday he slunk into chapel after the service had commenced and crept into Silas' box behind the door. Next week he was seen helping Silas to clean the chapel out, and it soon began to be prophesied that Alice Crawshaw and he would marry after all.

But they never did, for Jimmy's gentle sister died next year, and Hiram almost immediately emigrated, carrying with him one strange piece of luggage: a woman's crutch. Ever since then the collection at the " Sarmons " has been helped up by a bank order from the States, with which there always comes an unsigned note, inscribed " IN MEMORY OF ALICE CRAWSHAW."

The Knocker-up

141

The Knocker-up

THAT all-important event the " Sarmons " was approaching. The formal rehearsals for it took place in the chapel during the fortnight immediately preceding the great Sunday, but the real hard work of the band was done at the Clog Shop, and woe to the misguided customer who came to do business after the music had commenced.

It was the first practice of the season, and one by one the members of the band entered the shop, most of their faces wearing a caught-in-the-act sort of look, for their instruments had been taken down from their hanging-places on house ceilings to a feminine accompaniment of railing against all bands in general and the Beckside one in particular.

Each player as he arrived and began to tune his instrument, inquired—

" Hasn't Jethro come yet ? " and the later comers exchanged their query into—

" Wheer's Jethro ? "

Jethro, though not the leader of the band, was its moving spirit, and far away the best musician in Beckside. He was usually the first to arrive; but now, although Nathan, the smith, for whom they always had to wait, had come, there were no signs of Jethro.

At last Sam Speck offered to " goa an' fotch him," and whilst he is away on his errand I will tell you about the missing bandsman :—

He was a spare little man of about sixty years of age, and lived in a one-storey cottage, two steps below the level of the road, on the left-hand side as you went down towards the Beck.

He was the village knocker-up, and went his daily rounds with unfailing regularity every morning, except Sunday, between the hours of four and six. Over his shoulder he carried a long, light pole, with wire prongs at the end, with which he used to rattle at the bedroom windows of the sleepy factory hands until he received some signal from within that he had been heard.

Though employed and paid by the " hands," Jethro regarded himself as representing the masters' interests, and if a post was unoccupied or a loom " untented " when the engine started at six o'clock, Jethro felt that it was a reflection on his professional ability, and was ashamed and hurt.

This doubtless accounted for the extraordinary zeal which the old man put into his work. The knocker-up was expected to go and knock a second time a few minutes before six to stir up any drowsy one who might, per-adventure, have fallen asleep again, and into this second round, which was to many the real signal for rising, Jethro put all his resources. Not only the windows but the doors were assailed, and in addition he would give a word of exhortation in his thin piping voice—

"Bob! Dust ye'r? It's five minutes to six! Ger up, tha lazy haand (hound). If tha dusn't ger up Aw'll come an poo' thi aat o' bed."

At the next call he would drop into a coaxing tone—

"Lizer! Jinny! Come, wenches! You'll ne'er ha' breet een (eyes) if yo' lie i' bed like that."

After his rounds were finished, he would go down to the mill to report "quarterings" and sick cases, and to spend an hour with the fireman.

Jethro was a light-hearted, merry old fellow, who quoted Wesley's hymns by the yard on all possible occasions, and sang snatches of them in the still mornings as he went his rounds.

The knocker-up began his musical career as a fiddler, but on visiting Manchester on one occasion, and attending a great concert there, he came back bringing a trombone, and though there was considerable murmuring at the incongruity of introducing a brass instrument into a string and reed band, Jethro was so indispensable that nobody openly rebelled.

This trombone was Jethro's chief earthly pride and glory, and the source of untold pleasure to him. He was, in fact, often troubled with the fear that the very strength of his affection for the instrument was a sign of its unhallowed nature, and many of his spiritual conflicts were fought about this unfortunate trumpet.

"The dearest idol I have known," etc.,

was a favourite class-meeting verse at Beckside, but Jethro always sang it with painful misgivings, which gave an additional quaver to his tremulous tenor. In all pulpit utterances, "stumbling - blocks," "besetting sins," "spiritual idolatries," "false gods," and the like spelt "trombone" to Jethro, and all appeals for self-sacrifice brought up painful visions of a possible parting with that cherished instrument.

Once, indeed, it spent a Sunday night in the back garden, where its owner had thrown it in a fit of self-disgust at having played it in a public-house, where he had substituted for the sick trombonist of the Clough End brass band.

But the conscience-smitten knocker-up could not sleep whilst his beloved instrument lay among the cabbages, and he finally sneaked out about three in the morning, brought in his pet, went to bed again, and slept the sleep of guilty peace.

Now Jethro had an only son, grown up and married, who from the standpoint of the chapel was a very unsatisfactory character. Every Becksider, as I said before, believed in retribution, and the father was haunted with the suspicion that his son's prodigalities were judgments upon himself for his idolatrous love of his trombone.

By this time Sam Speck has returned from his search for the missing musician.

"Aw say, chaps," he cried, "there's summat up wi' th' owd lad;" and as the fiddle-bows stopped their scraping, he continued—

"He's sittin' afoor th' feire yond', and staring into't like sumbry gloppened, an' Aw couldna get a word aat on him."

The musicians looked at each other in astonishment.

"Wor he in a fit, dust think?" asked Jonas.

"Aw conna tell thi, but theer's summat wrung wi' th' owd lad."

Jabe and Long Ben posted off instantly to Jethro's cottage. Opening the door — for knocking was a sign of stiffness—they found him seated on a chair before an expired fire, with his feet on the fender and his body bent forward, so that he propped his chin with his arms, which, in their turn, were propped on his knees.   He never moved when the visitors entered.

"Wot's up wi' thi, Jethro?" asked Jabe, approaching him with some hesitation.   But the knocker-up neither moved nor spoke.

Long Ben took a careful look round the room, and finding nothing suggestive, he leaned against the mantelpiece so as to get a side light on Jethro's face, and then he said soothingly—

"Come! come! owd lad, wot's up?"

Jethro heaved a great sigh, and looked wildly round, whilst Jabe, getting behind the old man's chair, motioned to Ben not to speak.

"It's a judgment on me," cried Jethro at last.   "It's a judgment on me."

Ben was about to interrupt him, but Jabe scowlingly motioned him to desist.

"It's my own doin'. 'Be sure your sin 'ull find yo' aat!' An' it hez done! It hez done!"

Another pause; during which Jabe was going through every kind of pantomimic gesture he could think of to prevent Ben from speaking.

"Aw carried him to th' chapel when he wor three wik owd. He's been ta'n (taken) theer for twenty ye'r. When he'd th' fayver Aw fowt wi' th' Lord two neets an' a day, an' naa "—and the old man buried his head in his hands and moaned piteously.

Jabe and Ben drew chairs up, and sitting down one on each side of him, Long Ben asked gently—

" Come, owd lad, wot's it aw abaat ? "

Jethro lifted his head out of his hands, and asked, in a voice of tremulous surprise—

" Why, durn't yo' knaw ? " and Jabe and his companion answered simultaneously, " Neaw ! "

" Durn't yo'? Why, aar Jethro ta'n th' alehaase. O Absalom ! my son ! my son Absalom ! " and the heart-broken old man rose and stamped on the sanded floor in a passion of grief and shame.

The only public-house in Beckside stood on the left, a little below Jethro's house and close to the Beck - bridge. The innkeeper had died recently, and Jethro junior, unknown to his father, had got the licence temporarily transferred to himself. This young man could not have taken a more cruel means of inflicting pain on his old Methodist father than the one he had adopted, and whilst Jabe and Ben looked at each other with dull sad astonishment, Jethro walked about the house crying—

" Wot con Aw expect ? Didn't Aw let th' trombone tak' me into a public-haase mysel'? Aw never thowt it 'ud come whoam to me like this, but it hez! it hez!   My sin hez fun' me aat!"

Nothing that could be said or done seemed to pacify the old man, and his visitors felt that to mention the suspended " practice " would be to inflict pain.

For many a day after this Jethro went about disconsolate. His voice was scarcely ever heard in the silent road on a morning, and when it was it sounded like a sad wail. In spite of all that could be said, he was firmly convinced that his son's conduct was a sort of consequence of his own overweening devotion to the trombone, though he was never able quite to demonstrate the connection between the two. No amount of persuasion would induce him to play the trombone again, and he dared not go near the Clog Shop for fear of falling into temptation.

In a few days young Jethro moved into the Bridge Inn, and the knocker-up spent the whole of the removal day walking about in the road in front of the alehouse, but neither coaxing, nor flattery, nor reasoning, could induce him to step across the threshold.

But when the door closed at night for the first time on the new tenants, a haggard old man might have been seen kneeling on the steps and pouring out his soul in intense and tearful supplication.

Young Jethro's wife was a bonnie brown-faced lassie, who had been a great favourite with her father-in-law, and she had done everything that woman's wheedling could do to coax him into the house, but he vowed again and again that he would never cross the threshold.

Great, therefore, was Polly's astonishment one morning, when old Jethro entered the inn, but walked straight through into the kitchen.

"Hay, fayther, bless yo'! Aw *am* fain to see yo'," she cried, rising from her chair awkwardly; "come an' sit yo' daan."

But the old man did not move. He stood there in the middle of the room looking at his daughter-in-law with sad solemn eyes.

"Doan't ston' theer, fayther; sit yo' daan an' Aw'll make yo' some tay."

But Jethro took a short step backwards, and raising his hand, and looking for the moment not unlike an old Hebrew prophet, he said—

"Polly, if onybody 'ad towd me as my fust gronchilt 'ud be born in a alehaase, Aw'd a letten aar Jethro dee when he had th' fayver; he'd a bin safe then;" and then breaking down into a wail, and crying: "But it's a judgment on me," the old man hastened away.

Now the young landlord had not been much disturbed by his father's protests, for he had not noticed that the circumstance had taken the hold upon him which it had.

But two or three weeks innkeeping had opened his eyes, and so the account his wife gave of Jethro's visit made a deep impression on him.

Meanwhile the old man's melancholy seemed to deepen. All the efforts of his cronies to cheer him were vain, and as he evidently dared not go near the Clog Shop, the practices were seriously interfered with, not only by the absence of the leading spirit, but also by that of those who went to keep their old friend company.

One cold, dull morning—for the spring was late—old Jethro was seen hurrying up the road past the Clog Shop as fast as he could go, with a sack on his back. The sack might not have attracted any attention, but the suspicious haste with which it was being carried excited great curiosity at the cloggery, and Sam Speck followed very carefully to see what " th' owd chap wor up to."

After passing the chapel, Jethro slackened speed, and having turned the crest of the hill, he sat down on a heap of stones, whilst Sam was crouching behind the hedge and watching him.

The poor fellow looked very miserable, and after sitting for a minute or two he got up, looked stealthily around, then opened the sack, took out of it a long, green baize bag, containing the trombone, and, after concealing the sack in the hedge bottom, started off to Duxbury to sell his idol.

It was a seven-mile walk, and such an instrument was not easy to dispose of, and had to be carried about from place to place before a purchaser could be found. So terrible was the mental conflict going on within the old man that he forgot to take food, and started the long walk home in a fagged condition.

It was a weary tramp, accompanied by more than one Lot's-wife-like look behind him. The wind, strong and heavy, was all against him, the brooding grief of the last few weeks had drained his vitality; he began to feel very fatigued, then giddy; and finally, just as he drew near the place where he had concealed the sack, he staggered to the road-side in a dead swoon.

Luckily, however, Lige, the road-mender, was returning home from his work behind Jethro, and seeing him fall he hurried up, and in a short time the knocker-up was safe in his own bed. The doctor said it was a slight stroke, and Jethro must have been worrying about something, but as he had an excellent constitution no serious consequences need be apprehended.

Jethro's walk to Duxbury took place on

a Friday, and on the following day young Jethro sat brooding over late events behind his little bar, and it was evident he was very ill at ease.

On the Sunday he went twice to chapel, and after the evening service Jabe gave him that significant jerk of the head Clog Shopwards which was the recognised form of invitation to its councils.

The ordinary members of the Club treated him with marked coldness, but he sat the session out, and when the others rose to go, Jabe beckoned him back into his seat, and he sat down, knowing full well what was coming.

Long Ben also remained, and when they had gazed into the fire and puffed rather vigorously at their pipes for a little time, Jabe suddenly turned to the young landlord and said—

"Well, wot dust think to thysel'?"

"Wot abaat?"

"Wot abaat! Abaat aw t' trouble tha's gcen yond' owd chap o' yours."

"Haa did Aw knaw he'd tak' it so ill?"

"Neaw" (very sarcastically); "tha thowt 'as th' best owd saint i' Beckside 'ud feel a-whoam (at home) among pigeon-fliers an' cards an' ale-pot bottoms, didn't tha?"

The culprit was getting red, and so Long Ben put his hand gently on his shoulder, and said—

"Wot 'ud thy mother think if hoo saw thi, lad?"

Jethro winced, and Ben proceeded—

"We ne'er thowt as that Bible we gav' thi at th' schoo' 'ud find its road into a alehaase."

There was silence; the young man was deeply moved, and began to bite his lips, whilst a heavy sigh broke from him. In a moment or two Jabe said, very gently for him—

"Kneel thi daan, lad."

And down the three went, and there they prayed and prayed until the small hours of the morning, when young Jethro "found liberty," and went home with a new joy in his heart and a new power in his life. Next week he gave up the inn.

Some ten days after this the old knocker-up sat on a "long settle" which had been pulled up near the fire, though it was late in May.

Aunt Judy, who had installed herself head-nurse, had just been telling him about his son's conversion, for it had not been deemed prudent to inform him sooner. The old man's face was a picture. Delight, gratitude, and wonder seemed blended in it.

Then Judy excused herself for a moment and went out. She was soon back, however, carrying a mysterious bundle of clothes. This she "flopped" suddenly on Jethro's knee, and, pulling back the outer shawl, disclosed a fine three-days'-old baby.

"Theer!" she cried, "isn't that a whopper?

It's th' pictur of its grondad!   An' it's no' been born in a alehaase, nother."

What the knocker-up thought as he sat and looked at the wee one will never be known, but as he held his knees together lest the treasure they supported should be disturbed, Judy was startled to hear him burst out in his high piping voice and to a popular local tune—

"God moves in a mysterious way," etc.

After this the old man "came on" quite rapidly, and as the "Sarmons" were still three wceks off, he began to talk quite eagerly of being present at them "efther aw."

One evening some of his Clog Shop cronies paid him a visit. Jethro thought he noticed three of them as the door opened, but when he had made room for them on the long settle he perceived that there were only two—Jabe and Long Ben.

Jethro at once began to inquire eagerly about the practices, and his face became quite clouded as Jabe mentioned with most persistent frequency that they were "ill off for th' trombone."

The more the visitors talked the more uncomfortable Jethro got, and every now and again he glanced uneasily up at the empty hooks whereon his instrument used to hang. Then Jabe, glancing round the house as if making a most unimportant remark, said—

"We're thinkin of axin' Traycle Tim ta tak' th' trombone parts."

Now this was positively cruel, for Traycle Tim of the Clough End brass band was Jethro's great rival, and after gasping in a helpless sort of way, and glancing once more at the empty hooks above him, he said with a sigh—

"Ay, well! But Aw dunno want a trombone on the top o' me to keep me daan when Gabriel comes to knock us aw up."

"Gabriel?" cried Jabe; "why, he's a trumpet hissel'! Ay, an' he'll blow it too o' th' resurrection mornin'!"

This was a new idea to Jethro, and it evidently told; but, shaking his head, he replied, though not quite so decidedly as before—

"Ay! But a trombone isn't a trumpet, tha knaws."

"Yi, but it is. Th' new schoo'-missis says 'at trombone's ony a soart of a frenchified name for a big trumpet."

The new schoolmistress was a great favourite of Jethro's, and so, as Jabe expected, the second shot told even more heavily than the first.

Presently he said, "Th' trombone's a varry worldly instrument, tha knaws, Jabe."

"Nowt o' th' soart! They blowed trumpets at aw' th' anniversaries i' th' wilderness, an' i' th' Temple, an' th' owd prophet says 'at when th' millenium comes they'll blow the *great* trumpet, an' that means th' trombone—naa, doesn't it, Ben?"

"Sartinly!" said Ben, with tremendous emphasis.

Jethro sat a long time in silence; at last he said—

"Aw've happen made a mistak' efther aw."

"Of course tha hez," chimed in both his visitors.

"But yo see Aw'm feared o' lovin' th' trombone moar nor Aw love God, and God conna abide that."

"Ger aat, Jethro," interrupted Jabe; "Aw'm shawmed for thi. Did thaa iver tak' owt fra your Jethro for fear he'd like it better nor he liked thee?"

"Neaw," very slowly and ponderingly.

"Well then, dust think as God's woss nor us?"

"Aw never seed it like that afore," said Jethro, and glanced up again at the hooks, and then he went on—

"Aw wish Aw hed mi owd trumpet here!"

At that moment a most mysterious noise came from behind the long settle. It was intended to have been a royal blast, but Sam Speck's unaccustomed effort only evoked a gurgling, struggling sound.

It was enough, however. Old Jethro seized the instrument, and after holding it out to make sure it was really his own, he put it to his lips and sent forth a blast that brought the hands of his comrades to their ears.

It was really the old trombone. Nearly two days had Sam spent seeking it in Duxbury; and on the anniversary day, Jethro, with visions of tabernacle and temple in his mind, and the figure of the great Archangel in the background, blew away every lingering doubt and fear, and blew himself into contentment and hope and health again.

For Better, for Worse

I

The Dilemma

For Better, for Worse

I

The Dilemma

JOHNTY HARROP the " Minder " had got into difficulties, and although thereby he had demonstrated the sagacity and justified the prophecy of popular opinion in Beckside, this was not regarded as any palliation of his mistake. In fact, from the senators of the Clog Shop down to the frequenters of the Bridge Inn, the verdict had been " sarve him reet."

After the usual number of juvenile flirtations with the girls of the village he had eventually turned his back on them all and married a Clough Ender.

Now, as Clough End was a very modern mill village of no account whatever, but pretentious and aggressive in inverse ratio to its importance, its sedate and elderly neighbour, Beckside, had been compelled to treat it much as ancient Jerusalem treated Samaria, and no Clough Ender was of any account in the older village.

But Johnty's offence was aggravated by the fact that he was regarded as a very "likely" lad, and somewhat of a plum in the marriage market. So that feminine Beckside was scandalised at his lack of taste and decency in passing by his own people.

Moreover, the "elect" lady was a renegade Becksider. She belonged to a poor but somewhat proud and ambitious family which years ago had preferred Clough End to Beckside, which was, of course, an inexpiable offence.

When she was a girl, Susy Stones and her elder sister had shown a decided aversion to going to the mill, and so the Stoneses, who were all supposed to be cursed with "fawse pride," removed to Clough End, where the daughters became dressmakers.

Susy, the younger of these two, was undeniably pretty, a typical white-skinned, dark-eyed Lancashire lass, and whilst the Beckside girls felt that this gave a provoking justification to Johnty, the Clough End young men regarded him as an unscrupulous poacher.

As a mule-minder Johnty got good wages, and must have saved money, so that nobody was greatly surprised when he indulged a long-cherished purpose by taking the large four-roomed cottage next door to Long Ben's, so that he could begin housekeeping in the same house his mother had done, and in the house wherein he himself was born, although according to current ideas it was much too large for a newly-married couple.

Johnty filled the house with new and stylish furniture, but when Mrs. Johnty arrived she poured scorn on the chest of mahogany drawers with glass knobs, which her husband had bought with great pride, and insisted on its being exchanged for a new - fangled thing called a sideboard. Every housewife in Beckside was outraged, for a chest of mahogany drawers, especially with the added and uncommon glory of glass knobs, was the last ambition of every wifely heart.

Before feminine sentiment had got over this shock it was passed round in tragic whispers that Sue Johnty had got a sewing-machine, and though this was the first article of the kind that had been seen in Beckside, and every woman in the place was dying to inspect it, yet only a few of the baser sort ever made the attempt, all the self-respecting ones feeling that they would be morally compromised if by any means they should appear to be countenancing such unheard-of extravagance.

Very soon it became a fixed opinion in the village that Mrs. Johnty was a dressy, extravagant, wasteful woman, and for a time this was marrow and fatness to the Minder. It was clearly a case in which envy was at work, and the implied compliment to his own judgment in selecting a partner and to his wife's accomplishments greatly delighted him, whilst his wife's brightness and ability gave added zest to his pleasure, and her utter unconsciousness of the sensation she was making gave piquancy to the whole situation.

The Beckside women kept very much aloof from Johnty's wife, but imitated her in their best bonnets, and made their baby clothes as nearly like hers as possible; whilst the men shook their heads over her finery, expressed strong commiseration for Johnty, but straightened themselves up whenever she passed them, and followed her with unconcealable admiration in their eyes as long as she was in sight.

After a while, however, Johnty became uneasy. The strict ideas of domestic economy whcih obtained in the village, and in which he had been brought up, slowly began to assert themselves, and as his house became better furnished, and his two children better clothed, he began to seriously regret that he had commenced his married life by " turning up " practically all his wages to his wife according to well - established Beckside usage.

Having commenced, however, he found it difficult to stop, especially as his wife was so manifestly proud of the confidence reposed in her, and really gave him no opportunity of altering matters.

Little by little also, though he scarcely ever heard a word drop, the very pronounced opinions of the villagers on the subject began to percolate somehow into Johnty's mind, and very soon he suspected that the neighbours were on the lookout for an opportunity of discussing the matter with him, which, of course, made him more anxious to avoid it.

About this time the mill began to run short time, and Johnty took the news home to his wife with a heavy heart, and was confirmed in his fears of his wife's unthriftiness by the light way in which she received the news.

" Ne'er mind, lad," she said, " it's an ill wind 'at blows noabry ony good.   Tha'll be able ta tak' me an th' childer a walk a bit i' th' afternoons."

The next Friday she brought him a fancy pipe and a quarter of scented tobacco from Duxbury, and poor Johnty, though his heart was sad, was so entirely under the influence of this little wife of his that at her bidding he smoked the new pipe and tobacco the same night, feeling all the time as if it would choke him.

Mule-minding is piecework, and so, as she never thought of asking, Susy did not know exactly what her husband earned, and the Minder was strongly tempted to keep back more of his wages than he had previously done, and save it up for the dark day he felt sure was coming.

But instead of doing so, he went to the other extreme, and gave her almost every farthing he earned, to prevent her running into debt. This meant pinching himself in twenty little ways and running up small scores at the Clog Shop, and other places, as was usual when work was not plentiful.

When he came in from his work one day about this time his wife held up her wee mouth and displayed two new false teeth. Poor Johnty! It was so like this wife of his, and they really did so effectually remove the only weak spot on her beautiful face, that he hadn't the heart to say anything unkind about them, but knowing what a buzz of tattle they would cause in the village—false teeth being rare in Beckside at that time—he made a hasty tea and got out into the lanes to brood over his anxieties.

The Minder realised that the time for action had arrived, but how to act with the least possible disturbance was a problem that sorely perplexed him. As he walked he thought, and thought rapidly for him, so that all unconsciously in crossing the Padfoot fields. he overtook two women, Lottie Speck and an old flame of his, Martha Royle.

Martha was evidently excited about something, and craning out her long lean neck, she was saying to Lottie—

" An' theyn gowd plate on 'em, an' they tell me hoo's i' debt aw o'er Duxbury."

Then she caught sight of Johnty, blushed "as red as a peony," and began to talk loudly and excitedly about some totally different subject, in pretended obliviousness of his proximity.

The Minder passed them with a monosyllabic salutation, and turning at the first stile, took a short cut for the village.

The prospect of debt and of impending exposure was now added to his anxieties, for there was no room for doubt as to Martha Royle's meaning, and he shuddered to think of his wife and her two false teeth in the hands of this scandal-loving gossip.

Johnty made straight for home, and somewhat roughly demanded his supper. His plate of porridge was placed before him, and by its side, on a little white plate, was set a fragrant roasted apple, and his wife playfully plucked at his beard and called him " owd Grumpy " in a merry and altogether irresistible way.

But Johnty was in no mood for sport, and after eating his porridge he left the apple as a silent protest against extravagance, and went out again, for if the truth must be told he was afraid to stay alone with his wife just then.

Somehow, when Beckside men were in trouble, they seemed to gravitate by a sort of natural law towards the Clog Shop, and so the Minder, after walking aimlessly up and down the road past the chapel two or three times, turned in at Jabe's.

"Well! hast made owt on 'em?" he asked as he entered; but Jabe was not at his bench, as he expected, and turning towards the fireplace, he saw the Clogger sitting before the fire, and the clogs of some invisible wearer projecting out of the nook.

"Wor art talkin' abaat?" asked Jabe in answer to Johnty's question.

"Them owd clugs o' mine. Hast bin able for t' mak' owt on 'em?"

"Well, if Aw han, Aw'm abaat t' on'y mon i' Lancashire as could; an' if tha brings 'em here agean Aw'll chuck 'em on th' feire," and Jabe's short leg was riding up and down across the other at a frantic rate, whilst his lips pursed out and his eyebrows bristled quite threateningly.

"Aw'll pay thi for 'em o' Seterday," replied Johnty very humbly.

"Ay, if tha doesn't forget; but come here wi' thi; Aw want *thee*," and the Clogger moved to another seat to make room for the Minder.

"Wots cum o'er thi?" he demanded, as Johnty sank into a seat. "Tha used goa in for th' fanciest clugs i' Beckside afoor tha wor wed. Wot's up wi' thi?"

Johnty had recently fallen into the habit of feigning avariciousness and worldly cuteness as a cover for his wife's extravagance, and so he answered with an attempt at a cunning wink—

"A chap as hez his way ta mak' hez ta be curfull naa-a-days. Neaw, Aw've gan o'er smookin'; it's wasteful," he added, as Jabe passed him a corpulent brown effigy of Punch, which served the cloggery as a tobacco jar. The Clogger cast upon Johnty a slow, comprehensive, but quietly contemptuous look as he said—

"Oh, tha's started o' scrattin hez ta? Then that'll be whey tha hezna paid thy pew-rent this last two quarters."

Johnty felt there was something ominous in the Clogger's tones, but he prepared to brave it out, and replied—

"Oh, well, Aw'll fotch it up when we goa on full time agean; but if a chap's ta mak' owt aat he hez ta tak' cur of his brass, tha knows."

"Aw ye'r, tha tak's cowd tay to th' factory; Aw reacon that'll be to save tay-wayter money," continued Jabe. But though the tone was natural, it increased Johnty's misgivings.

"Ay!" he answered very slowly. "Aw— Aw liken cowd tay best, tha knows. Whot mak's me sweeat soa?"

Jabe gave a most mysterious grunt, and then after a few long, deliberate pulls at his pipe he looked steadily into the fire, and shaking his grey-fringed head, said with great impressiveness—

"It's an awful thing when a Christian mon starts o' lyin', Jonathan."

The Minder winced, flushed angrily, and then demanded—

"Lyin'! whoa's lyin'?"

The clogs protruding from the chimney corner crossed themselves, as an indication of quickened interest; but Jabe sat still, ignoring Johnty's question.

At length, turning and looking the Minder straight in the face, he said—

"Tha knaws as weel as Aw knaw at aw thy brass goas ta bey foine feathers for yon foine brid o' thine."

"Whoa says soa?" cried Johnty, and there was anger and fear and pathetic expostulation in his voice as he went on—

"Yo' aw talken like that, and yo' knaw nowt abaat it. Ther' isn't a cleaner, willinger, quieter wench i' th' clough, and Aw've ne'er ye'rd her say a word agean th' warst on yo'. Yo' owt ta be shawmed o' yo'rsels."

There was a low whistle of surprise from far into the chimney, presumably from the wearer of the obtruding clogs. Then Jabe, waving Johnty back into his seat, said, very mildly for him—

"Aw'm sorry for thi, lad, reet enuff; but whey doesn't tha awter it?"

"Haa con Aw?" cried poor Johnty, and

instantly could have bitten his tongue out as he discovered he had given himself away.

" Tha can be th' mestur i' thi own haase sure*li*," came from out of the chimney, and Sam Speck's face became visible through the smoke as he eagerly leaned forward.

" Ay ! as *thaa* used to be," said Jabe without looking at him, and at this reminder of his bygone domestic slavery Sam became invisible again except so far as his legs were concerned.

Then Jabe began with slow carefulness to recharge his pipe, saying as he did so—

" Hoo's a likely wench as fur as Aw knaw. But women's like horses,—the better they are, the mooar they wanten th' bit. Tha's nowt ta do but put thi foot daan an' be a mon."

There was such unusual gentleness in Jabe's voice that Johnty, encouraged to be confidential, leaned forward and said with a tremor in his voice—

" Jabe, hoo's as good as hoo's pratty. Ther' isn't a better wife i' th' countryside."

" Then, aw Aw've getten ta say is as th'art goin' t' reet rooad ta spile her. Aw tell thi, women conna stond it."

Then Sam, recovering from his rebuff, joined in the conversation, and soon Johnty was listening to story after story of the humiliating sufferings which men had brought on themselves by giving way to their wives, Sam's personal reminiscences being of a specially harrowing description. All this worked on poor Johnty's well-prepared mind, and he saw more clearly than ever where he had missed his way.

This thought dwelt the longer in his mind because it transferred the blame of the past to his own shoulders, and helped him to believe that in adopting the advice of his friends he would be really consulting his wife's best interests.

As he went home his spirits rose. It would only be one short, sharp struggle. And then it was for Susy's own good, and would prevent worse happening in the future. He was a man, and it was cowardly to shirk his responsibilities.

All this, together with the ingrained hatred of extravagance in which he had been trained, and his keen sense of wounded pride at the discovery that he and his wife were the village talk, decided him to " tak' th' bull bi' th' horns," as he phrased it, and end the matter that very night. There would be a storm, he expected, —the first of their married life. Susy was more than his match in argument, and he felt that the only thing to do was to turn bully for an hour as the easiest way of settling his difficulty.

Long Ben was standing at his garden gate smoking in the twilight as he passed, and it came into Johnty's head to consult his neighbour on the matter in hand, but remembering

Ben's mildness of temper, he feared that a counsel of gentleness would be given, which would frustrate all.

So he passed quickly on, and nerving himself to his great task, he opened the door with a noisy rattle, to keep himself up to sticking point, and stepped firmly across the threshold.

The house was in darkness except for the red glow of the fire-light, and looking round for his wife, he found her lying on a short sofa which she had drawn near the fire. She was fast asleep.

Now, in picturing to himself what he would do and say when he got home, Johnty had never imagined the possibility of his wife's being asleep, and when he found her in this condition he was quite nonplussed.

He paused a moment or two, reached up to the high mantelpiece and got hold of a candle, then hesitated and put it down again, and turning his back to the fire, stood looking at his little wife. She was in deep slumber, and looked somewhat tired. Her small, well-poised head was thrown back a little. The perfect white of her skin gleamed in the fire-light. The almost classically regular features were softened into repose, and the unhooked top of her dress gave glimpses of a round snowy neck, whilst her black hair drooped a little, and almost covered a tiny white ear.

She wore a light print dress, a very uncommon garment for a minder's wife's everyday use in those times, but which Susy had made herself and put on for her husband's pleasure, never dreaming how it might strike him.

But Johnty never saw the dress. He was looking down upon the unconscious Susy with a world of warring thoughts passing through his brain. As he looked he held his breath. Then he bent down and nearly touched her. Then he straightened himself again, heaved a great sigh, and finally, whilst his grey eyes gleamed again, he cried under his breath—

" H-e-y wench, but tha *art* bonny ! "

And then he bent down again until his breath touched her hair and murmured thickly—

" *Bless* thi ; *Bless* thi."

The sleeping woman moved a little, and Johnty hastily drew back whilst Susy tossed into sight a plump, round little arm, on which was a ridiculously small hand adorned by a wedding-ring. Somehow the ring attracted the Minder's attention. He stepped forward and knelt down on a mat by the sofa-side— for Susy was above sanded floors. Then he bent over and kissed the ring, murmuring as he did so—

" Aw'd dew it agean if Aw had ta dew it ta-neet. Ay, Aw'd do it if tha cost me ten times as mitch. *Bless* thi, *bless* thi."

He noticed that he was keeping the light from his wife's face, so he moved to get it on again, and then stood over the sleeping form regarding it intently.

" Hoo's welly loike an angil," he whispered. " Hey, theer's nowt fur wrung at th' back of a face loike that."

Then he moved round to the other side of the sofa to get a different angle of admiration, and standing here, he cried under his breath—

" If hoo hadn't a hed some bit of a fawt, hoo'd a bin a gradely angil, an' Aw should ne'er a known her."

Then he began to pray. Clasping his hands and turning his face towards the ceiling, he said—

" Lord, Aw tewk her fur better or for wur, an' theer's sa mitch o' th' better abaat her Aw'll ne'er mention th' little bit o' *wur* ony mooar. Let owd bachelors and henpecked widowers say wot they'n a mind. Aw winna; Aw winna ! "

And then he stooped down, and picking up his sleeping wife as if she had been a baby, he carried her, held to his heart, upstairs, and placing her gently on the bed and solemnly kissing the still placid face, he cried—

" Bless her ; hoo's chep at *ony* price."

For Better, for Worse

II

The Denouement

For Better, for Worse

II

The Denouement

When Johnty had left the Clog Shop fortified for the subjugation of his wife by the combined counsels of the Clogger and his satellite, Sam Speck sat rubbing his corduroys with his hands, and mentally basking in the beams of self-complacency.

That his own painful experiences had at last been turned to account for the benefit of a fellow - sufferer was at anyrate some consolation for the humiliation he had endured, whilst the *rôle* of counsellor, though somewhat new, was very flattering to his vanity.

Leaning against the chimney - back, and stretching out his somewhat bowed legs as far as they would go, he sucked away at his pipe in pleasing reflection. But with Sam to think was to talk, and so in a few moments he broke the silence by assuming an air of great meekness, and observing—

" Well, efther aw, it's summut ta be able ta gi' yo'r neighbur a bit o' help."

" Ay: aat o' th' fryin'-pon into th' feire," was the gruff rejoinder.

This totally unexpected retort fairly staggered Sam. His jaw dropped, a look of surprised mystification spread itself over his face, and at length he asked—

" Wot*ever* dust meean, Jabe ? "

Now, ever since Johnty's departure a course of reflection had been passing in the Clogger's mind of an exactly opposite character to that which moved in Sam's. He realised that at that very moment a painful scene might be enacting itself in Johnty's house. He felt how serious a thing it was to interfere between man and wife.

Then he began to remember how vague and unreliable was the evidence they possessed of Susy's weakness, saving only her superior taste in the matter of dress, which might, after all, be accounted for by the fact that she had been a dressmaker. And when he came to think of it, all the Stoneses were clever and smart, and Johnty had admitted that he had never asked his wife how she spent her money.

By this time things had assumed very serious shapes in his mind, and he had just begun internally to call himself and his fellow-counsellor very hard names, when Sam's conceited remarks broke on his meditation, and surprised out of him the exclamation which so excited Sam's amazement.

"Aw meean," he replied, in answer to his companion's last question, "as tha'rt a foo', and Aw'm a bigger, an' we're boath a pair o' meddlesome mischief-makkers. For owt we knaw," he added, "yon little woman's cryin' her een aat bi this time, an'"—

But here he broke down, dashed his clay pipe petulantly to the floor, and dragging out of his thick leather belt an enormous red handkerchief, he blew his nose with most suspicious violence.

Descending at one drop from self-complacent exaltation to a sense of meddlesome meanness, Sam was silent, and very soon sidled sheepishly off home, leaving the Clogger to sit far into the night torturing himself with self-accusations and visions of misery for Johnty and his wife.

All next day Jabe was very uneasy. Johnty sometimes went back to his work after dinner the longest way round for the sake of fresh air, and as this took him past the cloggery, Jabe, on the chance of seeing him,—as the day was unusually fine,—stood for nearly half an hour in his shop doorway, hoping to thus get some inkling of how matters had gone.

But no Johnty appeared, and Jabe spent a very miserable afternoon. By tea-time, however, he had made up his mind, and just before dark, after dressing himself with most unusual care,—going in fact to the extreme of a shirt-front in the middle of the week,—he made his way down to Johnty's house.

To his great relief, Susy looked as bright as ever, and welcomed him quite effusively. To his inquiry after her husband, she said that he had gone to Slakey Brow—a mile and a half away—after some celery plants, but would soon be back.

Jabe somehow felt immensely relieved, and would have excused himself, but Susy would take no denial. She put him in one of her new-fashioned easy chairs, and Jabe admitted to himself that these *were* easier than the Beckside straight-backs.

Then she got him a pipe, praised her husband's scented weed, and playfully compelled him to try it, charging the pipe herself, and even bringing him a lighted "spill."

When he had got fairly agoing, she rated him teasingly about not having been to see them before, and suddenly remembering something else, brought him a glass of "balm" wine, and insisted on his drinking to their happiness.

This unconscious coals-of-fire treatment made Jabe feel very bad indeed; but just then the baby—a sturdy, young ten months' old—awoke, and Susy brought him to Jabe to look at, and so bewitched him that, though he had scarcely touched a baby for thirty years, and felt dreadfully afraid of hurting it, he recklessly asked to be allowed to hold it, Susy, as he did so, stepping back and clapping her hands in admiration. She told him how well he looked "nossing a babby," and asked him if he hadn't made a mistake after all in being a bachelor—and the poor Clogger was never nearer confessing that he had in his life.

And then she began to talk to him artfully about himself, a temptation which no man can resist, and she did it so adroitly and unsuspectingly that Jabe was unconscious of the flattery of it, and would have felt very well pleased with himself but for the secret remorse that was stabbing him inwardly.

"Hay! yo' doan't know yo'r born till yo' get marrit, Jabe," she said. "Aw'm happier in a day naa nor Aw used be in a ye'r afoor we wor wed."

And this was the woman he had recommended should be subjugated!

It had come into the Clogger's mind that perhaps before Johnty returned he might get an opportunity of speaking a word in season to Susy, and he made this excuse to himself for tarrying, but before long, partly through shame at the way he felt he had misjudged the Minder's wife, and partly from the intoxicating influence of Susy's presence and innocent chatter, he had thrown all reflection to the winds, and was enjoying himself to the full, reckless of all consequences.

Johnty came at last. But strange to say, Jabe seemed to have forgotten what he came about, and departed presently without explaining his business.

"Naa, Aw expect [hope] yo'll not be lung afoor yo' come ageean, Jabez," Susy said as she opened the garden gate.

"Neaw, wench, neaw!" cried the Clogger, and hurried up the "broo" towards home.

When he had gone a few steps, and the door had closed upon Susy, Jabe stopped in the road and began to talk to himself—

"Jabe," he said, "tha's made mony a foo' o' thysel' i' thy toime, bud tha's ne'er made a bigger than tha hez this toime, tha prying, suspeecious, owd maddlin, thaa!"

Then he proceeded, and as he climbed the low "brow" his face began to light up with amused gratification, and an almost simpering expression came upon it, but he pulled up again and said—

"Whey, tha'rt i' luv wi' th' woman thysel', tha soft ninny, thaa!"

When Susy returned to her husband after seeing the Clogger off, she found him in the best of spirits.

"Aw mak' noa accaant o' frisky young bachelors comin' ta see thee when Aw'm aat

o' th' rooad.   He cut loike a redshank when
Aw turnt up."

"Hay," cried Susy.   "Isn't it a pity th'
owd chap's ne'er bin marrit?   He doesn't
know wot he's missed, does he?"

And as Johnty replied "Neaw," she continued—

"Bud Awst ax him daan here to his tay
sometimes of a Sunday.   He must be looansome.
Dust think he's bin crossed i' luv, Johnty?"

Johnty didn't know, but he ate his supper,
and then, to stifle returning scruples, smoked
out of his best new pipe and sat silently
speculating on Jabe's visit.

It was clear the Clogger had said nothing
to Susy, but he wondered why he had come
at all; and seeing he had come, what had
prevented him speaking either to his wife or
himself, or both?

But when Susy entered into a detailed
description of the visit, giving all those minute
particulars which only a woman can remember,
Johnty's face beamed with amusement, and he
went off to bed in a very comfortable frame of
mind.

Next day was Saturday, and the Minder
came home between one and two o'clock.

Just as he turned out of Sally's entry, a short
cut from the mill, he came upon a bill-poster
who was pasting an auction sale bill on the
nailed-up door of Long Ben's workshop.

Johnty paused a moment, and ran his eye carelessly over the bill, but presently came upon a paragraph, which brought all the gall back into his mind. It ran thus—

> "LOT V.—All that MESSUAGE dwelling-house situate on the roadside adjoining the premises of Benjamin Barber, carpenter, in the hamlet of Beckside, and now in the occupation of JONATHAN HARROP."

Several others were gathering round the bill, but Johnty had seen enough, and turned sullenly home. He could not trust himself with his wife just then, so he made for the back garden, ostensibly to examine the condition of the celery plants he intended to set that day, but really to cool down and get command of himself.

Johnty's house had been built by his grandfather, and had descended to his mother. Johnty himself had been born in it, and remembered with painful vividness the day when the mortgagee foreclosed and took possession, and widow and children had to "flit" to a smaller house.

It had been a joyful surprise to him when he found he could take the house on his own marriage, and he had cherished the hope that he might one day be able to purchase it. And now, instead of being owner, he knew he could not remain much longer even as tenant, for it was well known that Job Sharples, the pig-dealer, wanted to buy the cottage, and in fact all the property about it ; and when Job was in the market there was no chance for anybody else.

"Johnty, come lad. Thy dinner's waitin'," cried Susy from the kitchen door.

But the Minder was angry and surly, and never deigned an answer

Presently, however, he went indoors.

"Childer as corn't dew as they's towd gets their ears seaused" (boxed), said Susy playfully, suiting the action to the word.

But Johnty began eating his food in sullen silence. When dinner was over he walked to the front door, and stood moodily leaning against the doorpost, and smoking, ruminating bitterly the while on his troubles.

"Johnty," cried Susy, after a while, "art'na gooin' ta set them sallery plants ? "

"Neaw, Aw'm not," snapped the Minder.

"Haa's that ? "

And Johnty turned round and nearly roared out——

"'Cause we're getten ta flit."

"Flit ?   Wot for ? "

"'Cause th' property's gooin' t' be sowd next Frid-day," and a feeling of utter despair came over Johnty as he observed that his frivolous little wife was not stunned by the news.

Susy was perfectly aware how dear the house was to him, and how he had hoped some day to possess it, and yet in a few moments he heard her actually singing in the kitchen.

The next few days were spent by Johnty in moody gloom, all attempts on Susy's part to cheer him being sullenly rejected, and on Thursday, the day before the sale, the Minder came home in a worse frame of mind than ever, ready, in fact, to pick a quarrel on the smallest possible provocation.

But somehow Susy was prepared for him, and had sent the baby out so as not to annoy him. She had also adorned the tea-table with cress, and a nice bit of pig-seause (brawn).

" Johnty, con tha get off thy wark to-morn, dust think ? " she asked, as she put a second piece of brawn on his plate.

" Neaw ! " Johnty almost shouted, and then glared angrily at his wife, expecting her to say something that would give him cause for going further.

" Well, dunna shaat loike that. Aw want thi to goa a bit of an errand for me."

" An' hev' Aw nowt else t' do but goa errands for thi ? It takes me aw my time ta keep thi as it is."

There ! the rubicon was crossed, for the tone of Johnty's retort was even harsher than his words, and though he would have given worlds to have the word back, he kept up his hard look, and glanced furtively across the table to see what effect he had produced.

Every drop of blood seemed to have left

Susy's face, an injured and haughty look rose into her eyes, and rising to her feet, she bestowed one cold, hard glance on Johnty and fled upstairs.

To say that Johnty was miserable would be a very mild way of putting the case. He left his unfinished tea and went out, and after wandering aimlessly about for some time, turned in to the Bridge Inn. But he could not stay, and by nine o'clock he was back home again, and found his wife sitting sewing by the candle-light.

"Wheer dust want mi ta goa?" he asked, in a tone between apology and protestation.

"Noawheer; Aw con goa mysel'," and a second time Susy retreated to the bedroom.

When he came home to dinner next day he found, as he expected, that his wife had gone by the coach to Duxbury, and he felt painful misgivings as to his conduct, and was troubled with most unusual apprehension as to Susy's safety.

It was an almost interminable afternoon, and when six o'clock did come Johnty was almost the first man to leave the mill, although he worked in the top storey.

He heaved a great sigh of relief as he caught sight of his wife stooping over the cradle, and went up to kiss her, but she eluded him with an averted face, and went about her work.

The Minder ate his tea in silence, his mind

filled with conflicting emotions, whilst Susy hovered about the table and her husband quite strangely, but never gave him the chance to take hold of her, and carefully avoided meeting his eye.

There was a very tall jug standing on the table, a show-jug which Susy greatly prized, and which Johnty had never known her use before.

" Wot's i' this jug ? " he asked, to break the uncomfortable silence.

" Look and see," was the short answer, and Susy became instantly very busy amongst the baby-clothes. There was a small plate on the top of the jug, and Johnty lifted it down upon the table, and took the vessel up to explore its recesses. It contained a bundle of documents.

" Whativer's thoos ? " cried Johnty, and took them out and began unfolding them.

A moment's scrutiny showed him that they were the title-deeds of his house, with a hasty memorandum and a receipt for the price.

The sight nearly took his breath away and also his speech. But presently he found courage to ask—

" Wot's aw this meean, Sue ? "

" It meeans as tha'rt thy own landlord, if tha wants to know," and there was a distinctly no-compromise tone in Susy's voice.

" Me a landlord ! Haa con that be ? Whoa's bowt [bought] it ? "

" Aw have."

" Thee!   Wheer'st getten th' brass ? "

" No' fro' thee.   It tak's thee aw thy toime ta keep me, tha knows ! "

Johnty winced, and continued—

" Wheer'st borrad it ? "

" Aw've ne'er bin used ta borraing, Jonathan. Aw've saved it."

" Thee saved it ? "

And then the scales seemed to fall from the Minder's eyes, a great many things became clear all at once, and after a pause and a great relief-ful sigh, he rushed at his wife, and she ran upstairs again, and he after her.

He caught her before she got to the top, for she was not very good at climbing stairs just then, and took her in his arms and brought her down, stopping on every other step to kiss her burning and teary face.

Then he took her on his knee, and held her very close, and compelled her to tell him all about it.

There was nothing to tell, she said.   She knew how much he would like to own the house they lived in, for old associations' sake. She had a little bit of money when they were married, but thought, if he ever needed it, it would be so pleasant to give him a nice surprise ; so, as he never asked, she had never told him about it.

Since their marriage she had put something

by every week, and perhaps the fact that she was able to make her own and the children's clothes had helped her, as well as enabled her to make a pretty fair appearance. She had also made a few neighbours' dresses, but daren't tell him, because " he wor sa soft abaat " her.

She had learnt about the sale of the cottage quite by accident, and had already opened negotiations for a private purchase when the auction bills came out, and his alarm about having to flit had rather hurried her.

Oh what a happy man was Johnty Harrop then !

He made a full confession of all his suspicions, omitting only the Clog Shop incident. But he might as well have told that also, for when Jabe and Sam came to tea on Sunday by special invitation and heard the whole story, they confessed too, and Susy forgave them also with quite a queenly grace, and insisted when they had gone that their next baby should be called Jabez — as it very likely would have been, only it turned out to be a girl, and was christened Susan.

" Bullet " Pie

" Bullet " Pie

A LADY evangelist was conducting special services at Clough End, and Lige and Sam Speck had been to hear her, or, perhaps more correctly, to enjoy the unhallowed delight of seeing a woman in a pulpit. The " heckling " they received at the hands of the Clogger produced very complete repentance apparently ; but, alas ! the mischief was done, and the very next Sunday the fearful fruits of it were seen, for a woman actually got up in the Beckside after - service prayer - meeting and made a speech.

A speech, mark you ; not a prayer or an experience—these were not altogether contraband—but a speech, and a somewhat startling speech, too. Jabe had declared again and again whenever the disturbing question of female evangelists came up—

" There's ne'er bin a woman i' aar poopit sin' th' place wor built. Neaw, an' ther' never will be woll [while] Aw'm alive."

And now Beckside was suddenly brought down to the ignominious level of Clough End.

The offending female was the new school-mistress, and whilst some were of opinion that her official position gave her a sort of licence, Jabe and others held that such a person ought to have known better, and that her status aggravated the offence.

It was just at that time in late autumn when the temperature of the Sunday night prayer-meeting usually began to rise, and the prayers were most thickly punctuated with ejaculations. Suddenly one evening this misguided young woman rose in her place in the singing-pew, and, holding up her hand, cried in school-mistress style, " H-U-S-H ! "

Then, before anyone could rise from his knees and sit down, she gripped hold of the iron rod supporting the singing-pew curtain, and cried out in tremulous but earnest tones—

" Friends, why stand we here all the day idle ? Why do we keep on praying God to save sinners when the Brick-croft is full of sinners to whom we never go ? Christ said we were to go into all the world. Why don't we go ? " And then she paused, quiet tears swam in her eyes, and she sat abruptly down.

Sam Speck, who sat by her side, blushed a great red blush, and hid his head in his hands.

Long Ben opened his mouth as if to speak, and then in sheer astonishment forgot to close it, and sat gaping in a helpless sort of way, whilst his eyes glistened with suppressed excitement.

Others of the Clog Shop community glanced timidly round at each other, and presently Jabe from the back pew thundered out in his sternest tones—

" It's toime ta goa whoam, Bruther Banks."

Brother Banks, the preacher conducting the meeting, hurriedly closed it, and Jabe was seen limping homeward alone, with that exaggeration of his ordinary lameness which was a certain indication of internal disturbance. The rest of the counsellors followed in a slinking, guilty manner, as if they had been the transgressors and were coming for judgment.

Long Ben, however, who was the last to arrive, having shyly lingered behind to shake hands with and encourage the mistress, betrayed himself almost instantly, for, whilst putting on a look of portentous gravity, he allowed the corners of his mouth to twitch, and chuckled as he vainly hoped *sotto voce*, and was therefore considerably startled when Jabe, without sitting down, wheeled suddenly round and fiercely demanded—

" Who'rt lowfin [laughing] at ? "

But Ben's eyes only twinkled the more, and he filled his pipe with most exasperating deliberateness.

Somehow Jabe's pipe wouldn't light. The second " spill " burned his fingers ; the third lighted the pipe, but there was something wrong with the "draw"; and finally, in whisking round to give an annihilating answer to a question from Lige, he knocked the pipe against the chimney-corner and broke it. Then he sat down in a pet, and obstinately refused to smoke at all.

This was most ominous. The lesser lights of the Clog Shop looked at each other with apprehensive glances, but Ben smoked on in aggravating and aggressive imperturbability.

" Wee'st have a revival *naa*," he exclaimed at length—coming down rather heavily on the " naa."

" Ay," cried Jabe, rushing in at the opening for which he had been waiting, and laughing in bitter scorn. " A revival o' neyse (noise) an' Ranterism an' bosh ! Crowin' hens an' preychin' women 'ull mak' a bonny revival sure*li*." And his speaking leg actually kicked the hob of the fire-grate in its frantic excitement.

And then the others joined in, and soon the debate become fast and furious. For once Jabe was entirely alone. Encouraged by the daring stand made by Long Ben, the others, not even excepting Sam Speck, took up cudgels for the schoolmistress, which, of course, only exasperated the Clogger the more.

" By th' mon," he cried at the close of one of his tirades, " Hoo'll ger i' th' poopit next ? Bud if hoo does ! If hoo does ! " And finding no threat equal to the enormity of such a deed, he shook his fist in the air, and strutted lamely across the sanded floor.

In spite of all this, the revival did break out at the chapel, intermittently at first, but presently it settled down into regular form, under the direction of a lay evangelist recently engaged by the circuit.

Somehow the human credit of it was given to the schoolmistress, and as she made no further attempts at public speaking, but worked with exemplary zeal in twenty other ways, even Jabe suspended final judgment upon her, and admitted that she was a " varry dacent wench —*i' sum things.*"

The lady in question had had charge of the village school over the bridge and at the foot of the " Knob " for some months now. She was a plain-looking, yellow-haired girl of about twenty-five, whose face only became interesting when she began to speak to you. Then the great grey eyes filled with soft warm light, and the fair skin gleamed with kindliness, and the soft low voice worked upon you like a gentle spell. Nothing was known of her origin, except that she came from somewhere Gloucester way, and belonged to the Church.

But there was no church in Beckside. The parish church of Brogden was nearly two miles away, and the chapel-of-ease at Clough End was about the same distance. Most of her pupils went to the chapel, and as she was a sociable little body, and much interested in her scholars, she went too, and though startled and somewhat amused by what she saw, she soon discovered the deep spirituality underneath these surface incongruities, and became a most diligent attendant.

In a short time she grew quite interested in everything, read the *History of Methodism* out of the Sunday School Library, and asked Sam Speck (whose favour she won very early by calling him " Mister ") some very perplexing questions as to the wherefore of the various usages in vogue at the chapel. She was charmed with the class-meeting, and, being rather afraid of Jabe, became a member of Long Ben's class, and immediately captured that worthy's affection by the charming *naïveté* of her " experience."

Before long she caught the fever of Methodist aggressiveness, and became quite concerned for the religious condition of some of her neighbours, which explains the impulsive little plunge she made into exhortation at the prayer-meeting already described.

The Brick-croft, of which the mistress had spoken in her memorable speech, was a cluster of poor cottages, mostly single - storeyed, which stood on a flat piece of land along the side of the " Beck " and just behind the

Bridge Inn. The unregenerate part of Beck-side resided here. Almost every house, however small, had a pigeon-cote attached to it, and upon a good few of the low roofs were mechanical arrangements for the entrapping of " strags " (stray pigeons).

You never met a Brick-crofter but he had a pigeon in his pocket and a bull-terrier at his heels. Even the women were easily recognised in Duxbury by the fact that they invariably carried a sort of twin-lidded basket, commonly used for conveying pigeons.

The Brick-croft was the Beckside " far country." Whatever of broiling, drunkenness, or gambling disgraced the village was sure to spring from this unsavoury corner of it. The policeman lived on its outskirts.

The schoolmistress having to pass the outer border of the Croft every morning on her way to her duties, and having also to visit it frequently in search of her most truant scholars, grew quite alarmed for the state of the people and the surroundings amid which " her children " were brought up, and it was whilst listening to the seemingly earnest prayers of the chapel people, and brooding over the condition of the pigeon-flyers, that she was moved into making the speech which gave such umbrage to the Clogger.

During the week following, Miss Redford

held conversations with all the chapel people she could get hold of about the moral needs of the Brick-crofters, and was specially urgent upon Nathan the smith and Sam Speck, and these—immensely flattered by the lady's preference—at once began to stir up the rest.

The following Sunday an open-air service was held in the Croft, and whilst the men sang and exhorted, the schoolmistress went to the women, who stood in their doorways with aprons folded round dirty arms, and invited them to chapel.

One or two responded, and as they were old scholars of the Sunday School, they were easily impressed and coaxed up to the penitent-form. This was the beginning of the revival, and very soon special services of an exceedingly enthusiastic character were in full swing.

But the mistress was not content. Several women and two or three of the least notorious of the Brick-croft men had been drawn to chapel, but the main body of the pigeon-flyers was still untouched.

At last Miss Redford could rest no longer, and after dismissing the children one afternoon she retired into her little anteroom and dropped upon her knees. When she rose again she had pledged herself to make some determined effort that very night. Hastening home to her lodgings and making a hurried tea, she sallied forth to enlist assistance.

The smithy was next door but one to her lodgings, and Nathan had always been kind to her, but as soon as she expounded her plan he declared he was " up to th' een i' wark"; and so she passed on to Sam Speck's.

Sam, his sister said, was "at th' Clug Shop as yewzuall," and the mistress, who only guessed Jabe's sentiments towards her, but who regarded him with wholesome fear, could not muster courage to seek Sam there.

She turned back, therefore, and went into Long Ben's shop. The carpenter, when he heard her proposition, felt that his acts were recoiling on his own head, and half-wished that he had not triumphed quite so cruelly over his old friend Jabe. But before the schoolmistress had done Ben had pledged himself to call for her at half-past six and escort her round the Brick-croft, with the clear understanding, however, that she was to do all the talking.

Whilst the second hymn was being sung at the service that evening, and some of the worshippers were vaguely wondering what had become of the mistress, a commotion was heard in the porch outside, and almost immediately the dingy green door swung open, and in walked Miss Redford with moist

eyes and spilled over, and behind her came
more rough-looking men from the Brick-croft
including the two most hardened reprobates
in the place.

Long Ben brought up the rear, closed the
pew doors on the captured ones, and handed
them hymn-books with tremendous consciousness
that he was one of the heroes of the hour and
the object of much official envy.

This was the meaning of the hue and in the
days that followed first one and then another
of the saved Brier-eaters was 'added to
the Church' whilst the schoolmistress lived in
a seventh heaven of delight and Long Ben
struggled fiercely with a pride which he feared
was sinful.

But two or three of the most notorious of
the pigeon-flyers still held out—their ring-
leader 'Sniggy' Fendle in particular.

Sniggy a bye-name which had long supplanted his baptismal [illegible] was an undersized but thick-set middle-aged man, who
lived with his mother at one corner of the
[illegible]. He had been fined for [illegible]
more than once imprisoned at least once
for poaching, was the [illegible]-mouthed man in
the [illegible] and was gravely suspected of being
concerned in an affair which had all but cost a
gamekeeper his life.

In the [illegible] however he was fairly popular.
His bull-terrier had the most distinctly curved

front legs and the most murderous-looking head in the community. He knew more ways of snaring rabbits than a keeper; but chief of all his distinctions, he was the owner of that immortal pigeon, the "Bullet," which was glory more than enough for any ordinary man.

Other famous birds would come (fly) from Manchester; Tommy-o'-th'-Well's "Blue-cock" had come from London; but the incomparable "Bullet" had visited "forrin parts," and had flown home from Paris. But the highest distinction of this wonderful bird was its speed; and when, after one of its early victories, "Sluthering Jack," who had won five shillings by the achievement, said to the assembled sportsmen that "th' 'Dun-cock' owt ta be caw'd th' 'Bullet,'" everybody felt that Jack had had an inspiration, and that the bird had been finally and adequately labelled.

No one ever dreamed of competing with the "Dun-cock" now on equal terms, and all other aspirants to flying fame were valued by the distance they stood from Sniggy's "Bullet."

Emboldened by the security of his position as king of the Croft, Sniggy had shown the only discourtesy towards the schoolmistress which she received on her memorable invasion of that region, but the look on Long Ben's face as he stood behind Miss Redford, and the shamed way in which his mates dropped their heads at his insolent word, warned him of danger, and, to tell the whole truth, had awakened in him a shame which of itself prevented him from going to the chapel.

In the third week of the services, however, he ventured to join the rest, but even then nothing could be made of him; and when one night the schoolmistress's hopes were raised a little, they were subsequently dashed again by the fact that he did not turn up on the three succeeding evenings, one of which was Sunday.

Every day during this period Miss Redford called at Sniggy's, venturing alone by this time, but though on one occasion she almost followed Sniggy into the house, his hard-faced old mother assured her that he " worn't in."

Then she sounded his recently-converted mates, but they seemed afraid of him, and the only information she could glean was that he had pledged himself to fly the " Bullet " from Manchester against a Clough End pigeon for £20, giving the less famous bird a two-minutes' start.

Somehow this man got on the teacher's mind, chiefly, perhaps, because of the extraordinary difficulty of capturing him, and she was more than disappointed when for the fourth evening in succession Sniggy failed her.

Meanwhile the owner of the " Bullet " was himself in great trouble. As an old Sunday School scholar he knew enough to make him miserable, now that he had begun to think, and he confided to one of his mates that he felt " wuss nor he did when Billy Tinker stool th' ' Bullet.' "

On every occasion on which the school-mistress had called, he had been in, but had crouched behind the mangle, or rushed into the pantry, and up the plank ladder into the little dimly-lighted bedroom under the thatch. When the mistress stopped to talk he took his clogs off, stepped lightly over the attic floor until he was directly over the speaker's head, and then, lying on his stomach and applying his ear to a crack, he listened eagerly to every word that was uttered. Once, indeed, when Miss Redford had insisted on praying with hard, ignorant old Molly, he had sobbed until he was afraid of being discovered, as the visitor prayed for " Thy handmaid's son."

That night Sniggy gave his bull-terrier to the gamekeeper, shrewdly surmising how that functionary would dispose of it, and regarding it himself as a sort of compensation for many past injuries of which he was now painfully conscious.

Then he spent almost all the next night in the pigeon-cote wrestling with the question of the disposal of his birds, but always sticking fast when it came to the " Bullet," and edging off on the excuse of his approaching engagement with the ambitious Clough Ender.

Just as the prayer-meeting was closing on the fourth night of Sniggy's absence, and Miss Redford was listening to the final prayer with a sinking heart, Silas, the chapel-keeper, touched her on the shoulder and beckoned her out.

Arrived at the porch, she found Sniggy's mother with a shawl over her head, and a very sour look on her face, waiting for her.

"He wants yo' ta cum an' ha' sum supper wi' him, if yo' will," she said, in a tone which showed that she was far from approving of the invitation herself.

Now, during the revival, the poor fellows of the Brick-croft had taken all sorts of odd ways of showing their appreciation of the mistress's interest in them, and so she was not greatly startled at this extraordinary request.

"Thank you, Mrs. Molly," she said, calling the old woman by the only name she had ever heard of her having, "but won't you ask Mr. Barber to come as well?"

"Oh ay! He wants Ben an' owd Jabe tew, if they'll cum."

The mistress hastened back into the chapel and acquainted Ben with the invitation, leaving him to negotiate with Jabe, of whom she stood in great fear. In a moment or two both the stewards joined her, and all walked in wondering silence down to the Croft.

Two small tables of slightly different height, and covered with small white cloths put together to do duty as a tablecloth, stood in the middle of the newly-sanded floor, and Sniggy, washed and dressed in the best he had, but looking agitated and miserable, sat at one end waiting for them.

He bade them " mak' yo'rsels a' whoam " in gruffly solemn tones, and then, after seeing them all seated, he brought a " blazer " out of the pantry to screen the mistress's back from the fire, and, looking uneasily round, he said—

" Jabe, wilt' say a bit of a blessin' ? "

The Clogger did so, and then there was an awkward pause, during which Sniggy seemed to be struggling with some almost uncontrollable emotion. The quick woman's eyes of Miss Redford showed her that there was nothing on the table to eat except a little broken oat-cake at one corner.

" Naa then, bring it aat," cried Sniggy at that moment. And old Molly went to the oven and produced a rather small pie, which she immediately set before her son.

Sniggy seized the knife, rose to his feet, and then stood waveringly over the smoking dish, whilst the rest looked on with curious interest. But his knife dropped from his hand after a moment's hesitation, and falling back into his chair, he cried, with a sort of half-wail in his voice—

" Aw conna dew it ; Jabe, *thee* carve."

"Ar'ta badly, lad?" said Jabe, as he moved to take the pigeon-flyer's place.

"Neaw! Neaw! goa on wi' yo'r supper," was the answer, whilst old Molly disappeared suddenly into the pantry, from whence the mistress thought she heard smothered sobs coming, and Sniggy drew very close to the fire, as if he were cold.

"Art'na goin' to ha' sum'?" asked Jabe, turning to their host, after he had served the schoolmistress.

"Neaw, neaw!" cried Sniggy hastily, "bud help yo'rsels, aw on yer."

The dish turned out to be pigeon-pie, or rather a mixture of pigeon and steak, a very popular dainty in the Brick-croft, and the schoolmistress shrewdly surmised that they were eating some of Sniggy's own birds.

But it was a melancholy feast. Once or twice Miss Redford tried to start a conversation, but Jabe and Ben answered in monosyllables, and the master of the house cowered gloomily over the fire.

When supper was over and they were turning with feelings of relief from the tables, Sniggy turned to Jabe, who was nearest, and asked—

"Han yo' finished it?"

"Ay, lad."

"Ivery bit?"

"Ay! Except t' boanes."

Then there was a pause. Sniggy had evidently something more to say, but found it difficult to say it. By and by, looking from Ben to Jabe, and finally resting his eyes on the mistress, he stammered out—

" Yo'—*yo'n etten th' ' Bullet,'* " and burst into passionate sobs.

Poor Sniggy had realised very early in his spiritual struggles that the supreme conflict would be fought about his idolised pigeon. Again and again he had staved matters off by sacrificing his dog and his drink, and eventually several of his less distinguished birds, but it always came back to the same point. If ever he was saved the "Bullet" would have to go, and so, after a whole night's struggle, he at last nerved himself to the great sacrifice by the thought common in the Brick-croft that the schoolmistress " clemm't hersel'," and he would give her one good meal at anyrate. So with a terrible struggle he made the supper, achieved his victory, and soon after found spiritual rest.

The revival lasted some weeks after this. Many of Sniggy's companions followed his example, and soon the whole district was moved by the story of this wonderful work of God.

No Methodist revival is complete without a Lovefeast, and so on the last Sunday of the services there was a never-to-be-forgotten one instead of the Sunday evening service at Beckside.

The chapel was packed. All the Brick-croft

men "testified," and each in turn made grateful, if somewhat clumsy, allusion to " th' schoo'-missis," as the first human cause of their conversion.

Everybody was on "tenter-hooks" to hear the wonderful teacher speak, but in her retreat behind the singing-pew curtain she held down her head, and laughed and cried quietly to herself.

Presently Lige and Jonas Tatlock began to scowl and nod their heads excitedly in the direction of Long Ben's pew, and that worthy puzzled for a moment, suddenly heard several voices calling in loud whispers, " Th' missis," and, rising, he stepped up the pulpit stairs and said something to the preacher.

" Perhaps Sister Redford will say a few words," said the preacher, and then the school-mistress rose, and with her great eyes full of glory and her lips quivering with intense emotion, she looked timidly round on the many radiant faces upturned to hers. She tried to speak, but there was nothing of the schoolmistress about her that day, and her tones were low and timid.

" Speak up," people began to cry, and when every ear was strained to hear, the tense silence was broken by the well-known voice of the Clogger, crying in tones quivering with deep emotion—

" Bless thi, wench ; goo i' th' poopit."

A Diplomatic Reverse

A Diplomatic Reverse

WEAK people are great trials to their friends, and Long Ben was a frequent source of anxiety to old Jabe. Ben was so easily moved, and so rash when he was moved, that the Clogger told him every week of his life, " Thy yed's as sawft as a fuz-baw " (ball).

In financial matters Jabe regarded him as utterly incompetent. He was so open-handed towards the borrower, and so patient and hopeful towards his debtors, that he was informed by his chief mentor again and again, " Tha'll ne'er ha' nowt woll tha'rt wik " (living).

More than one Becksider had been disappointed of temporary loans from Ben by the sudden and peremptory interference of the Clogger, and Ben scarcely ever came to the Clog Shop without being catechised as to the state of his account with this or that slow-paying debtor. If Ben became reticent in any of these matters Jabe at once took the alarm, and by threatening and judicious " pumpings," and occasionally by plottings with Ben's wife, ultimately got the truth out of him, and sometimes saved him from loss.

Of late years, however, Ben, partly out of shy modesty, and partly out of fear of the Clogger, had developed a quite crafty slyness in his methods of rendering help to others.

" He's that fawse [cunning], wench," Jabe would confide to Mrs. Ben in their consultations on the subject, " He'd diddle Owd Scratch hissel', an' we ne'er knaw wot he's up to."

And the Clogger's difficulties were complicated by the view he took of himself. He regarded himself as of a naturally hard and unsympathetic disposition, with a terrible tendency towards grasping greediness. Financial operations were therefore very welcome to the old Adam in him, but very baneful, he feared, in their effects on his spiritual life, so that when Ben's weaknesses compelled him to act the part of an astute worldly-wise counsellor to his friend, it was done at great risk to his own soul.

Under these circumstances it will be easily seen how grievous a cross Ben's weaknesses were to poor Jabe. It must, however, be stated, if we are to make a full and faithful record, that the Clogger did not bear his cross either meekly or silently.

Jabe had been busy one day teaching his apprentice the art of clog-sole shaping, and as the work had been trying to both his back and his temper, he was resting and taking a quiet whiff, meditating the while on a little problem which was just then exercising his mind.

Four or five months before, Ralph Green, the cut-looker, had died, leaving a wife and five children unprovided for. There was the club money, of course, and Ralph, though delicate, had managed to put a little into the savings bank at Duxbury; so that it was well known that the bereaved family would be in no particular need for a little time.

But time had travelled quickly, and Jabe, reckoning it up, was startled to find that nearly five months had gone, and that therefore it was high time to make some inquiry into the condition of the family.

But Ben was in the way. If the subject were broached in his presence he would be sure to go right off and do something foolish, and something which, with his large family, he could ill afford.

And then Mrs. Green was not exactly a *persona grata*. She was a quiet, shy sort of woman. It was reluctantly granted that, as a wife and mother, she was "reet enuff," but as a neighbour she was close, reserved, and stiffly proud. Jabe, with the rest of the villagers, felt this, and he had difficulty in repressing a feeling of satisfaction that now, at anyrate she would be compelled to make friends of her neighbours.

At the same time, the Clogger justly surmised that, if help were given to the cutlooker's family, considerable care would have to be taken as to the mode of rendering it, or else it might be refused.

And then, none of the Greens were " members," so that to the strictly legal mind of the senior society steward there was a difficulty in the way of helping them from the chapel poor's fund. To further complicate matters, Jabe suspected himself of disinclination to help this case of need, which was another indication of the original desperateness of his nature, and entirely shook his own confidence in his power to rightly judge the matter.

Altogether the subject provided a very neat problem, which might have occupied two or three nights' discussion around the Clog Shop fire, and have given opportunities for the display of those fine forensic talents on which Jabe prided himself, but for that irritating and humiliating weakness of Long Ben's.

By this time the Clogger's pipe was out, and hung negligently between his lips, threatening every moment to drop to the ground. The apprentice, standing almost up to the knees in clog-chips, was perspiring over his work and inaudibly anathematising obdurate clog-soles, when there was a murmur of young voices outside, the " sneck " of the shop-door was gently and hesitatingly lifted, the door itself slowly pushed open, and in came two children, a boy and a girl. They carried a basket which seemed to contain something heavy, and after carefully closing the door after them, they dropped their burden upon the floor.

" Well, wot dun *yo'* want ? " demanded Jabe, taking his pipe out of his mouth, and scowling with a sternness he always assumed when talking to children.

For a moment or two there was no answer ; the boy looked at the girl ; and the girl, catching at her pinafore as if preparing to cry, looked back at the boy.

Presently, however, the girl seemed to repent of her tears, and making a resolute effort, which drove the blood from her thin cheeks, she stammered—

" Dun yo' want ta bey ony roppits [rabbits], Jabe ? "

The Clogger rose to his feet, and seemed about to explode upon his visitors, when the boy chimed in—

" Full-bred Spanish, yo' known ; nineteen inches across th' ye'rs."

" Roppits ! yo' wastrils," cried Jabe, in a grossly overdone pretence of anger ; " wot dew Aw want wi' roppits ? Tak' 'em aat o' th' place, or "—

But the girl plucked up courage, and dropping into a slightly wheedling tone, she said—

"Yo' met bey 'em, Jabe, my— We wanten th' brass."

"Brass! Wot dun yo' want th' brass fur?"

But a look of sudden resoluteness came into the eyes of the children, and the girl shook her head admonitorily at her brother, and then answered—

"We conna tell thi, Jabe."

"Yo' conna tell," shouted the Clogger; "yo' meean yo' winna."

And then, suddenly, as if to surprise something out of them, he asked—

"Does yur muther knaw as yur sellin' 'em?"

Another look of caution shot into the girl's eyes, but before she could speak the boy had answered, "Neaw."

"Neaw! Tha'rt a bonny mon ta cum sellin' roppits ba'at tellin' thy muther," cried Jabe, addressing the boy as evidently the less artful.

But the sister had telegraphed some kind of warning to her brother, and he stood and refused to answer a word. Then Jabe tried several other questions without much success, and finally said—

"Naa, then, Aw'm just wantin' a pur [pair] o' roppits like thoose," and he lifted the basket lid and glanced critically at the occupants. "Aw've a hempty pig-hoile daan th' garden yond', an' Aw want ta keep 'em in it; bud

Aw'st bey noa roppits off childer as corn't tell me wot they're goin' fur t' dew wi' th' brass."

The young rabbit - vendors breathed hard and looked at each other in dire perplexity, and then the girl glanced apprehensively at the apprentice, who, on perceiving that he was noticed, suddenly resumed his clog - shaping with demonstrative haste.

"Here, Isaac!" cried Jabe. "Goa daan th' gardin' an' mak' a place for these roppits i' th' pig-coite."

As soon as Isaac had disappeared on his invented errand, Jabe demanded the price ot the wonderful Black Spanishes, and on having two shillings each tentatively quoted to him, he pulled two half-crowns out of his pocket, and balancing them on his fingers, he said—

"Naa, then; wot dun yo' want th' brass fur?"

The children hesitated, looked longingly at the coins and then at each other, heaved great, anxious sighs, and then the girl ventured—

"Will yo' tell onybody, Jabe?"

"Tell onybody? Not *me*," cried Jabe, in a tone expressive of the utter impossibility of such a thing.

There was another pause, and then the girl drew a long breath, hesitated, took a step nearer the old Clogger, and then giving way suddenly, she fell forward with her head on his breast, and sobbed—

"We want ta give it my muther fur th' rent."

No Becksider of any experience would have believed it, but it is nevertheless true, that Jabe did not remove the little hot face that was buried in his bosom, and it was also true that whilst he was speaking to the brother, blushing and ashamed of his sister's tears, but hovering perilously near them himself, Jabe's arm somehow strayed round to the other side of the sobbing child, and as he talked he drew her tightly to him and held her there.

"Haa dust knaw thy muther conna pay th' rent hersel'?" he asked, looking at the boy, and speaking in tones of most unnecessary gruffness.

"'Cause Owd Croppy came for it yesterday, an' he sauced my muther, an' aar Lizer theer sleeps wi' my muther, an' hoo says hoo wur skrikin' welly aw neet."

As the reader will have surmised, Jabe's juvenile visitors were the children of Widow Green, and the interview just described brought painfully home to the Clogger the state of affairs at the cut-looker's cottage.

So with a brief, brusque admonition to secrecy, Jabe dismissed the children, and adjourned to the parlour for tea, previously telling the apprentice to take great care of the rabbits for a day or two.

Over tea and the pipe that followed, Jabe

matured his plans with difficulty. It was very provoking not to be able to take Ben into his confidence, and he resolved to punish that troublesome weakling by keeping him out of the affair altogether.

Only Ben was much more ingenious and inventive than the Clogger, and Jabe sorely needed a suggestion or two from him as to the quietest and most roundabout way of conveying the assistance to be rendered. Invention, in fact, was not Jabe's strong point, and he knew it, and so he was still chasing through his brain ideas that refused to be caught when the cronies began to assemble for the evening.

For a time he sat at his bench and took no part in the conversation. Presently, however, he pulled off his apron for the night, and joined the circle round the fire.

"Has ony on yo' yerd haa Phebe Green's goin' on?" he asked, with a laborious attempt at indifference which excited more curiosity than his most anxious tones could have done, and unfortunately woke up Long Ben, who seemed to be dozing far into the nook.

But nobody seemed to know anything, and Nathan the smith declared that "They met be clemmin' i' th' haase for owt as they towd onybody"; and Sam Speck said he "couldn't abide sitch fawse pride."

Jabe undertook a feeble defence of the widow, all the time keeping a vigilant eye on Long

Ben, who manifested a most satisfactory lack of interest. In fact, Ben only seemed to really wake up when Sniggy Parkin came in and announced that he was going to "tak' cur" (care) of his "owd woman," and, for a start, "Th' mangle's for sale!"

Now the sale of Molly's mangle was a matter of public interest. Wringing - machines were scarce in Beckside. Johnty Harrop's wife had got one, of course, and so had Jimmy Juddy's Nancy, and one or two others of the upper ten, but for the rest everybody took their clothes to the public mangles.

Until recently there had been two in the village,—one owned by Blind Alice, and patronised by the more respectable of the Becksiders, and Molly Parkin's in the Brick-croft, supported by the democracy. But some weeks before Blind Alice had been taken to the Asylum, and her mangle removed to Clough End.

The sale of Molly's machine therefore would create a sort of public crisis. It was agreed on all hands that the Brick-croft mangle must not leave the village, and Long Ben seemed so absorbed in the situation, and its possible developments, that Jabe rejoiced to think that Widow Green would drop for the time out of his thoughts. Meanwhile, what must be done for the Greens?

The next night proved so very wet that nobody turned up at the Clog Shop except

Sam Speck. But Sam was clearly pre-
judiced.

"Hoo keeps hersel' to hersel'; *leave* her to
hersel'," was his dictum.

Then Jabe opened his mind more fully, but
though they talked for a long time, the two
schemers could invent nothing better than a
tortuous and involved system of subsidies to
be given as occasion offered under various
elaborate pretexts. When they parted neither
was quite satisfied with the outcome of their
consultation, and Jabe was more and more irate
at Ben for his unavailability.

That same night, wet though it was, Ben
paid a visit to Phebe Green.

"Arta' in, Phebe?" he asked, opening the
door a little, and holding it.

"Ay," said a somewhat weary voice, and the
carpenter stepped inside, and reared his big
umbrella on the slop-stone to drip.

"Childer, reitch a cheer," said Phebe, and
when Ben had taken his seat, and given a sour-
sweet to each of the children, he stole a quiet
look round the house, and then glanced shyly
at the widow. She looked older and sadder
than of yore, Ben noted with a pang, and there
was that harassed look which sorrow never
brings to the face except when blended with
worry.

"Phebe, thee an' me's allis been thick, 'anna
we?" he ventured at last.

"Ay," said Phebe, but there was suspicion and rising resistance in her tones.

"Well, Aw want thi ta dew me a favour, ay, an' aw Beckside tew, if thaa will."

"Wot dust want?" asked the widow, still cautious and icy.

"Why, we're goin' t' be ba'at a mangle i' Beckside, an' Aw thowt sum on us met bey it in if thaa'd tak' it fur a bit, an' work it fur th' good o' th' village, thaa knaws."

Phebe, a tall, severe-looking woman, stood looking down upon Ben, white and motionless as a statue, and then the fountains of the deep seemed suddenly to open within her, and with a passionate cry she staggered to a seat, and leaning her head on the table, she sobbed out—

"O Lord, Thaa *art* 'the Father of the fatherless, and the Husband of the widow'! just when Aw were at th' fur end Thaa's sent me deliverance."

Presently her agitation subsided, and, looking up at the carpenter, she cried: "It's just loike thee, Ben Barber, bud thy wife an' childer 'ull ne'er want for nowt as long as theer's a God aboon us!"

"Aw see nowt ta tak' on o' that rooad abaat," said Ben, with a look of surprise which was not perhaps perfectly sincere. "If owd Molly's mangle went aat o' th' village it 'ud be Dicky Pink wi' aw th' Beckside cleean clooas. Th' childer 'ull be able ta turn fur thi."

" But," he continued, suddenly assuming a brisk business air to bring Phebe back to commercial matters, and with a thought also of saving her pride, " tha'll ha' ta dew aar manglin' fur nowt fur a month or tew if thaa wants th' mangle fur thy own."

When Ben had gone, having in leaving bound Phebe over to strict secrecy for a few days, the widow's children were amazed to see their staid, emotionless mother kiss them impulsively all round, with a series of hugs for the podgy baby, and caught some of their mother's gladness when they heard her say—

" Thank God, wee'st be able ta pay aar rooad naa, ay, an' put a bit of a stooan on yer fayther's grave an' aw."

Next night Jabe made a visit to the widow's with his first subsidy in his pocket, and was both surprised and encouraged by a new softness in Phebe's manner.

" Hay ! " he said, looking significantly at the two children with whom he had negotiated the purchase of the animals, " we 'an had sum wark wi' yon roppits. They'll dreive me off mi yed if Aw keep 'em mitch longer. Sithee, Jack ! If tha'll fotch 'em back tha'st have 'em for nowt, an' Aw'll give thi summat fur t' tak' 'em aat o' mi seet."

This speech, of course, had a very lively effect on young Jack's spirits, but quite a contrary one apparently on those of his mother, who thus learnt for the first time to whom the creatures had been sold.

A frosty silence followed.   Jabe had an uneasy sense of having blundered somehow, and so presently, discarding the subterfuges for which he felt so ill-fitted, he said, with a sigh of anticipatory sympathy—

" Well, wench, haa ar'ta goin' on ? "

" Pratty weel," said Phebe shyly; " wi' God's help an' my naybors' Aw think wee'st pull through."

The reply finished in so cheerful a tone, and Phebe herself looked so easy, that Jabe suspected there must be some recent cause for it, and beat about the bush for information. But it was no use, and so he retired in the hope of gleaning something at the Clog Shop fire.

But nobody responded to his very palpable leadings, and Long Ben's conduct was so unexceptionable as to disarm all suspicion of him.

Jabe was so ill-satisfied with the result of his first visit that he went to the widow's again the next night, but though Phebe was out and Jabe used his utmost artifices with the children, he got " noa furrader," as he grumblingly admitted to himself going home.

Next day he went again, resolving to have no more evasions, but to compel Phebe to accept his help, and even if necessary to scold her for her sinful pride.   But though Phebe was very kind, and even talkative for her, it was evident that she suspected his errand, and was bent on thwarting him, and so after staying a very long time he abandoned the entire scheme in sheer bad temper, and spitefully banged the door as he went out.

But next day the mangle was removed to Phebe's, and before night everybody knew of the new arrangements.

Jabe heard of it very early, of course, and sat over his work preparing for Long Ben the best "dressin' daan" he ever had in his life. But Ben evidently thought discretion the better part of valour, and did not turn up, for he knew that Jabe would suspect him of having arranged the matter.

Besides the absence of Ben, the conduct of the rest of the Clog Shop cronies was irritating. Jabe sat at his seat before the window some time after his ordinary hour for adjournment, and toiled on in moody unsociability, but the others—Sam Speck, Lige, and Nathan the smith—got as far as they could into the inglenook, and were whispering and breaking into sudden explosions of laughter, which they made great haste to suppress.

Jabe concluded they were rejoicing over the way in which Ben had out-manœuvred him, and bore it with ill-smothered wrath. When Lige and Nathan had gone, the Clogger drew up to the fire, and Sam, whose face wore a broad grin, at once looked preternaturally grave, but after struggling with himself for a few moments, overcome by irresistible inward merriment, he burst into an uproarious laugh.

The look Jabe cast on him would have frozen any mirth, however, and so, as soon as he could make a straight face, he leaned forward and said—

" Dust knaw wot they're sayin' abaat thi? "

" Aw nayther knaw nor care," snapped the Clogger, looking fiercely into the fire.

" They say "—but Sam got up and prepared for sudden exit, as he said it—" they say as thaa's started o' courtin' Phebe Green ; " and away Sam rushed, waking the echoes by his explosions of laughter as he crossed the road for home.

Vaulting Ambition

I
O'erleaping

Vaulting Ambition

I

O'erleaping

THE Clogger sat at a table under his parlour
window with Fleetwood's *Life of Christ* open
before him as a writing-pad, a very short
stumpy pen in his hand, smudges of ink on
his fingers and lips, and an irritated, indignant
look on his rugged countenance.

Seated in a chair beside him, and bending
so intently over him as to seriously incommode
him, and thus intensify his anger, was a long,
thin-faced woman of nearly his own age, who
wore under her shawl the " brat " of the ordinary
card-room factory-hand, which still had traces
of cotton " rovings " upon it.   This was Rachel
Walmsley, Jabe's cousin, a widow who lived by
herself in one of the small cottages between the
chapel and the Fold farm.

The two were occupied in writing a letter,
which was a very serious business, as the

Clogger hated writing, and Rachel could not even read. The letter was intended for the widow's only son Richard, a young doctor in London. Rachel usually wrote about once in three months, using Jabe as an amanuensis, and the composition of the letter generally produced a fierce conflict between the two.

Jabe, to whom the task was utterly abhorrent, was always bitterly sarcastic about some of the things dictated to him, and immovably obstinate about others, whilst Rachel was tormented with the suspicion that Jabe was not quite as scholarly as he pretended to be, and that her instructions to him were freely translated, and often cruelly abbreviated, by the penman to save trouble. The writing of this letter, therefore, was generally the occasion of a battle royal, out of which Jabe usually came with a complete loss of temper and self-respect, vowing with fierce resolution, " Aw'll niver write anuther woll my heart's warm."

On the present occasion, however, the letter was of more than usual interest, and Rachel was therefore more than usually trying, and Jabe was already in a high fever of irritation and disgust.

" Theer," exclaimed the widow, as Jabe, having over-dipped his pen, made a black spot on the letter, and then tried to remove it by using the end of his finger as a blotting-pad, " that's th' third blotch ta-neet, wun upo' ivery page.   That's a bonny letter to goa to a Lundon doctor, isn't it ? "

" Haa con Aw help it wi' thee mauling abaat me ? " shouted Jabe.   " Tha mak's me aw of a whacker " (shake).

" Whacker ? Ay ! that's thy ill-temper. Tha ne'er had a grain of patience sin' Aw knowed thi."

" Temper ? Of aw th' aggravatin' "—
But the Clogger stopped, took off his spectacles, laid down his stumpy pen, moved his chair from the table, and relighting an unfinished pipe, puffed away in grim silence, his weak member rocking up and down over the knee of the other leg at a frantic rate.

Rachel, knowing well with whom she had to do, and quite accustomed to demonstrations of this kind, waited quietly for some time, during which Jabe, sitting with his back to her, gave vent every now and then to an angry snort. At length she said mildly—

" Aar Rutchart [Richard] thinks a seet o' thee, Jabe."

Another snort from the Clogger, and a resumption of violent leg exercise.

" He'll be whoam afoor lung, naa, and ther'll be noabry praader on him nor thee, Jabe."

The smoke began to puff from Jabe's pipe in short, rapid whiffs.

" Didn't tha read as he wor thinkin' o' settlin' amung his own fouk i' Beckside, Jabe ? "

" Naa, Aw'll tell thee wot, Rachel," cried the Clogger, rising to his feet and limping to the table, " Aw'st finish this letter, if it dreives me maddlet ; but, mind thee, Aw'st write noa mooar, nayther fur thee nor yo'r Rutchart."

And with a visage of adamantine resolution, the Clogger picked up his pen and sat down again before " Fleetwood," demanding snappishly as he did so—

" Wot's th' next ? "

" Tell him fur t' moind wot he's doin' wi' them Lundon wenches. They're a fawse lot, an' "—

" But Aw've towd him that awready."

" Naa, thaa hezna."

" Then Aw said it th' last toime."

" Ay, bud that's three munths sin', thaa knows."

" Three munths ? Whey, Aw've towd him that i' ivery letter Aw've written this last five ye'r. Dust think th' lad's sawft ? "

" Hay, bud it 'ud be an awful thing, Jabez, if he browt a forriner ta Beckside."

" Lundoners ar'na forriners, tha lump-yed. Thaa'll be cawin' th' 'super' a forriner next, 'cause he cums fro' Lundon."

" Tell him theer's sum gradely nice wenches i' Beckside, an' "—

" Beckside ! " shouted the Clogger, rising out of his chair once more in amazement and indignation. " Dust think there's ony wench i'

Beckside as is fit for a Lundon doctor? He'll
live in a big haase, woman, wi' a brass knocker
upo' th' dur, an' a sarvant lass, an' he'll want a
wife as can talk fine and play th' pianney and
visit th' quality."

For a moment a look of exulting pride stood
on the faded face of the widow, but it disappeared instantly, and in its place came a look
of alarm, which developed rapidly into intense
anxiety. She leaned back in her chair, her
thin face became ashy pale, and at last she
said, quietly and huskily—

"His muther 'ull shawm [shame] him,
then?"

Jabe banged the pen down on the book
before him, and cried out in exasperated,
despairing tones—

"Hay, dear!" and then, suddenly turning
on Rachel, he continued, "If yo'r Dick's iver
shawmed of his muther, th' Longworth blood's
bred aat on him, that's aw! Shawmed of his
muther! His muther's a meytherin' owd
maddlin', iver ta think o' sitch a thing."

But the thought was evidently a new one to
Rachel, and rapidly took root in her mind.
She became so occupied with it, in fact, that
Jabe had no further difficulty in getting his
task finished, and was too rejoiced thereat to
notice the deeply pensive look on his cousin's
face.

Rachel had called at the Clog Shop on her

way home from the mill, and when she reached her own cottage the shadow caused by the words of Jabe deepened on her face, and tears dropped upon the highly-polished fireirons as she made and lighted the fire. When she sat down to tea, it proved a long and melancholy meal.

She had been made a widow by a mill accident some twenty years before, and had been left with one child, a bright little fellow of six. Several offers of marriage had been made to her, but she had peremptorily refused all, and lived alone with her child, who spent his time at Aunt Judy's when his mother was at the mill.

Richard had grown up a fine sharp boy, of more than ordinary promise; and so when he was about fourteen, and had long been pestering his mother to allow him to go to work like other boys, Rachel had got Jabe to write to her brother-in-law, a tradesman in Manchester, to inquire if he knew of an opening for the lad.

James Walmsley came to see Richard and his own old home at Beckside, took a great fancy to his fatherless nephew, and finally took him back with him. But, instead of finding him a situation, he had sent him to school again, and kept him there.

Then he discovered that Dick had a strong wish to be a doctor; and so, after many consultations with Rachel, he was sent to a college, and after a successful career had qualified some three years previous to the time of which we write, and the letter to which the one which had caused Jabe so much trouble was the reply had informed his mother that he was going a long sea voyage as a ship's surgeon, and that on his return he intended to come back to his native village and try to establish a practice in the neighbourhood.

Now, all this had been marrow and fatness to the widow. She had feared he would never come back and settle among his own. Years ago, when on one of his rare visits she had hinted at it, Uncle James had shaken his head and quoted the text about the prophet in his own country.

And then she was haunted by a terrible dread of his marrying some " forriner," and thus putting another barrier between them. But the fact that her heart's idol would not be the same simple, merry boy she had given up long ago with such terrible pangs, but a fine gentleman with " quality " ways and refined tastes, had never presented itself to her exactly as it did as the result of Jabe's words.

She was no sort of companion for a gentleman, she saw instantly, and she did not hide from herself that she would probably be a serious hindrance to him in society, and also, by her unfitness to manage his house and preside at his table, drive him into that very matrimonial market from which she longed to keep him.

For over twenty years she had worked and screwed and waited, sustained always by the dream of a strong, clever, prosperous son to love her and do her honour, and now the dream vanished into thin air. When he became a medical student she had given up all hope of his ever settling in his native village, and now, when her dearest wish was about to be fulfilled, and her boy was coming home, she felt she must begin a remorseless process of self-undeception and give up all she had lived for.

She blamed herself for not having thought of all this before. She understood now why " Rutchart " had pressed her so often in his letters of late to give up going to the mill. He had told her over and over again, in words that were milk and honey to her, that he was not of the marrying sort ; and now he would be compelled to wed because his mother was not fit to manage a house with a brass knocker on the door and a " sarvant lass " in the kitchen.

It was a long, sad evening for poor Rachel, and when she retired to rest it was but to toss and roll about in perplexity and utter disappointment.

Next night, however, Jabe noticed her pass the shop with a firmness of gait which was expressive of some change for the better in her mental condition, and after partaking of tea she fettled up the house rather more carefully than usual, and went out to " class."

Coming down the " broo " from the meeting, she invited the schoolmistress to make one of her occasional calls. The call included a " soop o' tay " and a bit of apple pasty.

Whilst they were sitting at the table Rachel said suddenly—

" Larnin's a foine thing, miss."

" Yes," said the mistress, wondering what was the precise purpose of the remark.

" Haa owd 'an folk fur t' be afoor they stoppen larnin' ? "

" The younger the better, of course; but people are never too old to learn, you know, Mrs. Walmsley."

" Ay, but yo' conna teitch an owd dog ony new tricks."

" Oh yes, we may all learn. ' Where there's a will there's a way,' you know."

But whilst the mistress was wondering what the conversation was intended to lead up to, Rachel suddenly changed the topic by asking—

" Are yo' comfortable, lodging wi' Bob Turner ? "

" Well, fairly comfortable; they do their best for me."

" Wod yo' like fur t' stop wi' me if Aw gav' up goin' to th' shop ? " (mill).

Rachel's house was a tempting little nest of a place, almost painfully clean, better furnished than most, and surrounded back and front with an old-fashioned little garden which had often excited Miss Redford's envy.

Rachel watched her visitor's face very narrowly as she asked her question, and saw instantly how welcome the change would be; and so without waiting for her reply she said—

" Aw want yo' ta cum an' live wi' me, an' atsteead o' payin' me owt, yo'n ta larn me ta be a lady."

An exclamation of surprise and amusement broke from the mistress's lips, but before she could reply Rachel had drawn her chair up close to her, and was pouring into her ears the perennial story of " aar Rutchart," adding, however, this time, several fresh items about his approaching home-coming, her own dislike of " forriners," and especially " forrin " women, and her desire to " fettle " herself up, so as to have some hope of keeping house for the doctor.

They talked for a long time, the schoolmistress evidently shrinking from the proposed task, and also objecting strenuously to the other terms of the arrangement. But Rachel would have her way.

" Yo' mun larn me my manners, an' haa ta talk foine and ta read an' write, an' yo' mun show me haa to tittivate th' haase up an' mak' it a bit loike a Lundon haase," persisted the older woman; and in the end, without the least faith as to the result, and with an uneasy sense of the ridiculous in the matter, Miss Redford consented to join Rachel in her little home.

Now, nobody was surprised when Rachel left the mill. Some even expressed the opinion that she ought to have done it long since, as it was well known she had saved a "tidy bit." Everybody approved also of her taking the schoolmistress to live with her, for, in the opinion of Beckside, nothing was too good for that young lady. Of course, the precise purpose of the new arrangement was carefully concealed, and it was only when it began to bear unexpected kinds of fruit that the neighbours remarked upon it.

One Sunday morning Rachel appeared at chapel with a gorgeously-bound hymn-book, which she made a show of using during the singing, and Sam Speck actually stopped in the middle of a fine bass run as his eyes fell on the widow using a hymn-book as big as the pulpit one, but much handsomer, and pretending to read it through gold-rimmed spectacles.

A week or two later she appeared in that surest sign of feminine greatness, a watered silk dress, to which was added a little later a fashionable mantle.

But the climax of outrageous innovation was reached when Rachel began to call her neighbours "Mister" and "Missis," and to speak in a ridiculous mixture of dialect and "fine talk."

Now, it must not be supposed that the school-mistress was responsible for all this. She saw it with pain and shame. When the widow persisted in her first proposals Miss Redford had acquiesced in the hope of being able in a quiet way to render her friend some assistance, or at anyrate to prevent her exposing herself to ridicule.

But she was soon in deep water. Rachel gave up learning to write after the third lesson, and proved but slow in acquiring power to read. In the art of making a fair show in the flesh, however, she effectually proved her true womanhood by comprehending and carrying out with astounding aptitude the gentle hints given by her instructress.

Before long, indeed, she got out of leading-strings altogether, took to going to Duxbury every week, where she bought her own garments, and was able to study at first hand the manners of the ladies she met with, and even produced afterwards slightly grotesque imitations of their toilets.

The mistress's efforts were confined almost entirely to checking Rachel's immoderate zeal, though once she went the length of openly opposing the purchase of an outrageous bonnet which a Duxbury milliner had called " so lady-like." They disagreed most of all, perhaps, on questions of colour. Miss Redford's diplomatic resources were strained to the utmost to prevent glaring offences, and she was driven back more frequently than she liked upon her one argument that never failed, " I'm sure the doctor wouldn't like it."

It must not be supposed that Beckside was indifferent to these things. They were intermittently absorbing themes of conversation. At the mangle-house, which was to Beckside women what the Clog Shop was to the men, Rachel's sudden rush into fashion was constantly canvassed and unhesitatingly condemned, and her " manners " and newly-adopted modes of speech called forth all Lottie Speck's unrivalled powers of mimicry.

At the Clog Shop the subject was discussed under difficulties, for Rachel was the Clogger's cousin, and for a time it was not known how he regarded the matter, whilst Jabe himself was too much disgusted to allude to it. Hints, however, were constantly being thrown out, and when one night Jabe said a word or two which seemed to invite discussion on the subject, he was told so many things that he boiled over with indignation.

Next day he called on the widow with his temper very insecurely under control. As he opened the door and stepped as usual over the threshold he noticed with rising scorn that the once carefully sanded floor was now covered with new carpet.

" Ay ! " he began in withering tones. But

before he could proceed he was met with the startling rebuke——

" Jabez Longworth, you should *knock* when you comes into folk's houses."

Arrested thus suddenly in his progress, and overwhelmed with what he saw and heard, Jabez stood in the middle of the room and glared around in speechless astonishment. Slowly his gaze focused itself upon Rachel, and transfixing her with an annihilating glare, he cried——

" Tha pride-brussen, mee-mawin, feathercock owd maddlin, tha, wot's up with thi ? "

But Rachel was on her dignity, and so, bridling up, she returned his fiery glare with interest, and replied, betraying her excitement by dropping into dialect——

" If thaa's ony manners thaa'll take thy cap off i' fouk's haases."

The Clogger stood back a step, surveyed Rachel slowly and deliberately from head to foot, and then with a tremendous thump on the table with his horny fist, he cried——

" Ay, Aw'll tak' my cap off an' mysel' tew."

" An', Rachel," he continued, after a moment's pause, " thaa niver hed much sense, but sin' thaa sowd thy sowl ta warldly pride thaa's lost wot bit thaa hed. Good mornin', *Missis Walmsley*," and, taking off his cap, he made her an elaborate mock bow, and stalked haughtily out of the house.

But Rachel was not to be turned from her purpose. Her dread of being an embarrassment to her son, and her fear of driving him into marriage with a daughter of the Philistines, acted as a stimulant to her energies, but whilst she certainly advanced rapidly in some things, her language was a bewildering medley, and her Sunday outfit was fearfully and wonderfully made.

At last there came a letter from the young doctor to say that he had landed at Southampton, and was going to London for a few days, but would be home in about a week, Rachel heard the schoolmistress read of the going to London with a pang, but soon forgot it in the excitement of preparation to welcome her boy.

Then came a second letter to say that Richard would reach Duxbury Station by the 4.19 train on Thursday, and for two nights poor Rachel never slept. Every few minutes she was asking her lodger if she thought "the doctor," as Miss Redford always called him, would like this or that article of dress or furniture, and the young lady was glad to have that opportunity of correcting several things which offended her taste.

On the subject of personal adornment, however, the elder woman was still untractable; and though the mistress's influence secured the omission of the more glaring ornaments, the proud mother was still more than sufficiently gorgeous when she started off, in a trap specially hired from Duxbury, to meet her son.

Now that the time had come she felt little of the elation she had expected, but in its place a nervous apprehension she found it difficult to account for. She was now certain that her boy would be too grand a fellow to care much for a factory-hand mother, whom he had only seen twice during the last seven years, and that since mixing in such grand society there would be nothing in Beckside to satisfy him.

Would he admire her plum-coloured satin dress in which she was meeting him? She was sure Miss Redford had been mistaken in recommending that plain shawl instead of the grand mantle. But, at anyrate, she had her gold guard on, and so she arrived at the station in a flurry of anxious misgivings.

Rachel had all a countrywoman's dread of trains, and stood a long way back when the express came in. In a moment she saw her son. Oh, what a fine fellow! What a fine beard he had grown! Here he comes! He has seen her, but after a hasty glance he looks farther down the platform. He doesn't know her! Then he turns toward her again. She starts forward with a cry, and in a moment he has hugged her to his heart.

But after a long, hearty embrace the young doctor holds her from him, glances perplexedly at her grand outfit, and seems uneasy and a shade disappointed, she fears. During the ride home, though he talked freely as of old, he seemed to be always looking at some part of her apparel, and appeared a trifle flat and disappointed, and even, she thought, distant.

But in a few moments Rachel had something else to think about. The day had been very warm, but during the last hour it had become sultry and thundery. Just as they were reaching the top of the hill out of Duxbury the rain began to fall, and in a few minutes it was pouring down. Rachel had " forgotten " her umbrella—that is, she had left it at home, because it was not fine enough. The doctor's had been left behind with his luggage, to come by Squire Taylor's cart. There was no shelter near, and the driver had scarcely any wraps. Such as he had were hastily dragged from under the seat, and wrapped round her shoulders, but, in spite of all, the poor widow reached home in a drenched and draggled condition.

The schoolmistress met them at the door, and exclaimed as she saw their soaked clothes, but as it was still raining heavily they made haste to get indoors, and the doctor insisted that " mother " should go and change at once.

But in the bedroom another scene took place.

Rachel was disappointed and thoroughly out of temper, and obstinately insisted on putting on her watered silk. But the schoolmistress, having taken her measure of the doctor, insisted that the widow's ordinary black stuff was the proper thing, and was so firm that Rachel had most unwillingly to give in. By the time she was ready to go down again she felt sick of the whole affair, and more than a little ashamed, and came into the wee parlour with a very penitent look on her face.

The doctor was stooping down pulling on an elastic-sided boot as she entered, but on hearing her footsteps he lifted his head. A look of surprised delight suddenly shone on his bronzed face, and jumping forward he seized her in his great arms, and giving her a tremendous hug, he cried, dropping quite naturally into the purest Beckside dialect—

"Hay! Aw'd a fine lady i' th' trap wi' me. But this is my gradely owd muther!"

Vaulting Ambition

II

Alighting

Vaulting Ambition

II

Alighting

SAM SPECK had often complained that there
had been an oversight in the building of the
Clog Shop.   There ought to have been a
window in the gable end of it, for that would
have commanded a view of the road up past
the chapel, and have immensely enhanced the
value of the Clog Shop as a coign of vantage
from which to supervise the public life of the
village.

And on the night of the young doctor's
return, Sam particularly felt the absence of this
outlook.   It was too wet to stand about outside, and too soon after his arrival to make a
decent excuse for calling, and yet Sam was
consumed with curiosity to see the doctor.
Lige, the road-mender, driven in from his work
by the rain, was also at the cloggery, and these
two — Sam in his character of cynic, and

Lige from sheer depression of spirits — were prophesying the certainty of the doctor's unapproachableness and pride, and prophesying all the more doggedly as their vaticinations produced very welcome declarations of an opposite character from Jabe.

As the evening drew on the company increased, and whilst some expressed themselves hopefully, the majority of the cronies belied themselves by endorsing Long Ben's dictum that " We conna expect owt else."

Jabe, however, stoutly held out, and whilst admitting the force of Ben's argument as to the length of time the boy had been absent, the character of the society in which he had mixed, and the appearance he would have to keep up if he meant to succeed as a doctor, he still expressed unbounded confidence in Richard, and predicted that they would find that he had not changed in the least.

In spite of all that Jabe could say, however, the company took a desponding view of the case, and Lige, the oldest person present, related numerous instances of persons who had left Beckside poor and unknown, and who either never acknowledged in after days the place whence they had sprung, or else returned occasionally and patronised the villagers with most offensive condescension.

To crown all, Jethro, the knocker-up, recalled the well-known instance of Tommy Royle, who, when he had risen to the dignity of mayor of a distant borough, brought his grand wife and a party of Corporation friends to see his birthplace, and made fun of the village and its inhabitants, even going to the length of chaffing Jethro himself, for the amusement of his fine friends, about the importance of Beckside, and Jethro's thin voice assumed its deepest possible tones as he impressively added, " Ten ye'r after, he wor i' th' bastile."

The relation of this oft-repeated tale in the present circumstances seemed to have a damping effect on the confidence even of Jabc, who relapsed under it into pensive silence, and as there was a long pause,—thc most painful of all things to Sam Speck,—he broke it by smiting his thigh and crying in tones of unalterable resolution—

" If Aw'd twenty childer, Aw'd keep 'em aw a-whoam [at home], if we'd ta eight [eat] porritch, and porritch to it."

Long Ben, as the family man of the party, seemed to dissent from this view of the case, but was so slow in replying that Jabe was just taking his pipe out of his mouth to answer, when the shop door sprang violently open, a tall figure rushed through the doorway, and putting a hand on the little counter and clearing it at a jump, alighted on a heap of clog chips on the other side. Turning to the company, the young doctor—for it was he—

cried out in tones welcome as music to those who heard them—

"Hay, chaps, haa are yo' aw?" and in a moment he was taking them by the hands and shaking them two at a time, and then beginning again and shaking again, he cried—

"Hay! bud Aw am *fain* to see yo' aw."

The effect was magical. Jabe straightened himself up and glanced proudly round on the rest. Sam and Lige looked embarrassed, but very happy. Jethro turned into the corner on the far side of the fireplace and blew his nose, and Long Ben had recourse to a dirty red cotton handkerchief. As it was summer time, there was no fire in the ingle-nook, but the cronies sat in a circle round it as though it had been the depth of winter.

Room was made for "Rutchart," and he was speedily installed as the guest of the evening. In the excitement of greeting, most of the pipes had gone out, and there was a general refilling as an introduction to proper conversation.

As soon as the doctor perceived this he cried, "Howd on, chaps," and diving into the pockets of a long loose coat, he produced a handful of gigantic foreign cigars and handed them round, crying as he did so—

"Noa pipes ta-neet. Th' mon as starts a pipe while theer's ony o' these left, Aw'll— Aw'll chuck him i' th' Beck!"

This terrible threat was quite unnecessary, however, cigars being at all times scarce things in Beckside, and foreign ones almost unknown, and in a few moments seven round red spots gleamed fitfully in the deepening twilight.

Yes, Richard Walmsley had come back to Beckside absolutely uncorrupted. He had the same merry twinkle in his eye, the same low but hearty laugh, and the same frank, open honesty in speech and act as he ever had. He talked about his voyage, and described the places he had seen and the adventures he had experienced, and passed for a moment under a cloud when, in answer to questions, his information about Methodist mission - stations proved to be scanty and bald.

But the cronies noted with grim satisfaction that the doctor spoke seldom and always very modestly of himself. Uneasy about his ignorance of missions in the presence of experts, he hastened back to his hospital days, and described scenes which were most satisfactorily blood-curdling. Then he said a few rather lame words about being glad to be in Beckside again, his confusion as he expressed himself being regarded as in the highest degree becoming.

Conversation afterwards became general, and at length, glancing hastily at a real gold watch which made Sam Speck's mouth water, he asked leave to retire, bargaining as he did so for a permanent place in the company, which was of course rapturously granted to him.

"Didn't Aw tell thi?" shouted Jabe, smiting Ben heartily between the shoulders, "th' Longworth blood breeds true, thaa sees."

"Aw thowt he'd a' bin a bit mooar of a gentleman," said Sam Speck, in a tone of dubious regret, and evidently forgetting his former and quite opposite fears.

"Gentleman!" shouted six voices at once, and Sam was glad to vanish, and escape the storm he had raised.

"Naa, Jonas," cried Jabe, as the company moved towards the door, "tha knows wot hymn we mun oppen aat wi' o' Sunday morning?"

Jonas looked a moment at the Clogger in perplexity, and then replied—

"Oh ay! But what if the preicher winna have it?"

"Have it? He'll *ha' ta* have it!"

And accordingly on the following Sabbath morning, with a full attendance of the choir and a quite unusual congregation, the Becksiders gave their old-time Sunday School scholar a most characteristic welcome, singing as he stood by his proud mother's side—

> "And are we yet alive
> And see each other's face?"

Now, Dr. Walmsley was not an exceptionally clever man. He had got the ordinary surgeon's qualifications, and had passed his examinations respectably; and that was all. But you couldn't have convinced Beckside of that. The postman had shown Sam Speck a letter, on the envelope of which was the doctor's name with no less than seven mysterious and imposing letters behind it——a fact which was duly communicated to the authorities at the Clog Shop, and discussed at becoming length. Clever or not, young Richard was soon as popular as either his mother or uncle could wish. He greeted the young men who had been boys with him as " owd lad," and called the girls by their Christian names.

He took the chair at the " Sarmons " tea-party, and the villagers laughed and cried together as he spoke in simple language of the days of " Auld Lang Syne." Jabe, as senior superintendent, lifted his head almost out of his very high shirt collar as he announced that " Dr. Walmsley " had undertaken to " teich th' little wenches " whilst the schoolmistress was away on her holiday.

Now, the Beckside neighbourhood, even if you included the whole of the Clough, embracing Brogden parish and Clough End, was not exactly a happy hunting-ground for an aspirant to medical fame. The inhabitants were mostly of tough constitution, and regarded hardness and stoical endurance of small ills as so indispensable a virtue that their applications for professional assistance were comparatively rare, and always reluctant. Besides this, they showed a marked preference for contraband, or, at any rate, irregular forms of doctoring.

Every housewife of any pretensions was something of a herbalist, and every cottage ceiling was adorned with numerous brown paper bags containing "yarbs" supposed to be potent for life or death; and there was no more important person in the village than Little Eli, who lived in Shaving Lane, and who, whilst doing a little occasional business as a barber, maintained himself chiefly by collecting, drying, and preserving herbs, and retailing certain mysterious but potent salves, ointments, and drops prepared therefrom.

For some years Eli had had no more constant customer than Rachel Walmsley, who prided herself on being a sort of valuable walking advertisement of the efficacy of Eli's celebrated "pain" drops, which she took as a cure for her rheumatism. But when the doctor had been at home a week or two, Eli lost his largest consumer, for Rachel, anxious for her son's future success, and scheming constantly to promote it, suddenly realised that Eli was an enemy and a stone of stumbling in her son's path.

"Aw'm fain aar Rutchart's come whoam," she would say, "if it's nowt but what he's done fur my pains." And when the person to whom she was speaking asked the question she intended them to ask, she would reply—

" Hay, wench, theer's nowt loike a gradely doctor efther aw. Aw've ta'n [taken] gallons upo' gallons o' Eli's drops, an' wot better wur Aw ? But th' fust bottle aar Rutchart gave me cured me—a—a—partly—wot." And then, after a pause, she would add, in an impressive whisper, " They tell me as Eli's toothwarch pills is nowt bud cobbler's wax."

After shaking a loose leg for several weeks, the doctor began to " shape " at practising. As his mother's house was small and low even for Beckside, and there was no suitable one empty, Jabe offered his parlour for temporary use, and Long Ben painted a neat board, on which was inscribed, " WALMSLEY, SURGEON." The doctor busied himself in sending to London for his remaining belongings and certain necessities of his profession, and when these arrived and were arranged on shelves in the parlour, with just the slightest bit of ostentation, the *habitués* of the Clog Shop were invited to inspect the extemporised surgery, and listened, open-mouthed, as the doctor explained the uses of the instruments and chemicals.

Jethro, the knocker-up, was regarded as a benefactor when, after a preliminary cough or two, he asked to be treated for " th' asthmatic." Then a bad cut on Ben's finger was submitted, and the way the doctor's deft fingers bathed and bandaged it made a profound impression. Then Sam Speck wanted a large wart removed from inside one of his fingers, and the howl he set up when the doctor, with a comprehensive wink at the company, dropped a drop of some terrible fiery fluid upon it, completed their satisfaction.

Very soon the young physician was getting a fair amount of practice, and so, after a serious consultation, to which Jabe and Aunt Judy were called, it was decided that a piece of land opposite the chapel should be bought, and Long Ben was requisitioned to prepare plans; and presently, after much profound debate both at the cottage and the Clog Shop, the house began to rise upon its foundations.

But Rachel realised now more clearly than ever that she could never take the place of the doctor's lady, and so she began to cast about to get him wisely married. The doctor must get " in " with the " quality," and so she thought of going to Brogden Church; but her fear of Jabe and also of her son compelled her to abandon that idea. Money was a *sine quâ non* she felt in this case, but she realised with distress that she had no connections with the upper-ten in the neighbourhood, and no means of establishing such connections.

Then she remembered, and was astonished she had so long forgotten it, that one of the ladies whose acquaintance she had made at

Duxbury on her fashion-studying expeditions had two daughters, and in a few days she had them over to spend the week-end with her. But Richard, though gallant enough to the maidens whilst they stayed, openly ridiculed both their dress and their manners when they had gone.

Next she thought of asking the schoolmistress, who on Richard's advent had gone back to Bob Turner's, whether she had any eligible friends whom she could invite to Beckside, and was busy maturing this idea in her mind when Aunt Judy came in one day, evidently laden with important news.

"Well, tha'll dew ba'at th' Duxbury dowdies naa," began the visitor.

"Judy Longworth, thaa'll have a nickname fur th' Almighty afoor lung! Dowdies! But wot shall Aw dew ba'at 'em fur?"

"Cause your Rutchart's fun' one nearer whoam, and a fine seet better tew."

"Nearer whoam?" cried Rachel, turning pale. "Whativer dust meean?"

"Well, if tha'd oppen thy een thaa'd see. If it had bin a lad o' mine Aw should ne'er ha' needed onybody fur t' tell me. Aw should ha' fun' it aat a munth sin'."

Now, as Aunt Judy was quite as curious as Rachel and almost as interested in the doctor's future, but had only been in possession of her great secret some ten minutes, it is to be feared that her statement was somewhat unscrupulous. But if she exaggerated for effect, she certainly had her reward ; for Rachel went white to her lips, put her hand to her heart, winced with a sudden twinge of her old " pains," and with terrible visions of Richard eloping with a factory girl, she fell back into her chair, crying, half in tears—

" Hay, wench, thaa's set me aw of a whacker! Speik, woman, speik ! "

" Speik !   Dust meean ta say as thaa's lived i' th' same haase wi' him an' doesn't knaw as he's i' luv wi' th' schoo'missis ? "

The look on Rachel's face as she slowly grasped the situation baffles description.   Amazed at the character of the news, and confounded by the fact that whilst she had been anticipating remote dangers she had never seen the nearer and more likely one, she was stunned, and sat looking at Judy dumbfounded.

Judy, in calm enjoyment of the effect she had produced, was just preparing to make a remark as a means of setting Rachel off again, when she was spared the trouble, for Miss Redford herself suddenly opened the door and stepped into the house, her pale face evidently flushed with pleasant excitement.

Before she could speak, however, Rachel started to her feet, and with red angry face almost screamed out—

" Stop wheer yo' are !   Haa con yo' for

shawm ta show yo'r face here? Pike aat o' th' haase, an' niver darken that dur ageean! Yo' "—

But the schoolmistress didn't hear the rest, having hastily retreated with surprise and distress on her face.

Aunt Judy called her back, but she sped on; so in hot indignation Judy turned upon Rachel, voicing the popular local opinion, and declaring " Hoo's as good as yo'r Dick ony day "—the " Dick " being a title never applied to the doctor, except in contempt.

This only inflamed poor Rachel the more; and for some minutes the battle raged hot and fierce, until at last, no match for the redoubtable Judy in word-warfare, and already condemned at the bar of her own conscience, she lapsed into silence, and allowed her visitor to retire with the honours of the conflict.

Now it happened that Judy was right, and the doctor had asked for an interview with Miss Redford, taking no pains to conceal his purpose in so doing, and so, as the prospect was very sweet to her, the mistress was in a flutter of happy feeling when she called upon Rachel.

The reception she met with rudely opened her eyes, and prompted her, after a severe struggle, to decline the proffered honour; and next day young Richard went back from the place of rendezvous a rejected man.

The mistress knew better than most people how deep and all-absorbing was Rachel's love for her son, and convinced herself that it was her duty to make the sacrifice for the mother's sake, and so in declining the doctor she did not even encourage his urgent supplication for a possible hope in the future.

That night the doctor went home a miserable man, and found, without particularly noticing it, a still more miserable woman. Rachel knew that Miss Redford would have been an ideal wife; but she had no money, and in Rachel's opinion that was a fatal objection. She was greatly exercised, especially as a fairly healthy conscience did its duty, and the doctor grew gloomier every day.

One night, after an unavailing attempt to move Miss Redford, or to get any explanation out of her, the doctor came home very late. He looked weary, and scarcely answered Rachel's inquiries, and the distressed mother went to bed to toss about and cry and pray.

Next day Richard went off to Duxbury, and did not return until the third night. He seemed more cheerful, however, and Rachel began to hope the worst might be over; when, to her dismay, he began to tell her of an assistant's place in Manchester that was vacant, and carried with it the chance of a partnership. Poor Rachel was at her wits' end, and to make things worse a neighbour brought her intelligence that the schoolmistress had given notice to leave.

The same morning Aunt Judy went to the Clog Shop, muttering and shaking her head as she walked. Having beckoned the Clogger into the parlour, where he followed her very leisurely, for it would never do to show any great concern about a woman's communications, Judy opened her budget by saying—

" Jabe, Aw've summat on my moind."

Jabe grunted with apparent unconcern, but in a few moments he was eagerly looking into his sister's face as she detailed the memorable interview in which she had taken a part.

When she had finished and received emphatic admonition to say " nowt ta noabry," she departed, and Jabe, after a vain attempt to resume work, put off his apron, and putting on his most uncompromising look, marched off to interview Rachel. She was almost glad to see him, and listened with chastened manner to his utterances. He certainly did not spare her, and when he left, the air seemed to be clearer, and Rachel began to see her way.

Next day, with a subdued and wistful look on her face, she made her way to the little schoolhouse, timing her visit so as to arrive just as the scholars were " loosing." The mistress, perched on a high stool at a desk, blushed quickly as she caught sight of her visitor, and

Rachel, stepping timidly up, said in penitent, apologetic tones—

" Will yo' speik to me ? "

For answer the mistress leaned over and kissed her.

Rachel was much moved, and for a few moments neither of the women spoke. Then Rachel took an aimless sort of look round the school, and dropping her head much as a guilty schoolgirl might have done, said very softly—

" Aw ax yer pardon."

Tears came into the mistress's eyes, and she bowed her head on the desk and sobbed quietly.

There was another long silence, and then Rachel, still standing by the high desk, faltered—

" Yo'—yo' can hev him if yo' want."

The schoolmistress shook her still bowed head very resolutely.

" Hay, bud yo' *mun* hev him."

Another shake of the head, another sob, and another painful silence.

Rachel sighed heavily, took a long troubled glance round the school again, and finally said, chokingly—

" *Aw* conna have him if yo' dunna."

But still the schoolmistress did not speak, and the older woman, clinging to the edge of the desk, continued—

" Aw know Aw've done wrung, but if ivver

yo're a hen wi' one chick yo'rsel' yo'll forgie me. Hay! *dew* have him, *dew*!"

And as she pleaded thus, she timidly slid her hand across the desk until it touched the little white hand of the mistress, and patting it coaxingly, she resumed—

"Aw gan his fayther up ta God twenty-two ye'r sin', an' Aw'll give him up ta yo'—if—yo'll hev him."

And then her head dropped upon the desk, and she began to sob as if her heart would break.

The schoolmistress tried to comfort her, and so the ice was broken, and they talked, and Rachel pleaded so urgently that when they left the school Miss Redford had consented to receive another visit from the doctor.

Next day all Beckside knew that young Richard was to marry their beloved schoolmistress.

"The Zeal of Thine House"

I

"When Greek Meets Greek"

"The Zeal of Thine House"

I

"When Greek Meets Greek"

In the September following Jimmy Juddy's wedding there was a change of superintendent ministers in the Duxbury Circuit. It was the middle of October before the new preacher came to Beckside, his first visit having been reserved for the "Trust Sermons" Sunday. He had come from a circuit near London, and had never been in Lancashire before, the only piece of information retailed about him being that he was a great chapel-builder.

Such descriptions of the good man as had reached Beckside were strangely conflicting. Some said he was a thorough gentleman and a polished speaker, others that he was rather too high and mighty for Lancashire. In this division of circuit opinion Beckside realised its responsibility, and prepared itself to give the preacher a very careful hearing.

The little he had heard of Beckside prepared the preacher for amusement, and he was a little nonplussed therefore when Jabe and Long Ben received him in the vestry with impenetrable and icy stolidity. To counterbalance this, however, he was cheered when the service was over by Lige, the road-mender, who, in his Sunday attire, looked a very imposing person, and who met him at the bottom of the pulpit stairs, and exclaimed, " That's th' best sarmon we'n had i' this chapil for mony a ye'r."   And the minister did not know that Lige had expressed the same opinion of nearly every sermon he had heard for many years.

It was Long Ben's turn to take the preacher that day, and that worthy over the after-dinner pipe imparted to his visitor as a profound secret the disturbing information that he would have to get a new steward in his place at Christmas. Well, there was nothing remark-able in that piece of news, but it was impressed more than usually upon the " super's " mind by the peculiar action of Ben's plump, red-cheeked little wife, who happened to overhear the closing words of Ben's speech. For she shut with a bang the drawer into which she was putting the tablecloth, shook her cap-strings quite violently, and then remarked, apparently to the big brass-clasped Bible on the drawer-top, and in a tone between amusement and irritation—

" Hay, dear !   Owder and softer ! "

Now, the " super " was not quite sure in his own mind whether the remark, which he only imperfectly understood, applied to the good lady's husband or himself, and was glancing inquiringly from one to the other of them when Ben invited him to have a walk up to the Clog Shop.

There, more pipes were smoked, though the minister was not a disciple of St. Nicotine ; and when Sam Speck came in and took Ben out to hunt up some negligent Sunday School scholars, Jabe informed the "super" that after twenty-four years' service he had made up his mind " wilta shalta" [whether or not] to "cum aat at Christmas."

This second resignation made the minister think he smelt a rat, and so he inquired whether there was anything wrong in the Church.

" Neaw," Jabe replied, " we're reet enough, but Aw mean wot Aw say," and he puffed away and looked a very sphinx of stony mystery.

The minister was a little annoyed, and went rather early to the Sunday School to inspect and address it. When the children were being dismissed, Nathan, the smith, drew him into the vestry ; and having carefully closed the door, informed him that he had been seven years in the office of chapel steward, and had only kept on holding the office to oblige the "supers" who had been there before the present one, but that now there were so many young ones coming up he should retire at the end of the year, especially as he wasn't very good at keeping accounts—and the new minister did not know, of course, that account-keeping was Nathan's hobby, and that it was his constant boast that he had never been more than ninepence wrong in all these years.

All this was perplexing, not to say irritating, to the minister, and when he reached his armchair at Ben's, he heaved a little sigh as he sat down.

" Yo're siking [sighing], mestur," said Mrs. Ben.   " Is summut wrung wi' yo ? "

" No, I'm all right ; but what are all these good men resigning for ? "

" Bless yo' ; is that aw ?   They allis [always] do it when a new mon comes. Yo' munno tak' ony noatice on 'em ; they'd be a fine sight mooar bothered nor yo' if yo' did."

Then she bustled back into the kitchen, and Ben coming in from the garden, the minister heard him called " lump-yed," and told that it would " sarve him reet if he *wor* turn't aat."

Now the " super " was a shrewd man, and laid these things up in his mind.

After the evening service the minister went to the Clog Shop for supper, and was formally introduced to the members of the Club.

When supper was over and the pipes were in full work, Jabe with a characteristic movement of his short leg, and an assumption of modesty which did not at all fit him, asked—

"Well, wot dun yo' think of aar chapil, Mestur 'Shuper'?" And every man in the company tried to imitate Jabe's expression of grateful modesty in anticipation of the only answer which could possibly be given.

The new minister seemed most unaccountably embarrassed, and was about to give an evasive reply when old Lige burst out—

"Yo 'hanna [have not] seen a prattier chapil i' yo'r life, naa, han yo'?"

The minister smiled rather oddly, and did not quite succeed in keeping a contemptuous tone out of his voice as he inquired—

"What style do you call it?"

"Style! it's th' A 1 style, an' nowt else," cried Lige excitedly, whilst the others held their pipes at arm's length, listening intently.

The minister looked wicked, and there was the ghost of a scoff on his face as he asked—

"Well, but is it classic, or Gothic, or what is it?"

"G-o-t-h-i-c," shouted Lige with lofty indignation. "Neaw, it isn't; it's gradely owd Lancashire, that's wot it is—wi' yo'r classics! an' yo'r Gothics!"

The minister laughed, and as he had over a mile to walk to catch the circuit conveyance at the four-road ends, he excused himself and went away.

But he left behind him a most painful impression. For the first time in its history the beauty of the Beckside tabernacle had been called into question, at anyrate by implication. And the offence had been committed by the superintendent minister, of all persons !

The talk in the Clog Shop parlour was long and very serious ; and though Jabe kept up for some time a show of defence of the ecclesiastic, it was very half-heartedly done, and he admitted to Sam Speck when the rest were gone—

" When he talked abaat his Gothics, thaa could 'a knocked me daan wi' a feather."

Next day all Beckside knew that the minister had scoffed at the chapel ; and the feeling of indignation was quickened when Silas, the chapel-keeper, made it known that when the minister came to the week-night service on the following Tuesday he had gone round the chapel laughing at the high-backed pews, putting his stick into the cracks in the gable wall, and talking of ventilation until Silas said—

" Aw welly brast aat on him."

Every time the " super " came to Beckside, he dropped hints about the chapel which conveyed the impression that he thought it past redemption.

Then a local preacher told Sam Speck under an inviolable bond of secrecy that he had heard the " super " call the chapel a " ramshackle old building." But as Sam always made mental reservations in favour of the Club in his promises of silence, this most offensive expression was soon common property.

Under these circumstances, when the Annual Trustees' Meeting came to be held in the following January, feeling ran very high, and the minister, unconscious of the sentiments of his flock, very speedily made things worse. The possibility of danger to their tabernacle put everything else out of the heads of the Church officers, and not a word was said on the question of resignations. This was a time to " hold on," everybody felt.

When the routine business of the meeting had been got through, the minister leaned back in his chair and said—

" Well now, brethren, what about this building ? It was all right, I dare say, seventy or eighty years ago ; but it won't do now. It is behind the times. What do you say to a new chapel ? "

Nobody spoke, but Long Ben and Nathan began to stare hard at the fire, and the rest became absorbed in some mysterious matter going on on the ceiling.

The circuit steward from Duxbury, who had come with the minister, and was present as auditor of accounts, then took up the tale.

" You know, brethren, this is a box ; simply a box ; and (with a very demonstrative sniff) a very musty box too."

Nobody spoke.

A non-resident Trustee, who had also come in the circuit conveyance, next broke in—

"You know we must move with the times, friends. What was good enough for our grandfathers is not good enough for us."

Another long silence.

"Come, friends," said the "super" in the chair; "What do you think?"

No answer.

"Will some one propose that we meet again this day three weeks to take into consideration the advisability of building a new chapel?"

Another pause.

Presently Jabe rose to his feet, turned slowly round, picked his hat off the peg above his head, and deliberately limped down the whole length of the vestry to the door amidst a dead silence.

After another minute's pause Long Ben got up and went through exactly the same performance as his colleague, staring steadily before him as he marched out. Then Lige followed, and then Sam Speck. Only one local Trustee was left; and as the minister sat back in his chair, watching the scene with amazement, Nathan followed the rest.

One behind another, like a procession of ducks, the Trustees made for the Clog Shop, and there held long and excited debate on the crisis. Everybody agreed that Jabe's mode of treating the matter was the correct one, and did him credit.

Presently the circuit trap was heard driving past. This seemed a sort of relief, and crowding as far as possible into the ingle-nook and lighting their pipes, the conspirators discussed the situation in all its bearings, whilst the fire-light cast flickering shadows on their faces.

The chapel was compared to other edifices of the kind in the neighbourhood, very much to its advantage. Long Ben dwelt with affectionate pride on the labours of the committee who had cleaned and decorated it for Jimmy Juddy's wedding, and the "super" was denounced as a stuck-up cockney, a formalist, and finally by Sam Speck as a Puseyite—the last epithet being all the more popular because of its being only faintly understood and altogether inapplicable.

The minister's talk about "Gothic" was held up to derision, and it was confidently prophesied that "he wouldn't stop his time aat."

Presently Sam, who was in a state of mental elation in consequence of his late brilliant feat in nomenclature, asked from behind clouds of tobacco smoke, which rendered him invisible far into the chimney nook—

"Well, wot mun we do?"

This gave the conversation a new turn, and brought forth a number of extraordinary proposals. None of them, however, met with general approbation, chiefly because of their inadequacy to express the seriousness of the occasion or the magnitude of the superintendent's transgression.

At last, however, all criticism was silenced; and perfect, and, in fact, vociferous unanimity was secured, by the paralysing suggestion that Jabe should resign all his offices at once.

Yes! That would do. Action so astounding would bring conviction even to the callous heart of the new " super."

When it was first proposed as a bare possibility, Jabe, though he thought it not decent to say much, let it be seen that he regarded the suggestion as a truly heroic one, but when the others began to discuss it as a really practicable thing he was a little staggered, and left to himself would probably have been content with something less drastic.

But he was the leader of the revolt—first in honour and first in danger. Desperate diseases require desperate remedies; and so, though he postponed final decision as long as he could, the infectious confidence of his comrades stimulated him, and he was soon trying to wear modestly the honour of being the hero of the hour, and every now and again was dropping mysterious hints as to the startling effects of their *coup* on the offending dignitary.

At first it was decided that the awful act

should take place on the "super's" next visit, an idea which Jabe strongly supported; but Sam Speck and old Lige contented that that was too long to wait, the moral effect of the deed depending on its following promptly on the occurrences of the night.

Next day was the Duxbury market, and it was decided that Jabe should send all his books and other insignia of office, accompanied by a formal written resignation, by Squire Taylor's market cart in the early morning.

Then the company dispersed; and Jabe, when the stimulating effects of friendly presences was withdrawn, found it strangely difficult to make up his mind about the note. Writing was not the easiest thing in the world to him at any time, and composition generally took time, but this evening he was slower than usual. A sudden thought about the dear old chapel, however, and the "super's" sacrilegious suggestions about it, brought the necessary resolution, and after spoiling several sheets of paper he finally produced the following laconic epistle—

 "SIR,—
  "I resine all my offices.
   "Your brother in Christ,
    "JABEZ LONGWORTH."

During the next two or three days the Clog

Shop Club sat in almost perpetual committee. Highly coloured pictures of the stunning effects of Jabe's resignation on the minister were painted by Sam Speck and Lige, and anticipations of what that dignitary would do were canvassed all day long by those who came and went from the ingle-nook.

Sam Speck expressed an intense desire to see the minister arrive " wi' his tail between his legs," as he phrased it; and, as the others shared his curiosity, and, with the exception of Lige, were their own masters, very little work was done for some days.

But the " super " gave no sign.

The Trustees' Meeting had been held on a Monday, and when Friday arrived and neither letter nor message had been received, and Jabe's books were still at Duxbury, everybody became very serious, and Jabe was evidently labouring under deep anxiety. It was concluded at the Clog Shop on Saturday night that the " super " would be sending the books back together with a note by the local preacher who was coming on the morrow.

When Sam suggested that a note would not do, and that in an affair of such magnitude nothing but a visit in person would suffice, he was somewhat seriously reproved by his elders, and reminded of his disqualification for sober counsels on the score of juvenility.

The preacher arrived on Sunday morning,

and was met by the stewards in the usual way, and when it was clear that he had brought neither books nor message, Long Ben looked anxiously at Jabe, who wheeled round in the vestry and limped out into a little back lane, and was absent from service for the first time for many years.

This was probably as dark a day as the old Clogger had ever spent, and when the usual Sunday night deliberations in the parlour produced not a single ray of light, Jabe went to bed to spend a sleepless night.

The next day he was snappish and bitterly sarcastic. Customers did their business in the fewest possible words and departed; and the ingle-nook conspirators endured Jabe's temper very meekly, regarding it as a special and richly deserved judgment on themselves.

By Wednesday Jabe's crustiness had gone, however, and the Clogger's aiders and abettors in rebellion noted with consternation that he had become excessively but sorrowfully amiable. A patient, resigned, but terribly sad look sat on his face. He sighed heavily every few minutes, and stuck to his work with a sort of dull desperation.

On Thursday he positively refused to smoke; and on Friday, whilst he still sat on his bench, it was observed that he was constantly gazing through the window with a far-away look of melancholy on his face.

Late on Friday he and Long Ben sat up in deep and secret conclave, and before daylight next morning Jabe had started to see the " super " at Duxbury.

Now, the minister was a clever man, and prided himself on his knowledge of human nature. His silence on the question that so greatly agitated the Beckside Trustees was the silence of policy, and a smile of triumph crossed his face as Jabe was ushered into his study on Saturday morning.

" Good morning, Mr. Jabez. Glad to see you ! Sit down, sir ! "

But Jabe, with a grave, sad face, remained standing, and overlooking the minister's out-stretched hand, and too deeply troubled to notice his ill-concealed look of victory, he said—

" Mestur ' Shuper,' Aw've done wrung."

" Wrong, Mr. Jabez ? I hope not ! In what way ? "

" Aw've left a good shop [situation] and a grand Mestur, just because one of my work-mates didn't agree wi' me."

" I don't understand you."

" Dunno yo' ? Well th' Lord's let me work for Him till Aw thowt He couldn't dew ba'at me, but He's shown me as He could. He can dew better ba'at me nor Aw con dew ba'at Him, a fine sight."

The minister began to have misgivings as to his skill in judging character.

" Is it about the chapel ? " he inquired gently.

" Neaw.   It's abaat them books as Aw sent back. Aw've come ta humble mysel' an' ta ax for t'books back, an' if my Heavenly Father 'ull forgive me this time aw th' 'supers' i' Methodism shanna drive me fro' my pooast ageean."

The minister began to feel small.

" Yo' see, Mestur, yo'rs is a changin' life. Yo've seen hundreds o' chapels i' yo'r time, an' if God spares yo' yo'll see hundreds mooar. But us at Beckside yond' hev' ony wun little Bethil ta think abaat, an' when yo'n been ta'n to a place as little childer, an' ne'er been noa wheer else mitch, an' when yo'n getten yo'r fost glimpse o' Calvary theer, an' aw th' peeps into th' New Jerusalem yo'n iver hed, why yo' luv' that spot, yo' know, an' theer's sum on us i' Beckside as luvs ivery stooan there is i' th' building, an' we'd dee for it if we mud" (must).

" Mr. Jabez," interrupted the minister, gripping the Clogger's hard hand, whilst his eyes gleamed with unfamiliar tears, " Forgive me, sir, forgive me ! Would to God I loved Him and His cause as you do. I honour you from my heart."

And the minister asked Jabe to pray with him as a son would ask a father. And then with wet eyes he went out and told his wife, and brought her in to see his latest teacher. Then they both asked Jabe to stay to dinner, and the " super " sent for the circuit conveyance, and drove Jabe back to Beckside, charging him on the way to keep silence about his visit.

When they reached the Clog Shop he went and saw Long Ben and Nathan, and it soon became known that all was well again, the minister cleverly contriving that it should be understood that Jabe had conquered him—as indeed he had.

"The Zeal of Thine House"

II

"To Be, or Not to Be"

II

" To Be, or Not to Be "

THE new " super," whose attack on the Beckside chapel has been recorded, was too wise a man to push his plans in the face of such determined opposition, and consequently abandoned the whole project; and it is only consistent with the nature of things that, when the minister had finally given up the idea, those who had so resolutely resisted began to see something in it.

Jabe had poured scorn on the suggestion that the pews were not altogether what they ought to be, but somehow they never either looked or felt quite as cosy afterwards, and he caught himself very nearly admitting that they were deep and stiff-backed.

Long Ben, who had been so proud of the work of the painting and decorating committee which " fettled up " the chapel for Jimmy Juddy's wedding, presently became troubled with inward doubts as to whether the result justified the effort, and Sam Speck had to be severely reproved for expressing the treasonable wish that the chapel didn't look quite so much like the mill engine-house.

In proportion, however, as these doubts took root in their minds, each became more and more demonstrative in repelling attacks on the old building, and more and more emphatic in praising its many excellences.   At the same time each man was conscious of an uneasy suspicion of the loyalty of his friends in the matter.

To have heard the conversation as they stood outside and watched Silas lock up on Sunday evening, you would have thought that their admiration of the edifice was higher than ever; for whilst before the "super's" ill-starred proposal the chapel came in for occasional commendation or defence, just as circumstances required, now there scarcely ever passed a Sunday night but, on their way to the Clog Shop parlour or home, some one of the officials would be sure to turn round just where he could get a last glimpse of the building and say—

" Ther' isn't a cumfurtabler little chapil for twenty mile raand."

All the same, a slow progress of disintegration was going on in the minds of these authorities, a process of which this excessive admiration was but too certain a sign.   The fact was the Becksiders had a great respect for the superintendent minister, whoever he might be, and the present one—the new chapel suggestion apart—was so popular with them all that unconsciously they had been deeply impressed by his opinion. The way also in which he had borne himself when opposed, and the good sense he had displayed in not resenting opposition, commended him strongly to their judgments, and one or two of them had gone so far as to secretly regret the part they had played in his recent defeat.

Not that anyone ever spoke of the matter. The "super" regarded the question as closed, and apparently the officials did the same, but they were all nervously afraid of some one suddenly springing the question upon them again, and thus compelling them to avow their modified views.

The lesser lights were particularly uncertain about Jabe. Judged by his utterances, there wasn't the slightest chance of a new chapel whilst he lived, but they were not quite sure, some of them, that his loud protestations were not a trifle overdone, and they were strengthened in their suspicions by the Clogger's very apparent admiration of the " super."

These feelings were deepened by the fact that Jabe announced to them, one evening, that the " super " had been an architect before he entered the ministry, and had built at least a score places of worship in the course of his public life. Evidently Jabe and the preacher had been talking of chapel-building.

One Sunday night a stray remark by that rash young man, Dr. Walmsley, gave Long Ben a long-looked-for opportunity, and five men stopped in the middle of long pulls at their pipes, and held their breaths, as Ben alluded for the first time openly to the forbidden subject in the presence of the minister.

But the "super" knew his men by this time, and did not rise to the bait, and every listening smoker breathed a sigh of relief.

When he had gone, and the company had settled down to the regular Sunday evening topic, and Lige had finished a highly-flattering criticism of the sermon, Jabe once more brought all talk to a standstill.   For, tilting back in his chair and balancing it on its back legs, in sublime indifference to the subject under discussion, he said, apparently to a half-consumed ham hanging on the joist near the door—

" If ever we *dew* have a new chapil i' Beckside, yon's th' mon as Aw should loike ta build it."

There was a long silence.   Not a word was said in reply, and when the conversation was resumed it was on the old topic of the evening's sermon.   All the same every man went away that night with the feeling that the new chapel was now at anyrate a possibility.

Next week was the Circuit Quarterly Meeting, and as usual, Jabe, Long Ben, Nathan, and Sam attended as the representatives of Beckside.

Just before the meeting closed, the " super," with a palpably gratified air, announced that a very interesting communication was about to be made to the meeting, and called upon Brother Ramsden, of Clough End.

This gentleman, who was to Clough End what Jabe was to Beckside, and who had been, for him, unusually quiet all evening, with a look of immense importance, rose at the call of the chairman, and after justifying his reputation for jocularity by a number of more or less appropriate witticisms, formally asked the permission of the meeting to build a new chapel at Clough End.

" An' Aw whop (hope)," he concluded, " as it 'ull stir aar Beckside friends up ta get aat o' yond' owd barn o' theirs."

All eyes were at once turned towards the Clogger and his friends, but Jabe closed his mouth very tightly, pursed his lips, and looked across the room into vacancy; and the others feeling, as Sam Speck afterwards admitted, " as if cowd wayter wur runnin' daan my back," shot glances of quick inquiry at Jabe, and imitated his look of stern gravity, as if in rebuke of the frivolity of the speech to which they had just listened.

The Clough Enders, who had to pass through Beckside on their way home, got into the coach with the Clogger and his friends, and were, of course, full of their new scheme. Soon they drew Long Ben—as a practical man—into the discussion of a draft plan of the proposed structure which they had brought with them.

This was too much for Sam and Nathan, whose curiosity proved stronger than their dignity, but Jabe with folded arms sat bolt upright in the far corner of the vehicle, not deigning to notice the plans or show the slightest interest in the conversation.

There was always a full attendance round the Clog Shop fire on the evening of the Quarterly Meeting, and on this occasion every possible seat was occupied. Jimmy Juddy, Sniggy Parkin, the Doctor, and even retiring Ned Royle, being there to hear the news.

The air with which the Clogger walked through the shop into the parlour to change his Sunday coat announced more plainly than words that there was something unusual to tell, and the company present was preparing itself for a feast of succulent intelligence and discussion when Sam Speck, who had stayed behind to say " Good neet " to the Clough Enders, suddenly burst into the shop and spoilt all by blurting out in excited eagerness—

" Chaps ! th' Clough Enders is goin' ta hev' a new chapil."

Instead of the sensation he expected Sam received a decided snub. The news he brought was unwelcome, but his manner of serving it up was inexcusable. Matters of this kind were not to be flung at them as if they were mere items of ordinary gossip, and so instead of looking at each other in amazement, as Sam had expected, they carefully avoided catching each other's eyes, and sat looking into the fire with a decidedly non-committal look on their faces.

At this moment Jabe reappeared, and everybody felt that now the subject would receive becoming treatment. But first the Clogger held a consultation with his apprentice on some matter of business, and the company was divided between impatience to hear his story and admiration of his artistic *sang froid.*

Then he sauntered idly to his seat by the fire, and commenced to charge his pipe, attempting as he did so to start a discussion on the probable age of the vehicle in which he had just travelled. But nobody assisted him, though all admired his magnificent self-possession.

The pipe duly lighted, he at length commenced his regular description of the events of the day. But he was most aggravatingly deliberate. Not a detail was omitted, though he must have seen with what impatience his needless elaboration was received.

Then he diverged into a discussion with Sam Speck as to whether the average contribution per member from Brogden had been 1s. 4½d. or 1s. 5½d., and when the latter figure was eventually accepted he branched off, for the special edification of Sniggy, into an exhaustive description of the financial system of averages which obtained in the circuit.

The company listened with growing but carefully-concealed impatience to this digression, marvelling uncharitably at Sniggy's lack of comprehension, and all looked relieved and hopeful when, with a long-drawn " Well," Jabe prepared to resume the main current of his story.

But just at that moment his pipe went out, and every man in the company watched with painful interest as, after trying three matches, he finally discovered that the fuel was exhausted, and proceeded with exasperating deliberateness to refill and relight it.

As a rule the members of the Club were proud of the prodigious memory of their chief, but for once they could have wished it had been a little less tenacious and precise, for the speeches of the officials seemed long and tedious affairs indeed as Jabe reported them.

At last, however, the statement for which every one was waiting with a burning impatience could no longer be withheld, and so propping himself against the shoulder of the ingle-nook, and drawing it out as if it were a hardship to have to give such an utterly unimportant detail, he said—

" An' then Hallelujah Tommy said summat abaat a new chapil at Clough End.   But Aw ne'er tak's mitch heed ta wot that gaumless says."

But nobody was deceived by this painful pretence of indifference, and in a moment or two Sam set every tongue wagging, and got rid himself of much pent-up excitement by crying—

" Ay! an' it's ta hev' churchified windows, an' a pinnicle."

Soon the discussion waxed hot, the interest being intensified by the fact that though they were only discussing the Clough End chapel, a far more important question was felt to be in the background.

By long-established custom the Club sat an hour longer than usual on Quarterly Meeting nights; but though it was late when they began to separate, Long Ben, often one of the first to leave, lingered behind, and when he and the Clogger were alone and had sat for some minutes silently looking at the dying chip embers in the fire, he turned to Jabe and said, with an anxious sigh,—

" Aw'm feart wee'st ha' ta give in, lad."

And the sigh which accompanied the Clogger's reluctant " Ay " was longer drawn and deeper than Ben's.

It was customary in the week of the Quarterly Meeting to hold a united fellowship meeting instead of the ordinary classes, and at such gatherings Silas, the chapel-keeper, was generally a prominent figure. But the night after the events just described Silas was dumb, and neither long pauses nor nods, nor even nudges, had any effect.

" Th' dumb divil's getten howd of sum folk," said Jabe significantly, as he, Ben, and Silas were passing along the side of the chapel homewards. But Silas only held his sharp, sallow face a little higher, and gazed sideways at the rising moon.

As they were turning the corner to the front of the chapel, however, Jabe pulled up, and whipping round at Silas in the rear, he demanded sternly—

" Wot's up wi' thee ? "

" Up ! " shouted Silas, a look of fierce aggressiveness springing into his face ; " Up ! " he repeated, and seizing his companions by the arms he pulled them back into the little graveyard and cried—

" We're goin' t' have a new chapil, Aw ye'r."

" Well ! wot if we are ? " demanded Jabe.

" Well, if there's a new chapil ther'll be a—a," and Silas's voice became tremulant, " there'll be a new chapil-keeper, that's aw."

The two leaders looked Silas over slowly from head to foot with a mournfully curious look.

" Dunna meyther thysel', lad," said Ben soothingly, as he put his hand gently on Silas' shoulder.

" Meyther mysel' ! " cried the chapel-keeper

almost in a scream, and springing away from Ben's touch, " Aw've ta'n cur of this chapil for welly forty ye'r, an' Aw'm th' poorest mon among yo', but Aw've ne'er ta'n a brass fardin o' wages aw th' toime. Wot have Aw done that fur? Wot have Aw lived i' th' little damp chapil-haase fur aw this toime? "

The leaders moved uncomfortably, and had a guilty, self-reproachful look.

" Dunna, Silas! dunna, lad! " said Ben, in a mournful, coaxing tone.

" Dunna! " shouted the agitated apparitor, and, pointing to a grave close under the chapel wall, he continued in high, protesting tones—

" Sithee, my owd mother lies theer, an' aar Kitty, an' little Laban, an' yond' "—pointing across towards the boundary wall—" yond' lies my own bonny Grace an' her little un. An'," he continued, wheeling round, "here's thy fayther, Jabe, as poo'ed mi aat o' th' Beck when Aw were draandin', and theer's owd Juddy, as poo'ed me aat o' the horrible pit an' the miry clay. Ay," he went on, standing up and wildly waving his hands around him, " they're aw here. An' Aw live wi' 'em, an' they live wi' me. An' when Aw feels looansome an' daan i' th' maath, Aw comes aat here an' sits me daan an' sings aw by mysel'—

'Come, let us jine our friends above
That hev obtained the prize.'

An' Aw'st ne'er leave 'em. Aw'st ne'er leave 'em till Aw goa an' see 'em gradely."

And, out of breath with his exertion and excitement, the poor chapel-keeper sank back and propped himself against a gravestone.

By this time Ben was in tears, and Jabe, trying ineffectually to swallow something, looked first at one grave Silas had pointed out, and then at another, with a miserable convicted look on his face and certain strange twitches about his mouth.

" We met poo' it daan, an' rebuild it, thaa knaws," suggested Ben hesitatingly, from behind his pocket-handkerchief.

" Ay ! for sure," chimed in Jabe.

" Poo' it daan ! " cried Silas, in new agitation ; " that's woss nor aw. Sithee, Jabe, Aw'll show thee summat as thaa's ne'er seen afoor. Aw nobbut fun it aat mysel' t'other day."

And, taking Jabe by the elbow, he led him forward to where, close to the ground, in a dark corner all green and mouldy, was a stone in the wall. Then he plucked a handful of grass and briskly rubbed the face of the stone, and then, striking a match and holding it near the stone, he made Jabe kneel down and examine it, pointing as he did so to certain indistinct marks on the face of the stone.

" Con ta read it ? " he queried eagerly, but Jabe did not answer ; but, kneeling on the grass, he kept looking carefully at the scratches until they slowly formed themselves into a scrawling legend, evidently made by the point of some sharp instrument—

Ebenezer—
John Longworth

Jabe continued to scrutinise the inscription, which was very faint, and had evidently been hastily done, until Ben came and knelt at his side and assisted in the work of decipherment.

"It's reet," said Silas, when at length they rose to their feet. "It's just loike his writing i' the burrying-book."

The three men stood looking down at the stone, and presently Silas resumed—

"Naa, that's it. Thy fayther 'ud nobbut be a lad when he put that in—just converted, Aw reacon, an' thaa talks o' poo'in it daan, docs ta?"

"An'"—throwing open a window as he spoke —"yon's th' owd poopit as Adam Clarke preached in, an' Sammy Bradburn. Aw reacon thaa'll poo' that daan. An' yond's th' penitent-form [communion-rail], wheer thee an' me, an' sum 'at's up aboon, fan peace i' th' Great Revival. Thaa'll be poo'in' that daan, wilta?

Well, yo' con dew as you'n a mind, but t'owd Book says, ' Thy servants shall take pleasure in her stones and favour the dust thereof.' An' Aw dew ! Aw dew !"

And, leaning his dark face against the old wall caressingly, as a child to its parent, he concluded—

" Aw love every stoaan in it, ay, an' th' varry dust we're treidin' on."

Deeply moved by what they had heard, the two leaders somewhat hastily bade Silas " Good neet," and as they were going down the " broo " each turned round and took a long, lingering look at the edifice they had just been discussing, sighing heavily the while ; and that same week, without any spoken word having been used, but by such processes as were perfectly understood amongst them, it penetrated into the minds of the Beckside Methodists that whatever else was done there would be no new chapel.

" The Zeal of Thine House "

III

" Of His Necessity "

III

" Of His Necessity "

LONG BEN, Jabe, and the " super," with their heads close together, were bending over certain hasty lead-pencil drawings, engrossed in earnest conversation.

" Howd ! howd," cried the Clogger, interrupting the minister, " Yo' munna talk like that. Th' on'y chance o' gerrin' it through 'ull be fur t' keep them names aat. If yo' talken abaat Roman ex's [esques] and Gothics ta aar chaps yo'll ruin th' job, an' wee'st ha' wark enew as it is."

" Aw think we'd better let th' owd winders a' be," chimed in Ben ; " bud yo' con mak' a fancy frunt if yo'n a moind. On'y dooan't caw it by ony fancy names."

" Very good," said the " super," with a sigh of disappointment. " I'll do the best I can, and you must pave the way for me."

" An' ther' mun be noa steeples, nur pinnacles, nur hangels' yeds, nur Chineese wark abaat it," persisted Jabe.   And, as the "super" nodded slowly, Ben gently added, "An' we mun ha' noa thrutchin, an' wilta-shalta wark.   If they winna they winna, and we ar'na' fur t' hurt even ' one o' these little ones.' "   And the tremolo cadence of anxiety in the carpenter's voice disarmed a momentary irritation in the minister's mind.

This conversation took place on a Sunday afternoon.   The two officials having made up their minds that, though the old building must be preserved, some heed must be paid to the wishes of those who pressed for improvement, had requested an interview with their ecclesiastical chief, of which the words recorded above were the closing parts.

They had explained to him the exact situation, and after a stealthy visit to the chapel ostensibly to address the scholars, but really to survey the premises, the "super" had hastily sketched a plan which had the tentative support of his subordinates, the understanding being that he was to prepare detailed drawings and submit the whole scheme to a meeting of trustees, Jabe and Ben undertaking to prepare the way as best they could.

Now, since the memorable scene in the chapel-yard, Silas, only an occasional visitor before, had taken to attending regularly at the

Clog Shop, evidently apprehensive lest, in his absence, some conspiracy might be hatching for the injury of his beloved chapel. And as Sam Speck had recently taken to openly advocating a new building, thereby manifesting a dangerous independence of judgment, the Clog Shop confabulations often developed into stand-up forensic fights between the two, the other members of the party only making occasional contributions to the debates.

On the Sunday night in question, the discussion on the " super's " sermon lasted rather longer than usual, a passing reference of his to Socinianism having produced itching curiosity on the part of the irresponsibles, and evasion and impenetrable mystery on the part of those who were generally recognised as authorities.

Presently, however, Long Ben, who was generally supposed to dislike the subject of the new chapel as provocative of strong words and stronger emotions, actually introduced the question himself.

Sam Speck, astonished at this manœuvre, and hoping, though with misgivings, that he had made a convert, at once launched out in commendation of the enterprise and pluck of the Clough Enders, and the grandeur of their new building, at least as far as its plans were concerned.

Of course Silas, the chapel-keeper, at once

accepted the challenge, and was soon giving Sam a Roland for his Oliver.

To the surprise of everybody, Long Ben and Jabe immediately took sides with Silas, and out-Heroded Herod in their denunciation of any idea of erecting a new sanctuary.

Sam was dumbfounded, and Silas, whose only reliable supporters hitherto had been Lige and Jethro, rejoiced over the new converts with many a quiet chuckle. Sam looked crestfallen, and Jonas Tatlock and Nathan the smith, his chief supporters, frowned and looked at each other in sympathetic resentment.

Presently Long Ben, contemplating with peculiar steadiness the candle on the table, and with the most guileless expression of countenance he could command, remarked—

" Th' Independents hez a gradely nice chapil at th' Hawpenny Gate."

" Ay," added Jabe reflectively, as if the idea were perfectly new to him, " specially sin' it wur rebuilt."

As nobody followed this subtle lead, Ben resumed—

" Le'ss see ; when wur it fettlet up ? "

" Nine ye'r sin', cum th' frost of February," said Lige, who prided himself on chronology.

Nobody, however, seemed to take any particular interest in the matter, for the Halfpenny Gate was four miles away, and the chapel only an Independent one, and Jethro was just beginning to hum a tune preparatory to starting a hymn, singing being not an uncommon practice when topics of interest were scarce, when Jabe observed—

"It wur th' poorest chapil i' th' country-side afoor it wur enlarged."

"Soa it wur, lad," replied Ben, apparently only just remembering the fact, and then, after another pause, he went on—

"Aw'm nor i' favour of new patches upo' owd cloas as a general thing, but it's aw reet i' *sum* cases, and saves boath brass an' fawin' aat."

Now, Sam Speck, indignant at the unusually emphatic manner in which the recognised heads had opposed his new building scheme, was giving but a sulky and indifferent ear to the conversation, but happening to lift his head at this moment, he caught a gleam in Ben's eye which came as a revelation to him, and catching at the suggestion hidden under Ben's last remark, he cried out suddenly—

"That's it! By th' mon, that's it! Chaps, we'll enlarge th' owd 'un!"

And those crafty schemers, Jabe and Ben, affected to consider this as a totally new idea. They tilted back their chairs and studied the joists intently, and then slowly shook their heads, as if to say that they thought very little of the scheme, and, at anyrate, saw serious difficulties.

And their attitude had exactly the effect they expected. Gentle opposition only wedded Sam the faster to his idea, and made him the more fruitful of arguments in favour of it.

Silas also—a much more serious difficulty than Sam—was deceived by the manœuvre, and, as the only person present who knew the exact measurements, supplied details which strongly confirmed Sam's proposal, and very soon found himself getting angry at the inconvinceableness of the arch-conspirators.

At length, after long argument, Jabe, in dubious, hesitant tones, admitted that " Ther' met be summat in it," and with that the assembly dissolved, Sam full of the double glory of invention and conquest in argument, and the two stewards demurely content.

The following Friday the "super" held the Trustees' Meeting and expounded his scheme. The old building was to be left intact, except that the front was to be taken out and brought forward, thus giving about forty extra sittings in the chapel. The vestry at the back was to be pulled down and a schoolroom erected in its place. The old woodwork of the chapel was to be removed into the school, but the pulpit and communion-rail were to be left intact; and when, after describing his scheme in outline, the "super" unfolded a number of beautifully drawn and coloured plans ("as good as picters," according to Sam Speck), and invited examination, seven self-consciously important men drew up to the table and proceeded to scrutinise the designs with as much of the air of experts as they could manage to put on. They hung long and lovingly over the " picters," and when the " super " returned that night to Duxbury he had full authority to proceed, and left behind him a body of men who spent the rest of the evening marvelling at the extent and versatility of his gifts.

A day or two later completed plans were sent, and lay on the Clog Shop counter for public inspection, and for the next fortnight Beckside Methodism sat in almost perpetual committee over these latest examples of the minister's skill. By the end of that time, there was scarcely a person concerned even remotely in the matter who had not given judgment in favour of the scheme. There was one excep-tion, however, and though it would ordinarily have been regarded as of little moment, yet after what had passed in the graveyard, Jabe and Ben were honestly distressed at the ominous absence of Silas.

The " super " was coming over to a public meeting for the purpose of raising funds on the Friday, and Wednesday night had arrived, but the chapel-keeper had given no sign. Glowing descriptions of the new designs had been given him by those who knew nothing of what had occurred between him and the leaders. Twice, after putting the plans in a conspicuous place on the counter, Jabe had sent for Silas on some invented business in order to draw him into a criticism of the scheme, but without success, and to have directly broached the question would have been to court failure.

Thursday, the day before the great meeting, arrived, and no satisfactory evidence was forthcoming as to Silas's attitude. In the quietest part of the afternoon of that day, however, whilst Jabe was busy upon a new pair of clogs, Silas suddenly presented himself. He wanted a clog-iron on, and he wanted it on in a great hurry, and, catching sight out of the corner of his eye of the plans, he turned his face toward the opposite wall, and became intensely interested in a quite venerable advertisement of patent blacking.

Jabe took most extraordinary pains with that clog-iron, and succeeded in making the operation last quite a long time. In the meantime, Silas, affecting the most restless impatience, fidgeted every moment about the shortness of time.

Presently Jabe began dropping hints, and putting leading questions, but Silas would not be caught, and when the iron had been replaced, and another one that Jabe discovered to be "loosening" had been made secure, and the repairing process could no longer be prolonged, he handed back the clog to its owner with a petulant jerk.

Silas, on his side, now that the opportunity of departure was provided, seemed suddenly to have been seized with a fit of lingering, and manifested a reluctance to depart strangely inconsistent with his former feverish impatience.

At this moment a new idea occurred to Jabe, and, catching sight of a pair of clogs, evidently waiting to be taken home, he cried out—

" Hay, dear ! that lump-yed of a Isaac's goan to his tay ba'at takkin' Jethro's clugs wi' him. Sit thi daan, Silas, an' moind th' shop woll Aw nip daan an' tak' em. Th' owd lad conna cum aat till he gets 'em."

Silas, forgetting his previous haste, complied with ill-disguised alacrity, and almost before Jabe had closed the shop-door, he was bending eagerly over the erstwhile invisible plans. He had a good long look at them, for Jabe was an unconscionable time away, and when he did return he found the plans apparently as he had left them, and Silas still engrossed in the subject of patent blacking.

Jabe attempted to draw the chapel-keeper into conversation again, but without success. Silas remembered his forgotten haste, and departed with demonstrations of impatience, leaving the Clogger wrestling with a sense of defeat.

In the evening Silas joined the company round the fire, and appeared very attentive when anything referring to the renovation scheme was introduced; and, when he had departed, Ben nodded his head sagaciously across the fireplace at his friend, and re-marked—

" He's cumin' raand nicely, tha sees."

The following night the great meeting was to be held. The "super" was to take the chair, and for some days consultations had been held, challenges given, and thinly-veiled exhortations addressed by the Becksiders one to another with a view to promoting liber-ality.

It was getting dark on the Friday even-ing as the "super" reached the top of the hill going down to the village, and his reverence was just tightening rein to steady his steed down the rough incline when a man came out from behind a gate - post and cried, looking cautiously round as he did so, " Whey! "

It was Long Ben, and as he came close to the trap the "super" noticed a look of appre-hensive caution on his face. After the heartiest of greetings, and another anxious glance towards the village, he said, dropping his voice almost to a whisper—

" He's bin agate on me ageean ; he winna le' me gie nowt."

" Who won't ? " asked the " super."

"Whey, him!" jerking his thumb in the direction of the Clog Shop. "He says Aw'm nobbut fur t' gie five paand!" And Ben's long face lengthened considerably with an injured, resentful expression.

"Well, can you afford more, Mr. Barber?" asked the "super," who knew enough to justify the question.

"Affooard! Wot's affooarding to dew wi' it?" cried Ben, now fairly roused. "This is fur th' Lord's haase, isn't it? Aw *mun* affooard, an' Aw will, fur oather him or yo'!"

"Well, but, with your family, Mr. Barber"—

"Family! that's just it. Dew yo' think my childer 'ud loike fur t' goa theer, an' gie nowt towart th' fettlin' on it? Neaw, neaw, mestur, we'est dew it if we 'an ta clem [starve] fur it!"

"And does Mr. Jabez want to stop you?"

"Stop us? Ay, does he. He says as if Aw give a hawpenny mooar nur five paand he'll stop th' job."

"Well, what do you want me to do?"

"Aw've getten a bit of a plan fur chettin' him, if yo'll help me."

"Well, what is it?"

"When yo' begin ta read aat th' subscriptions yo' mun read aat 'Ben Barber, five paand,' an' then a bit efther yo' can say, 'A Friend, twenty paand,' dun yo' see, an' theer's th' brass," and Ben handed the minister five five-pound notes.

A few minutes later the " super " and Ben entered the Clog Shop in company, and Jabe seeing them together, glared fiercely at Ben and demanded—

" Weer'st bin ? "

But Ben merely sauntered to his seat with his hands in his pockets, and began humming a tune.

" Tum, tum, tum," cried Jabe, mocking the carpenter's music, and evidently in the worst of humours; " tha's summat ta ' tum, tum ' abaat, tha has."   And eyeing him with a look of mingled suspicion and disgust, he suddenly demanded—

" Hast browt that writin' papper ? "

" Hey, neaw ! " cried Ben in sudden remembrance; " Aw'd cleean forgetten it," and he hurried off homeward.

Jabe watched him disappear with distrustful, uneasy looks, and then, turning with a heavy sigh to the minister, he cried despairingly—

" Aw'st ne'er mak' nowt on him, Aw con see. Aw've bin trying forty ye'r, an' Aw'm furder off nor ivver ! " and then on sudden recollection he changed his tone and said, " But Aw want ta hev a word wi' yo', Mestur Shuper, afoor we goa."

" Proceed, Mr. Steward."

" Naa, when yo' starten a talkin' abaat brass

ta-neet, yon sawft ninny 'ull be up on his feet an' givin' away his childer's meit afoor we know wheer we are.   Well, Aw'm gooin' fur t' stop him.   As soon as yo'n oppened aat, yo mun read aat, 'Jabez Longworth, twenty-five paand,' an' then, afoor he has time fur t' speik, yo' mun say, 'Ben Barber, twenty-five paand.'   An' if yon mon gets up on his lung legs yo' mun stop him, an' if he gets up twenty toimes yo' mun stop him,—and theer's th' brass."   And Jabe handed fifty pounds to the minister in gold and notes.

The "super," touched, amused, and a little embarrassed by the conflicting confidences of these two friends, was about to reply, when Ben returned with the writing materials, and all three adjourned to the chapel.

A goodly company had assembled, and, after a formal opening, the minister proceeded in a clear and forcible speech to explain the scheme and solicit subscriptions.

"I have received one or two subscriptions already," he said, "which I will read :—

"Mr. Benjamin Barber, five pounds.

"A Friend, twenty pounds."

There was an exclamation of smothered wrath from Jabe, but the minister proceeded :—

"Mr. Jabez Longworth, twenty-five pounds.

"Mr. Benjamin Barber, twenty-five."

The meeting looked mystified.   Two subscriptions in one name sounded very odd. Long Ben sat in his side pew with his eyes closed, and his face void of all expression, and Jabe, after emitting from tightly-pursed lips certain indescribable sounds, suddenly rose to his feet, and glaring over the heads of the people, across the whole length of the chapel, exclaimed, shaking a podgy finger at Ben—

"Thaa thinks thaa's dun it this toime, dust na? Bud Aw'll be straight wi' thee yet, tha long lump-yed, thaa."

The minister was shocked at this very un-parliamentary language, and was about to intervene when his attention was diverted by a scuffling sound in one of the middle pews, where Sam Speck and Nathan seemed to be having some trouble with Silas the chapel-keeper, who was tightly jammed between them.

More subscriptions began to come in. Dr. Walmsley, in his own and his "dear wife's" name, offered a thankoffering for a good mother, followed by smaller gifts from the ladies themselves. Then came Jonas Tatlock and Johnty Harrop, followed by poor Phebe Green from the mangle-house, who wanted "to thank God for being a friend to the widow and sending her some more friends."

"Ten paand, Mestur Shuper," shouted Nathan the smith, still embarrassed by that mysterious conflict in the middle pew.

" An' me ten," chimed in Sam Speck, apparently out of breath from the same cause.

Then a sudden hush fell on the assembly as Sniggy Parkin stood up, in evident emotion.

" Aw—aw hevn't getten gradely straight yet, friends," he stammered, " bud if yo'll trust me twelve months Aw'll gee two paand ten fur th' schoo'-missis, God bless her " — (loud Amens)—" an' two paand ten fur this blessed owd place wheer Jesus washed my sins away."

Then came smaller contributions from others of the reformed Brick-crofters, each accompanied by some rudely-tender reference to " th' schoo'-missis."

A pause followed, and Lige, the road-mender, started off singing, " Ther'll be na mooar sorra theer."

And when that was got through, Job Sharples, the niggardly pig-dealer, rose. There was breathless silence as he opened his pew door and walked up to the communion-rail, behind which the minister sat, and put down on the table a coin.

Then he smiled patronisingly on the minister, and walked back to his seat. Several persons rose in their seats and leaned over to see what the coin was. " A sovereign," passed in whispers round the chapel, and expressive looks were exchanged.

As the whispers reached the back pew Jabe rose from his seat, paused to draw himself to his very fullest height, and then kicking savagely at the disobedient pew door, he limped down the whole length of the chapel, took the coin from the table, and, stepping with a haughty mien to Job's seat, he placed the coin on the narrow book-rest with a loud click, saying as he did so, in tones of inexpressible scorn and irony, " Thaa conna affooard it, Job," and then, with his nose very much in the air, he limped back to his pew.

A second time, at a moment of intense interest, that mysterious noise came from Sam Speck's pew, and taking advantage of the momentary distraction, Job snatched his cap from one of the pegs against the wall and hurried out.

A few more subscriptions were now announced, including quite reckless sums from Jethro and Lige, and once more that unruly disturbance in Sam Speck's neighbourhood broke out. A sharp sound, like the rending of cloth, was heard, and Silas, the chapel-keeper, with a flapping rent in one of his coat-sleeves, came struggling out of the pew, having evidently escaped with difficulty from the restraining hands of Sam and Nathan.

With his long, thin hair waving about, and excitement and triumph in his look, he rushed up to the table, and dragging out of his pocket a large tobacco-box, he opened the lid and emptied the contents before the minister. It was a strange collection. There were several dim and dirty threepenny and fourpenny pieces, a number of green-mouldy coppers, two crowns, a few other odd silver coins, and three little greasy packets containing a half-sovereign each.

" They say Aw munna give nowt 'cause Aw'm sa poor," he cried, in his wild way. " They say as they'll send it back if Aw dew. Did th' Lord stop th' poor widow fro' givin' 'cause hoo wur poor ? Did He send *her* mite back ? Neaw ! An' *He* winna send *mine* back, if *they* dew. It wur aw as hoo had, and He took it ; an' it's aw as Aw have, an' He'll tak' mine. An' Aw daar ony on yo' ta stop me." And poor Silas sank sobbing upon the communion cushion.

" Friends," said the minister, with wet eyes and shaking voice, " Silas, like the widow, has given more than we all, for he has given of his necessity."

"The Zeal of Thine House"

IV

Raising the Wind

"The Zeal of Thine House"

IV

Raising the Wind

THE Clogger sat in a high-backed arm chair, very close to the parlour fire. He had a huge "comforter" round his neck, the ends of which passed up over his ears and met in a knot at the top of his head. One side of his face was swollen. Though the weather was cold, he was without a coat, for Beckside gentlemen seldom wore their coats indoors; but his shoulders were covered by a heavy shawl. He had on his knee a jug containing ale-posset—a very popular local cure for colds—and near him, on the oven top, another jug containing " cumfrey tay."

He held his head a little on one side in a pensive manner, and had a pathetic, self-pitying expression on his face. He had got wet through two or three times lately whilst out begging for the chapel, and this was the result. He had now had several days of invalidism, which had tried his temper very severely, and at last had reduced him to pensive and sorrowful resignation.

"Aw've towd thi mony a toime as Aw shouldn't be a lung liver," he said, in melancholy, whining tones, to Aunt Judy, who was nursing him. "An' tha secs Aw'm reet. Aw'st dee abaat th' same age as my muther did."

"Dee? Ger aat wi' thi, tha owd mollycoddle. Yo' felleys is so feart if owt ails yo'."

"Judy," he replied, shaking his head with profound solemnity, "yo'r Jabe's dun." And then, after another pause and a sob, which he did not even try to conceal, " Aw'st ne'er see th' chapil oppened aat."

Judy was in difficulties. She did not in the least share the patient's fears, but she knew that to refuse to believe in them would only make things worse. So she tried to get up an argument with him on the comparative virtues of ale-posset and "cumfrey tay," and roundly declared, in the hope of arousing a spark of the old combativeness, that the preference of men-folk for ale-posset was a suspicious circumstance to her.

But even this did not succeed, and Jabe was commencing to give some directions as to the disposal of his worldly possessions, when Judy had a sudden inspiration, and broke in—

"Hast yerd wot Sue Johnty's bin propoasin'?"

"Neaw, wench," replied the Clogger, but with just the faintest gleam of curiosity in his eye. "Aw've noa interest i' warldly things naa."

"Hoo says hoo can see a hunderd paand in it, at ony rate," said Judy, stealing a sly look at her brother's face, and knowing that if anything could rouse him it would be the chance of hearing of means to raise money for the chapel renovation scheme.

"Well, hoo's a loikely wench is Susy," Jabe replied. "Wot's hoo been sayin'?"

"Hoo wants us to have a buzaar." And Judy gave a sort of anticipatory wince, and shot a glance of quick apprehension at the Clogger, as she dropped out the last word.

"Wot?" shouted Jabe, jumping to his feet, and upsetting the jug of ale-posset as he did so. And for the next five minutes poor Judy had poured upon her a torrent of abuse and reproach.

The attack would doubtless have lasted longer than it did but for the fact that Jabe's excitement burst a huge gumboil and effectually closed his mouth for the time, and the doctor, coming in a little later, found him faint and exhausted, but still "breathing out threatenings."

For the next three days Jabe sat in semi-state in his parlour, passing through the various stages of convalescence, and telling over and over again the story of Sue Johnty's wicked and worldly proposal, and though many disagreed with him, and some had even given a conditional adhesion to Mrs. Johnty's scheme, nobody dared to say so in the Clogger's presence.

Jabe had never seen a bazaar, but he regarded them as the last sign of worldliness and pride in a church, and declared again and again during those days of convalescence—

" Aw'd sooner see th' bums [bailiffs] i' th' chapel fur debt nur pay it off wi' brass fro' Vanity Fair."

This episode seemed also to increase his animosity towards the opposite sex.

" Women an' trubbel cam' into th' warld together, an' they'n bin together ivver sin'; bud Aw'll watch 'em at this."

But poor Jabe was only human, and turned pale with a sense of approaching discomfiture as on the first day after he resumed work he lifted his head and saw the schoolmistress (now Mrs. Dr. Walmsley), Nancy of the Fold farm, and the irresistible Mrs. Johnty Harrop approaching the shop.

It was a long tussle in the parlour that afternoon, and when the ladies retired they had a subdued and resigned air about them which seemed to indicate defeat, but it was only the meekness of a great sense of victory, for that very night Jabe, by tortuous and difficult processes, understood only by the initiated, caused it to be known that he was sacrificing his principles for peace sake, and that the bazaar would be held.

In a few days all Beckside was working and begging for the sale. It was intended to be held in the following February, and as the time of opening drew near, the whole neighbourhood became excited about it. Church people from Brogden offered to help, and the families of the two brothers who owned the Beckside Mill took hearty interest in the enterprise.

Jabe and his confederates became positively nervous about it. A bazaar had never been held nearer than Duxbury, and our friends had many misgivings. Most of the arrangements were in the hands of the ladies, and one or two of them were wilful and quite irresistible women, who did not even consult the dignitaries of the Clog Shop, and every few hours Sam Speck brought tidings of fresh arrangements of an utterly unheard-of character, until, when the Sunday before the great event arrived, Jabe was almost ill with suppressed excitement.

The sale was to last two days, and the local preacher who was appointed on the preceding Sunday brought a note from the "super" containing hints for the management of the affair. At the close of the note he remarked that as the schoolhouse where the bazaar was to be held was over the Beck-bridge, and rather lonely, it would be well to get someone to stay in the building all night, as a protection against fire or thieves.

This suggestion was a perfect boon. After having had to stand aside and act as mere camp-followers in the affair, the Clog Shop authorities suddenly found themselves in charge of an important department, and proceeded to discuss the situation with undisguised relish.

As soon as the question was raised there were numerous volunteers, and it seemed at one time as if there was going to be difficulty in settling who should have the honour of defending the schoolhouse—Sam Speck, whose father had been a parish constable, and had bequeathed an old truncheon to his son, and Lige the road - mender, who often at the Clog Shop fire told remarkable stories about his achievements as gamekeeper's substitute in days gone by, being the most clamorous.

As the debate proceeded, however, it widened out somewhat, and in a short time the bazaar was forgotten in the breathless interest with which the circle listened to stories of footpads, burglars, and highway robbers.

By this time Sam and Lige seemed to show some uneasiness. From thieves the conversation seemed to pass quite naturally to ghosts, and by the time that Jonas Tatlock had told once more his never-failing story of the sexton who fell asleep one night in Brogden Church, and was awakened by a ghost which touched his hair, leaving a white tuft amidst a plentiful shock of brown, every person present was most satisfactorily thrilled, and the sudden falling together of the embers in the fire sent a shock through the whole company.

In the silence that followed every man seemed to be inwardly resolving to swallow his own preferences and to waive any claim he might have to the hitherto coveted honour. And so, when conversation on the immediate question was resumed, Sam and Lige found that all competition for the perilous honour they claimed had ceased, and they were likely to be left in unchallenged possession.

Then Sam became suddenly generous, and intimated that he really didn't mind very much if anybody particularly wanted the honour.

But nobody did, and some hints dropped by Lige about the dangers to his "asthmatic" in being out late were ignored; in fact, the more generous Sam and his companion showed themselves, the more self-sacrificing became the rest of the company, and Sam, at anyrate, went home that night anathematising his own long tongue.

But real self-sacrifice brings its own reward, and so the valiant volunteer guardsmen were comforted next day by the discovery that they had achieved fame as heroic spirits. All day on Monday they were receiving offers of loans of firearms of almost every style and age, whilst bludgeons and cudgels were tendered wholesale, and Micky Hollows, from the Gravel Hole, offered an ingenious man-trap with powerful springs of his own invention.

This popularity, of course, had its effect on the two daring spirits, and when the policeman sauntered into the Clog Shop on Monday night, and volunteered to assist them, his offer was slightingly — almost scornfully— declined.

The next day, " Poncake Tuesday," was the opening of the bazaar. All passed off well in spite of the fuming and agitation of Jabe, and when the first day's proceedings were over, and it was announced that £93, 17s. had been taken, everybody went home tired but happy.

As the buyers and sellers dispersed, much interest was excited by the arrival of Sam and Lige to mount guard over the building and its valuable contents. Sam carried a thick cudgel over his shoulder, and a pistol sticking out of each pocket, whilst Lige had an old gun, one of his own long-handled stone-breaking hammers, and an old-fashioned powder-flask, whilst he led by a chain Long Ben's big yard dog " Tenter." Feeling that admiring and even envious eyes were upon them, the watchmen marched towards the stove in the middle of the schoolhouse, and very self-consciously proceeded to arrange their weapons in order.

When the general public had gone, Jabe, Ben, and a few of the others stayed behind with the watchers, and smoked a social pipe whilst they recounted the successes of the day. When they talked of going, Sam, who seemed somehow to have laid in quite a stock of new or revised stories, began to tell them faster than ever, putting into the relation rather more than his usual animation. Then he invited them to taste a brew of hot coffee, which he proceeded to make; and so it was past midnight when the last lingerers departed, and the valiant defenders of church property were left alone.

For a time they stood in the road listening to the retreating footsteps and voices of their friends, and then to the banging of doors which followed, but in a minute or two all was quiet, and an eerie stillness seemed to be in the black darkness.

So the watchmen went inside for the comfort and company of the dog. Then they smoked, glancing uneasily up at the high windows every now and again, and holding their breath to listen at the slightest sound.

After a while Sam began to examine his weapons, and showed unmistakable signs of nervousness, while Lige took frequent pulls at a large can of warm ale, which was kept in condition by standing near the stove. The dog stretched himself out on the floor to sleep.

Presently Lige began to nod, which made Sam quite angry, and he tried to draw him into conversation. But it was no use; the road-mender was overpowered, and was sinking every minute or two into slumber, in spite of his own and Sam's efforts to keep him awake.

The stove was a closed one. They had been recommended for safety's sake to use a lantern instead of a naked light, and so the room was almost dark, and the articles that hung about made all sorts of strange deep shadows, and assumed all sorts of suggestive and terrifying shapes.

Sam grew so apprehensive that he dared not look round. It was the very longest night he had ever spent. How cold it was getting, and how awesomely quiet. Would morning never— Bang !

Sam must have been dozing, but this bang brought him instantly to his feet. He snatched up the pistols, held them straight over his head, shut his eyes, and fired. One of the pistols kicked and hurt him, and he jumped back and yelled.

The shots were followed by the furious barking of the dog, and by Lige falling from his seat and lying on his back, where he remained shouting, " Murther! Thieves! Fire!"

Then the dog, frantic with excitement, jumped at Sam, who sprang back and fell over the small table on which the lantern was standing, and extinguished the only light they had.

" Help! Murther!" shouted Sam.

" Fire! Fire!" shouted Lige, and then they both lay panting on the floor in the powder smoke until the dog ceased barking, and all was still again.

Presently they heard a scraping sound on the walls outside, which set the dog barking again, and then there was a bang at one of the high windows. A minute later, Sam, venturing to lift up his head, saw a man with a lantern trying to open the window.

" Thieves! Help!" shouted Sam again, and began to grope on the floor for a weapon, the dog the while going nearly frantic. All at once the window flew open, a puff of cold air entered the room, and the thin, squeaky voice of Jethro the knocker-up was heard crying—

" Sam ! Liger ! wotiver's ta dew ?   Are yo' kilt ? "

In a few minutes Jethro had lowered his lantern into the room on the end of his handkerchief, and by its light Sam rescued Lige from the débris and opened the door, when it appeared that Jethro, getting up early to prepare for his rounds, had remembered the lonely watchers, and had made them a can of hot coffee, but that in the darkness he had stumbled against the door with the butt-end of his knocking-up stick, and had made the sharp bang which had startled Sam so terribly.

The next day nearly all the goods were disposed of. The handsome total of £204 was realised, and the graver spirits of the Clog Shop were of opinion that it was worth while to have had the bazaar, if only for its chastening effects on the irrepressible Sam.

But Sam and Lige escaped more easily than they otherwise would have done, because another matter attracted public attention. The bazaar had made Beckside popular, and the struggles of the villagers with their chapel scheme evoked sympathy in quite unexpected quarters.

One day the younger of the two gentlemen who owned the mill sent for Jabe to the office, and proposed to him, by the help of a party of musical friends from Duxbury, to give a grand concert in a temporarily empty warehouse belonging to the mill. The proceeds were to go to the renovation fund. As soon as the scheme was described to him Jabe saw in it a grand opportunity for the Beckside string band to display its talents, but the master, after long and skilful fencing, managed to convince the Clogger that, however desirable, this was scarcely practicable.

When Jabe announced the arrangements to his friends he was almost unanimously reproached for never having proposed that their band should give concerts. They might have had the schoolhouse for the asking. But when it was clear that he had actually discussed the question of the band assisting at the forthcoming performance, and had allowed himself to be beaten, he was regarded as having seriously compromised himself.

The concert promised to be a very grand affair, and, to crown all, the day but one before it was to take place the master brought news that the famous Madame Bona, a great professional lady singer, who happened to be singing at Whipham, a town a few miles the other side of Duxbury, had sent a special message to say that she had heard of the Beckside concert and its object, and would like to sing at it without fee.

This being noised abroad the fame of the lady created quite a rush for tickets, and when the evening arrived the big warehouse, swept

out and decorated for the occasion, was crammed.
The reserved seats were filled with the local
gentry, many of whom had never even seen
Beckside before, and on the front row of the
cheaper seats sat the members of the Clog
Shop Club.

The small but select band from Duxbury
came in for very severe criticism indeed from
these authorities. Jethro, as chief, sat bolt
upright with his eyes closed, every now and
then making expressive grimaces as the per-
formers offended his delicate ear; and, when the
overture was finished, Sam Speck leaned back-
ward to a Duxbury man who was sitting
behind, and pointing at Jonas Tatlock, whispered—

"Ther's a mon theere as 'ud fiddle the'r yeds
off."

After three or four pieces had been got
through, a rustle in the front seats and a
general buzz of excitement announced the
advent of the great singer. Most of the Clog
Shop cronies stood up to see her come in; and
when she did so each turned and looked at his
neighbour with a surprised and shocked expression, for the lady was in evening dress.

It was the first time most of them had seen
a lady thus attired, and it so irresistibly
suggested the theatre, and other wicked places,
that Jabe and Ben sat suddenly down and
buried their faces—hot with shame—in their

hands, whilst the rest looked at each other with embarrassment.

But the lady began to sing; and as her full, rich tones rolled down the room even Jabe lifted his head to listen, carefully avoiding, however, looking at the singer. In a moment or two he began to frown, and, finally, turning to Jethro, he cried in a loud, angry whisper—

"What's hoo mee-mawin abaat?"

"Huish, mon," cried Jethro, who was as perplexed as his friend, but had his reputation to think of. "Aw fancy yon's that new Tonic Sol-fa as thaa's yerd abaat."

But Jabe only shook his head in weary disapproval, and though the "quality" applauded the Italian song, and even the crowd clapped, the chapel authorities received it in frigid silence.

One or two band selections having been played, a well-known and somewhat old-fashioned violin solo was given, which, as it came within the range of their own knowledge, received from the village critics a modified approval.

Then the lady appeared again and sang an English love-song, and, though its sentiments made Jabe's lip curl, its music found a way to his heart, and he led off the clapping for their bench. The others somewhat coldly joined in, and Sam Speck stood bolt upright and stared at the singer with all his eyes, although she

was, according to Beckside standards, un-
dressed.

Towards the close of the concert the lady
sang once more, and was rapturously encored.
When she responded it was noticed that she
was without music, and signalled to the accom-
panist that she would dispense with his assistance. What was she going to do? Every
eye in the great throng was upon her; even
the bench of critics was compelled to look at
her.

And there she stood. Something seemed
to be moving her, and she tried to commence
but could not. Then she folded her hands
behind her, school girl fashion, threw back her
beautiful head, and a moment later there came
warbling through the hot air the old familiar
strains of Beckside's favourite Sunday School
hymn—

> "Around the throne of God in heaven,
> Thousands of children stand."

The audience was spellbound; and as the
singer sang on, a great flush of feeling passed
over hundreds of faces in the cheaper seats,
and all were listening entranced, when suddenly
the thin, shrill voice of Jethro pierced the air
with a vibrant, long drawn out " G-l-o-r-y ! "

The singer faltered; tears suddenly swam
into her eyes; she stopped, swept a long, low
curtsey, and hurriedly retired—whilst the back

benches, led by Jethro, took up the broken refrain and sang it to the end.

The reserved seats even had been touched by this unrehearsed item, and as the assembly broke up the only topic of conversation was the great singer's last song, and her unheard-of breakdown.

The Clogger and his friends filed off, duck fashion, to the shop, each man feeling as he wiped his eyes that they had something worth talking about for once. The pipes had all been charged, and Jethro was just opening the conversation, when a carriage was heard to stop outside. The door opened; a rustle of silk and a waft of scent came floating into the shop, and the great Madame Bona swept towards the ingle-nook.

"Well, gentlemen; how did you like my song?" she asked, still manifesting signs of emotion.

"God bless yo'!" shouted two or three at once.

"God bless *you*, for you taught it me," replied the singer.

Every man rose to his feet in amazement.

"Yes, old friends, you taught it me. And in my strange life now, that and other things you taught me, keep me from going entirely wrong. I've heard of your sacrifices for the dear old chapel, and I want you to know that there are others out in the great world who love it too, and will thank God for it for ever."

And slipping a heavy purse into Jabe's trembling hand, she made another sweeping curtsey, crying, as she did so, " God bless you, and God bless the chapel ! "—and was gone.

"The Zeal of Thine House"

V

At Last!

"The Zeal of Thine House"

V

At Last !

DURING the renovation of the chapel the Clog Shop became a sort of General Office. The Building Committee, which had been formed by a strictly temporary enlargement of the Trustees' Meeting, was supposed to meet in Jabe's parlour every Friday evening, but in reality it could never be said to have suspended its sittings, and the Friday night meetings became mere perfunctory ceremonies which formally closed the week's work.

The "super" had informed them that to be strictly in order all decisions must be confirmed by the Trustees, and the fortnightly meeting of that body, though brief, was a solemnly important affair, and invested the members of it with much of the same sense of dignified responsibility that supports the Lords Commissioners when delivering the Royal Assent which makes a mere " Bill " an Act of Parliament.

Now, Silas the chapel-keeper had been made a committee-man, and had not the least idea of allowing his office to become a sinecure. Sometimes, indeed, his functions seemed in danger of clashing the one with the other, the chapel-keeper getting in the way of the committee-man or *vice versâ*, which led to some mental perturbation.

Silas, however, had an adequate idea of what was required of him, and, as he had also much leisure and more zeal, he was a most prominent member of the Building Board. Vested with his new authority, he became a sort of self-appointed inspector of works of the most lynx-eyed and incorruptible character, and a thorn in the side of the workmen.

On that memorable Monday morning when Long Ben and his workmen arrived on the premises to commence operations, they found Silas waiting for them at the gate dangling his keys in his hand, and evidently fully sensible of the honour and responsibility vested in him.

As he inserted the key into the front door, he turned round and eyed the two tool-laden apprentices with suspicious and admonitory looks as he said—

" Naa, yo' lads, nooan o' yo'r gams. Yo're no' gooin' in to a menadgerie or a alehaase, mind yo'."

When they began the work of removing the front pews Silas found himself in difficulties. If he stood by and watched the workmen, every stroke of the hammer sent a thrill through him, and their light-hearted manner made his blood boil, but if he left them he was tortured with apprehensions of the sacrilege they might be committing.

Presently in the pleasant excitement of the work one of the boys began to hiss a tune through his teeth, and in a few moments the hiss grew into a whistle.

"Wot!" shouted Silas, coming in from the graveyard, and glaring fiercely at the offender whistling. "Thaa gaumless wastril, dust know wheer thaa art?"

A day or two later, as a high wind was blowing and the chapel became very draughty, the other apprentice ventured to put on his cap, and was unconscious of the enormity of his crime until the cap was sent flying from his head, and Silas stood over him shaking his fist and shouting—

"For shawm o' thysel. Wheer hast bin browt up?" and then turning to the other workmen, who were sheepishly removing their head coverings, he gave them an up-to-date exposition of the awful examples of Uzzah and the rash men of Bethshemesh.

Later on Silas was haunted with suspicion that smoking occasionally took place in the vestry, and had elaborated the most ingenious plan for discovering the offender when a much more serious difficulty presented itself.

When the bricklayers arrived one morning to commence pulling down the back premises preparatory to building the new schoolroom, Silas discovered that Pot Dick, an avowed sceptic from Brogden, was amongst the number. He saw him arrive with silent amazement, and as Dick was passing round towards the back of the chapel to commence work, Silas stopped him—

" Wot ! Thee ! Sithee, if thaa puts a finger upo' thuse owd stooans Aw'll—Aw'll chuck thi o'er that waw."

As Silas was slight and painfully thin, and Pot Dick a burly sixteen-stoner, this terrible threat only made the bricklayer smile.

But at that moment Long Ben appeared on the scene, and the outraged chapel-keeper at once attacked him. Ben seemed inclined to argue the point, and so Silas fetched Jabe and Sam Speck, and, after a long wrangle, he carried his point, and the master bricklayer was requested to remove the obnoxious workman.

Encouraged by this victory, the chapel-keeper stood guard over his beloved charge, and so lectured and badgered the workmen that Ben's position as chief contractor became a very difficult one indeed.

As the new part of the building began to rise on its foundations, Silas also took upon himself the role of chief exhibitor ; and getting possession somehow of a number of technical building terms, he amazed and mystified the villagers by entirely incomprehensible descriptions, in which pullasthurs (pilasters); mullions, corbills (corbels), and cornishes frequently appeared, whilst strange visitors went away profoundly impressed with the transcendent abilities of " Aar artchitect."

When the front window was nearly finished Silas made a grand discovery, and for several days every person visiting the building was taken across the road to get a view of the window, and was then informed under inviolable bonds of secrecy, " They tell me as that winder's pure Gostic. Brogdin Church winder's a sky-leet to it."

To the workmen, however, Silas became a perfect terror. If they inadvertently trod on a grave or laid anything upon the packing-sheets covering the pulpit and communion-rail, he was down upon them with unexampled fierceness ; and a joiner who absently began singing " Rule Britannia " was not allowed to forget his enormous transgression for weeks.

At last the badgered labourers began to resent these things. Murmurs broke out, protests were made, and one Saturday, after paying the wages, Long Ben adjourned to the Clog Shop in a very perplexed frame of mind.

He sighed heavily as he sank into his accustomed seat and began to fill his pipe, but as the others were deep in a discussion as to whether *Sovrenity* (Sovereignty) or *Wheat and Tares* would be the best tune to commence with on the opening day, he was unheeded.

In a few moments, however, unable longer to contain himself, he burst out—

" Aw'll tell yo' wot it is, chaps.   If iver th' chapel's ta be oppened aat, yo'll ha' ta muzzil yond' awd crater i' th' chapil yard."

Every eye was turned instantly on the speaker, and as he leaned back in the chimney-nook with a decided " I've had my say and mean it " look on his face, Jabe drawled out as he poked his little finger into the bowl of his pipe—

" Ay, rots is allis daan o' tarriers."

Ben vouchsafed no reply; he was too busy with his own thoughts.   At length he observed—

" Wee'st ha' ta get him aat o' th' rooad some rooad."

" Ay ! " said two or three at once, and laughed incredulously at the absurdity of such an idea.

" Aw shouldn't loike fur t' be th' mon ta mention sitchen a thing to him," said Sam Speck.

"Yo' couldn't poo' him aat o' Beckside just naa wi' horses an' cheynes" (chains), said Jabe with deep conviction.

"But there are other reasons why he should be got away at once," broke in the doctor, who was present. Everybody turned to look at the speaker interrogatively, and Long Ben asked somewhat eagerly—

"Wot dun yo' meean, doctor?"

"I mean that unless he gets a complete change at once we shall lose him."

There was a long pause, during which surprise deepened into anxiety on every face as they looked meaningly at each other, and Ben's gradually assumed a very conscience-stricken expression.

But just then Silas appeared on the scene, and though to those who had heard the doctor's statement he looked more worn and haggard than ever, he at once commenced an animated discussion on the to him obnoxious proposal to put a patent ventilator on the roof.

In the midst of the debate the doctor rose to go, and Jabe and Ben followed him out.

"Dun yo' meean it, doctor?" asked Ben anxiously when they got outside.

"About Silas? I *do* mean it. It is a very serious case. It is only his interest in that old building that is keeping him up."

Ben heaved a great sigh, and began to pull his straggling beard very nervously, whilst Jabe, turning his head away and gazing far away up the hill, asked in a husky voice—

" Dun yo' think as th' owd chapil-haase 'as hed owt to dew wi' it ? "

" Think ?   I'm sure of it."

The two stewards shot quick glances at each other, and instantly dropped their eyes to the ground, and as they stood there rubbing the dust with uneasy feet, remembrances of Silas' long and voluntary services and of appeals he had made for improvements in his little cottage came home to them, and added bitterness to the sorrow of the moment.

At last Jabe broke out—

" He mun goa, chuse wot he says and chuse wot it cosses (costs).   He mun be ta'n away if he winna goa."

To this the other two agreed, and Jabe and Ben went back to the shop.

Next morning Silas was not in his usual place at the schoolhouse, which was the temporary place of worship, and it was soon known that he was in bed, with the doctor attending him.   He seemed to rally, however, about Tuesday, and after the week-night service Jabe and Ben went to have their tussle with the patient, taking the minister and the doctor with them.

The chapel-keeper heard the proposal with

intense indignation, and refused peremptorily to have the question discussed. When, however, the doctor and the minister had spoken seriously to him, and he began to fear having to give way, he lost his temper, accused Ben of interested motives, called him a "fawse owd schamer," and then gave himself away by threatening him with all sorts of dire vengeance when he came back.

Ben endured his chastisement with great meekness, and said coaxingly—

"If tha'll goa to th' sayside we'll say no mooar abaat th' ventilator, an' tha'st tak' a pictur' o' th' chapil wi' thi. Sam Speck shall goa wi' thi fur company, an' tha'st come back i' toime fur th' oppenin' aat."

Visiting the "sayside" was not so common in Lancashire in those days, and Silas and his friend were the only Becksiders who enjoyed the luxury that season; but neither the distinction thus achieved nor the load of little comforts that were heaped upon him to take with him, nor all the promises of his friends to write to him compensated, in Silas' mind, for his painful separation from his beloved charge.

All the day before his departure he followed Long Ben about, instructing, cautioning, and even threatening him, until Ben was glad when evening came; and next morning the coach was kept standing some time outside the chapel, whilst Silas gave his final directions.

A few days later Jabe sat dozing in the ingle-nook, with Ben as his only companion.

" There's twenty-five paand wrung between thee an' me," said the carpenter

Jabe responded with an unintelligible grunt.

" Aw think Aw've fun a way o' squaring it," continued Ben.   " Th' doctor says he'll gie me ten paand and Nancy-o'-th'-Fowt 'ull gie me anuther, an' wi' that twenty-five th' job's dun."

" Wot's dun ?   Wot art talkin' abaat ? " cried Jabe, waking up and rubbing his eyes.

" Pooin' Silas' haase daan, an' buildin' a betther afore he comes whoam," was the reply.

Jabe stopped in the middle of a vast yawn, transfixed Ben with his eyes, as if to look him through, and sat gazing thus at him whilst the whole project was passing in review before his mind.   He saw at once the discrepancy between Ben's figures and the probable cost of the new cottage, and did not need the least hint as to how Ben, who would of course build it, meant to make up the deficiency.

With this exception the proposal was exactly to his mind; and so after stipulating that the matter should be kept out of the weekly letter to Silas, so that " Th' owd lad can come back to a grand surprise," he gave his consent to the scheme, and, in fact, came so near to paying Ben a compliment for his thoughtfulness that that worthy had some difficulty in concealing his surprise.

In course of time the chapel drew near to completion. The date of the opening was fixed. Band practices in preparation for the great event were in full swing, and Ben was pushing rapidly on with Silas' cottage. Letters of painful elaborateness were received weekly from the absentees, which, whilst they contained innumerable questions about the progress of the renovation, very pointed and peremptory messages to the committee, and impatient demands as to when they might come home, gave only the most cursory information about the patient.

At last, word was sent that Silas might return, and two days later the old coach landed him and Sam at the chapel gate, where a knot of Beckside worthies had gathered to welcome them. Silas had to be helped out, and a glance of sad meaning passed round as the onlookers scanned his yellow face.

But Silas scarcely saw them. Disengaging himself from Sam's arm, and waving his friends back for a moment he leaned on his stick, and, standing in the middle of the road, drew a long, heavy breath, as his shining eyes feasted themselves on the now finished chapel front.

" H-a-y, bud *isn't* it grand ! " he cried out at length, and then, dropping his stick and waving his hands over his head, he cried, " ' Beautiful for situation, the jye of the whole earth is

Mount Zion.'   Hay, chaps! Clough End's a coil hoile [coal house] to it."

Then he entered the chapel yard, passing his new cottage without noticing it, and after looking eagerly and delightedly at everything, he turned to the graves, and cried as if addressing the occupants—

"John Longworth! Juddy! Mother! Wot dun yo' think o' this?   It's welly as foine as yo'r own place, isn't it?   'Beautiful for situation, the jye of the whole earth is Mount Zion.'"

But Silas' excitement had exhausted him; and as he sank down upon a gravestone, Long Ben came forward and led him towards his house.

Aunt Judy and Mrs. Johnty Harrop were in possession, and whilst they had polished up all the old bits of furniture that were worth keeping, and had arranged them as nearly as possible in the old places, they had added a great many new things, and waited to have their reward in seeing Silas' surprise.

When he approached the house and first realised what had been done, his face was a picture.   Perplexity, astonishment, and delight followed each other on his withered face, and passing inside he dropped into a big arm-chair, the gift of the schoolmistress, and burst into sobs, crying out through his tears—

"'Mooar nor we can ask or think.'   'Mooar nor we can ask or think.'"

The opening service was a never-to-be-forgotten triumph. The Chairman of the District preached. The band achieved its most complete success. The anthem given by the united band and choir filled the preacher with most satisfactory astonishment, and all the visitors, with the exception of a few envious Clough Enders, expressed their admiration of the improvements.

After the evening service the "super" announced that the collections had far exceeded expectations, and that, in fact, the chapel was opened without a penny of debt upon it, at which glad tidings congregation and choir, and band and committee, and all combined sent up such a Doxology that Jethro declared —and surely we could have no better judge—

"Aw thowt Aw wur flooatin' into heaven."

And Jethro was nearly a prophet for others, at anyrate, if not for himself, for when the congregation was dispersing Aunt Judy came hurrying into the vestry and beckoned Jabe and his co-steward out. Silas, it appeared, had been quite carried away by the last Doxology, and the excitement had been too much for him, so that, after opening the doors for the people to pass out, he hurried to his cottage and fell down in a dead swoon.

The doctor, who was, of course, on the premises, was in almost instant attendance, but from the first gave little hope. And Jabe and the rest passed in a moment from elevated delight to fear and sorrow. Silas was laid on a long settle, and everything that could be suggested was got or done to relieve him.

After half an hour's anxious waiting he moved a little, and presently opened his eyes. But, instead of noticing any one, he fixed his gaze on the opposite wall.

Suddenly his countenance brightened. He moved his hand as though he would have pointed, and cried—

"Hay, wot a big 'un! This is niver aar chapil!"

And then he paused, and presently broke out again—

"Bless thi, Grace! Has thaa come to th' oppenin'? An' yo', muther? An' yo', John Longworth? Wait till they oppen th' dur. Naa, then! naa, then!" and as he spoke Silas' chapel doors *did* open, and the dear old saint entered into the joy of his Lord.

THE END

PRINTED BY
MORRISON AND GIBB LIMITED, EDINBURGH